Maximum
DARE

VANESSA FEWINGS

Cover created by: Najla Qamber @NajlaQamberDesigns

Cover Photo Model: Bernardo Velasco

Formatted by: Champagne Book Design
Editor: Debbie Kuhn

ISBN: 978-1-7337742-9-1

For those in need of healing.

Chapter
ONE

Daisy

THIS WAS A BAD IDEA.

Like one of those things that makes perfect sense in your mind but once you've done it, it's perfectly non-sensical. I clutched the fancy gold envelope to my chest, catching a glimpse of my reflection in the bar's long mirror. I looked worse than I'd imagined, my expression revealing my guilt—and my pain. The dark circles under my eyes were reminders of what had been done to me.

The moment Morgan Hawtry had set her sights on my man, my life had been obliterated. Everything I'd believed to be true was a lie. Seeing the two of them together had left my heart paralyzed.

And this swanky lounge would prove a decent setting for more heartbreak if Nick didn't even register my presence.

On numerous occasions, I'd passed by Isobel's Bar, but had never actually ventured inside. Nick had preferred our local pub—the kind of place where he could sit quietly and not have to chat with strangers.

I tried to ignore the warning in my head that being here was a mistake. At twenty-three, this little adventure felt like being back at Uni, where we had made bad decisions and put it down to naivety. But even back then I'd never done anything like this.

I buried the golden envelope in my handbag to hide the evidence of my thievery and then nudged my glasses up my nose to act like I hadn't just plucked it out of Morgan's Prada handbag. I'd taken advantage of those moments when she'd been distracted with her tongue in my boyfriend's mouth.

Okay…ex-boyfriend, but there was still a chance he'd come back.

I needed to believe this.

Nick had to realize this woman was bad news. Surely he'd seen the numerous selfies of her committing idiotic acts of danger. She'd posted countless images of her recklessness. More recently, she'd leaped off seaside cliffs during a holiday in Greece, gotten too close to a rhino at a zoo, zoomed down a city street on a Vespa without a helmet, and last week, she'd filmed herself getting a tattoo of a scorpion on her bum—her birth sign.

The Queen of Social Media had stolen something of great value to me. She'd stolen *him*—the best thing that had ever happened to me. The man I'd been living with up until three weeks ago, when I'd found the note that told me he was leaving…that he needed time to figure things out. He'd not revealed the real reason.

Thanks to Morgan's Instagram page, I'd discovered he'd left me for her. She'd posted a photo of her new beau and it had been the love of my life.

She was impossible to compete with. Morgan was quite simply stunning. Not only out of my league but out of my universe.

I'd left work at Harvey Nichols and driven all the way here from Knightsbridge in rush hour traffic to make it to

Isobel's before the new couple bailed and headed off to another party—something Morgan was famous for, since her popularity knew no bounds.

I tried to ignore the many glances from the lounge's überposh crowd in their high-society fashions, their snarky looks aimed at my simple black minidress. Or maybe they'd guessed Nick's ex had arrived and was on the verge of making a scene.

Both Nick and Morgan had looked uncomfortable when they'd first spotted me. If my strategy worked, Nick would take me aside and want to talk with me about why I was here.

That was my *in*—my chance to warn him.

None of his mates from his football team were here. The only reason I'd found out about this party was because I'd seen Morgan showing off about the event on Facebook.

Turning up like this probably seemed a bit stalkerish—but trust me, this was about saving a man who'd once saved me…back when all I'd known was grief. This was me looking out for Nick now, making sure he didn't blow up his life for a girl who could never truly love him. It was easy to see why she'd hunted him down. Nick was a rising football star destined to follow in his dad's iconic footsteps.

Why did he have to look so adorable with his tousled dark blond hair and expressive grey eyes? Chiseled features made him stand out even in this freakishly good-looking crowd, along with his athletic physique. I was now entering the hating phase…the I-can't-bear-to-be-in-the-same-room phase. Yet Nick still made my insides do a flip-flop.

The last few weeks had been crushing in so many ways. The house we'd shared in Bermondsey was going to be sold. Moving out was inevitable because Nick was now living with Morgan in her Chelsea high-rise.

That girl was my opposite: Tall and blonde and a first

prize winner in the genetics lottery. I was a brunette with blue eyes who wore round-rimmed glasses—my look was more the girl next door. Not wild and sexy like Morgan, a woman who chased after endless fun and thrived on surprises.

Before she'd stolen my man, I'd followed Morgan's make-up tutorials posted for and viewed by millions. She had two speeds—partying fashionista or poolside babe.

My speed was literally in reverse. There was no competing with a woman who was an expert at wooing men with her fake charm. And I'd never have the kind of money it would take to look like her. She indulged in cosmetic surgery to tweak imperceptible imperfections, giving her a flawless, airbrushed appearance that was hard to imitate.

Nick was destined to become another "Most Hated" post on Morgan's Instagram page after she'd tired of him and moved on. It was inevitable. That was her thing.

I couldn't let it happen to him.

A few minutes alone with Nick and I'd be able to show him the evidence I'd found on Morgan's social media pages to prove she was bad news. He seemed oblivious to the long list of exes mentioned in her blog posts—whimsical fancies who formed the fodder for her emotional breakdowns and at the same time garnered her more followers.

But even knowing all of this, I still hesitated—guilt for stealing that envelope niggling at my conscience.

Don't do it.

Don't lower yourself to her standards.

Rummaging around in my handbag, I retrieved the envelope ready to slip it back into Morgan's Prada purse.

Oh, no!

They were leaving.

Hand in hand, Nick and Morgan waved goodbye to

the crowd like they were a celebrity couple. My worried glare tracked their movement along the other side of the window.

Having not quite used up my stalker quota for the evening, I decided *what the hell* and grabbed my parka from the barstool, pulling it on. I followed them out and was hit with a blast of freezing cold January wind that stung my face.

A limo was waiting for them. A chauffeur wearing a grey suit opened the back door in a formal gesture so that Morgan could elegantly slide into the back.

Nick stopped short of climbing in behind her to pin me with a look of disbelief. My humiliation rose with each faltering step and I forced a weak smile to reassure him.

It's just me, your ex. The girl with no life who refuses to let you go.

I gathered the courage to sprint forward, holding out the envelope. "She dropped this—"

SLAM!

My glasses went flying as I collided with a rock-hard male body. My cheek squished against a woolen coat as my body fell heavily against his, a flood of pheromones rushing through me from his heady cologne. It reminded me of endless nights filled with sordid pleasures. At first I was reluctant to look up, afraid I might be disappointed after that incredible preview...

"Hi, there," he said, his tone amused, his accent seductively foreign.

Dazed, I peered up at his face. He was too tall to kiss, this dark stranger with a three-day stubble. His masculine scent stirred a forbidden desire deep inside of me and I couldn't speak for a moment. He was so damn gorgeous. His temples revealed just a hint of grey—making me think he was in his thirties. His hypnotic brown eyes crinkled with kindness as he gave me a dazzling smile.

"Thank you?" I finally said. The response had made sense in my head.

He must have found it humorous, as I saw his full, kissable lips quirk up in a smile—a smile that suddenly faded as he glanced over my shoulder.

Someone from behind me gripped my arms and dragged me away from him, forcing me to trot on unsteady heels towards an SUV. I had no choice but to move in that direction, feeling dizzy as the world whooshed by.

My handbag slipped off my shoulder and landed on the ground as that someone then shoved me against the front of the vehicle, pushing me forward until my cheek pressed against the hard metal of the car bonnet. I tried to push myself up, but my hands were suddenly drawn behind my back and I was held down, incapacitated—and vaguely aware that the handsome stranger was watching.

My cheeks ablaze, I cringed at the thought that Nick was seeing this, too.

I lifted my head a little and saw Morgan climb out of the limo. She whipped out her iPhone and pointed it in my direction.

The flash was blinding.

Chapter
TWO

Max

"WAIT RIGHT THERE!" I CALLED AFTER MY brother as he climbed into the back of a limo. *God, it's cold.*

I could see my breath forming white puffs in the air. January in England was never kind. I rubbed my arms in a failed attempt to warm up. Nick was bailing on his own party. The bastard didn't even have the courtesy to wait for me. Considering I'd flown in from Brazil, this was not cool.

But before I headed over to Nick's car, I first needed to deal with the woman who'd slammed into me. My driver, Carl, had the situation under control as I approached. He was currently holding the girl with her face pressed against the hood of the SUV.

"Você está bem?" *Wait, I'm in London.* "Are you okay?"

"Yeah, I'm having a blast!" she snapped.

"Do I know you?" I tilted my head and saw expressive blue eyes peeking out between locks of long brown hair. Even with a scowl, she certainly didn't look like a threat.

"I was trying to get to my boyfriend," she said.

"Nick?" I stood up straight and shot a glare through the

dark tinted windows. My brother was in the back of that car with a blonde, no less.

"He's *your* boyfriend?"

"We live together."

That was news to me.

"Well, we used to," she added. "He's my ex now."

I motioned for Carl to let her go and she immediately picked her handbag up off the ground. When she straightened, dark curls tumbled over her shoulders and caught in the breeze.

"Come onto the pavement," I told her.

She was pretty, even ethereal, with big soulful eyes and pink sensuous lips. Her long curls enhanced her youthful appearance. I tried to fathom why my brother had ditched her.

Her smashed glasses lay in front of me on the pavement. I picked them up and handed them back, trying not to cringe. She took them with a nod of thanks and then turned them over, frowning at the damage.

Carl handed her an envelope. "This is yours, too?"

She shook her head. "I was trying to return it."

I braced for the onslaught that might be coming my way, expecting her to object to the way my driver had treated her. Half the bar was gaping at us through the window.

I refocused on her. "You're not hurt, are you?"

She rubbed her wrists. "It's how I like to spend my Friday nights…an evening of total humiliation topped off by being manhandled by a complete stranger."

"Sorry about that."

"What did I do wrong?"

"You came at me rather fast. Carl's my driver and he doubles as a bodyguard."

I'd be shaking him off after tonight. He usually drove my

mother. She had insisted he usher me around after my arrival in London.

"I didn't see you," she said, slipping the ruined glasses into her purse.

"I'm rather hard to miss." She looked annoyed, so I held out my hand to shake hers. "I hope you'll accept my apology."

She wrapped her fingers gently around mine and squeezed, sending a shiver of delight into my palm and up my wrist. When she finally let go of my hand, I had the urge to shake off the tingling sensation.

What was that feeling exactly?

"I'm Daisy."

"Max."

"Nick's brother?" She blushed.

Her sweetness had eased the tension in the air. If she hadn't been connected to my brother, I'd have swooped in at once. I couldn't understand why Nick had kept her hidden away. I was struck by her grace. The way she threw a reassuring wave to Carl was endearing.

"Can you wait here?" I asked.

When she nodded, I made my way over to Nick's limo. I rested a hand on the open passenger door and leaned over to glare at my sibling in the back seat. "You're leaving?"

"Hey," said Nick. "You made it!"

"Is that meant to be funny?" I pointed a thumb at the bar. "Are you going back in?"

He gestured to the woman sitting beside him. "This is Morgan."

His weak diversion made my jaw clench with frustration.

"You must be Max?" she cooed.

"Nice to meet you, Morgan." I returned my focus to him. "I've flown thousands of miles to be here."

"I appreciate that. You're here for a couple of weeks, right?"

I took a deep, calming breath, reminding myself that, while Nick could be infuriating, it wasn't really his fault. He was still dealing with his father's death. More recently, I was concerned his grief was affecting him in new and interesting ways. His phone calls to me had dropped off and Mum had shared how worried she was about him. Nick and I shared the same mother, though that was where our similarities ended.

I loved my half brother, but Nick was always pushing his boundaries.

Twenty-six years ago, my mother had been swept off her feet by one of England's most prominent football players—Nick's dashing father. The only solace for me as a kid was that I loved football, so me staying with Mum during the holidays was always something I looked forward to. Growing up playing football with an icon in the garden had soothed this boy's hurt feelings.

Still, the divorce had left behind shards of pain that had never eased. I was only seven years old when my mother left us...left my father to die from a broken heart. I'd never revealed that to anyone—least of all my mother.

My unfailing obsession with football was now encouraged by this asshat. Nick was a talented player. I both envied and admired him at the same time. I felt envy for the time he'd had with my mum after she'd left me in São Paulo. And I felt inspired by him because he was set to follow in his dad's footsteps and become an icon himself.

Which was probably why I decided to give Nick a pass this time...another in a long line of passes. "Come back in and update me on how it's going with you joining Manchester United."

"I really don't feel up to it," he whined. "Anyway, you prefer Brazil's national football team."

"Not as far as you're concerned. I love hearing about…"

I saw Morgan's expression and it hit me—Nick probably had an erection and they were heading off to shag. There was no negotiating with these two.

Nick brightened. "Are you staying at the Waldorf Astoria?"

"Yes." The hotel was closer to his place than our family estate. I'd hoped to spend some time with him. "I thought we might hang out?"

He smirked. "I'll hang out with you tomorrow at Mum's during the party."

"What party?" I cringed at Mum's never-ending attempts to introduce me to high society girls. In her mind, her thirty-three-year-old son should be married by now. Didn't she know she'd put me off marriage…tainted my desire for that level of commitment? I'd witnessed too much heartache in my dad to ever romanticize love.

Not so for my brother, who was always flirting with someone. From the way Nick couldn't keep his hands off Morgan, I could see he was infatuated with the stunning blonde.

"We really need to go," he whined again.

"See you later, then." I let out a sigh of frustration because there was no arguing with him. "Nice to meet you, Morgan."

She fluttered her eyelashes and I wondered if that ever worked on the weak-minded. From the way my brother was besotted, the answer was clearly yes.

"Phone." I held out my hand.

"I've already asked Morgan to delete the photo," said Nick.

I glanced back at Daisy. "She's your ex?"

He nodded. "Have no idea why she came here."

Not only was he bailing, he was leaving me to deal with his mess.

Great.

"Phone," I insisted.

Morgan rolled her eyes and handed it over.

With a few swipes, I deleted the photo of Daisy. I didn't trust these kids. If that photo was released with me in them, it could cause quite the scandal. Still, Daisy seemed like a sweet girl caught up in my brother's emotional baggage. She looked like the type to go away quietly.

I handed the phone back to Morgan and turned to Nick. "See you tomorrow night. Don't be late."

"Oh, I'm staying for the whole show," he said with a grin.

"Our family is not a show."

It *was* a show.

What with my hotheaded Brazilian mum and Nick's side of the family, the entire evening promised to be full of entertainment—more like a horror show, actually.

Nick waggled his eyebrows. "By the way, thank you for taking care of *that*."

"Daisy?"

He nodded. "This is out of character for her."

"Boring as hell," muttered Morgan.

"She's not boring," said Nick. "She just plays it safe. All. The. Time."

I ignored that. "Happy birthday, bro."

"Thanks for being here, Max." He gave me an affectionate glance before reaching over and shutting the door in my face.

Their car pulled away from the curb.

I swore under my breath.

I'd landed at Heathrow a few hours ago and had raced to check into The Waldorf so I could change and make it here on time. So much for trying to beat the Friday night traffic and be the good brother.

I headed back to Daisy with my game face on. Negotiating with a jilted ex was the last thing I'd had on my agenda for this evening. A nice cold beer had been in my future. A quiet evening fighting jet lag and catching up. Anything but having to deal with *this*.

"Hi." I smiled at her warmly. "Nick sends his apologies for leaving."

She looked surprised. "I think Morgan took a photo of me."

"Nick had her delete it."

"He did?"

"I made sure of it." I gestured to Carl. "Can you wait in the car, please?"

We watched him get comfortable in the driver's seat.

"Carl's a bit overzealous, I'm afraid. Your glasses…perhaps I can give you something for them?"

She gave me a thin smile. "You must not visit often? I've never met you before."

I visited frequently—every few months, at least. But Nick had kept Daisy a secret from me, even though they apparently had been living together. It made me wonder why he'd not introduced us. My mother would certainly have mentioned her.

She seemed nice enough for our family.

I glanced at my watch. There was enough time to get back to the hotel and put in a few hours of work.

"I'm so embarrassed," Daisy said softly.

"No one saw."

"Everyone saw."

13

Not that it mattered now, but I still decided to ask. "Why did you come here?"

"I needed to talk with Nick."

"About?" I suddenly realized she might be a little more challenging to handle. "Are you wanting money?"

"Excuse me?"

"I'm just trying to figure out why you're following my brother."

She let out an irritated sigh. "Well, it's been fun, Max, but I think I'll call it a night."

"How are you getting home?"

"Same way I got here."

"By Tube?"

She looked over at a blue Mini Cooper parked on the curb across the street. "My car's over there."

"Let me give you a ride home. Can you even drive without your glasses?"

"Probably not. Now, if you're quite finished accosting young women…"

Quite the sucker punch after I'd been the only who'd been decent to her. Daisy had this annoyingly cute pouty mouth. I wanted to give it a good hard kiss as punishment for her attitude toward me.

"Daisy, may I advise you to stop finding yourself in the same place as my brother. These things can get out of hand."

She gave me a *what the fuck* look that may have scorched a lesser man, and pulled her broken glasses out of her purse.

When she put them on, I pointed at the spider-webbed lenses. "Surely you can't see through those?"

She pivoted away from me and headed off.

And then walked right into a lamppost, smashing her face against the pole.

Chapter
THREE

Daisy

"**C**AN I GET YOU ANYTHING ELSE?" ASKED MAX.

He sat beside me in the back of his SUV, throwing glances of quiet contempt my way—unless I was misreading his broodiness.

"I'm fine, thank you." The driver had found a cold pack in their first aid kit and it was making my face numb.

The humiliation was endless.

I should never have had the brief thought earlier, after seeing my boyfriend at Isobel's with Morgan Hawtry, that things couldn't get any worse.

Things had gone downhill so fast I was still spiraling. Having to be driven home by Nick's arrogant brother had rounded out the evening's fuckery quite nicely.

Nick had mentioned he had a Brazilian half brother. Though he'd not shared how dreamy he was. This man was so hot I could feel the burn coming off him. His foreign accent was doing strange things to me. Making me all flustered. Or maybe it was because Max had asked the driver to turn the heat all the way up.

I'd had to peel off my coat and set it aside.

Max may be devastatingly attractive, but I could never fancy someone who acted this formal and stuffy.

"You'll be home soon," he muttered more to himself than me.

Other than the ache in my throbbing nose from hitting that lamppost at warp speed, I was actually feeling better. Max was a pleasant distraction—even if he was distant and cold and obviously hating every second of doing the right thing.

He was doing his brother's dirty work by getting me out of the way, so I didn't make a bad scene worse.

He'd been right about my glasses. They were toast thanks to his driver thinking he'd stepped out of a Keanu Reeves film.

But my pride had suffered the most, seeing Nick with *her*. I was still trying to ignore the crushing pain in my chest.

I lowered the cold pack and gently touched my bruised nose. At least I hadn't broken it after walking straight into a lamppost—the one with a sign proclaiming that spot as the most fun place in London.

"I live in Bermondsey," I said.

"Carl knows."

But apparently they'd had no idea I'd been living with Nick. There were so many possible reasons why he hadn't told them. Maybe it was to protect me from his weird family... though clearly Morgan was being proudly showcased to them and the rest of the entire world.

This did nothing for my confidence. I was merely the shop girl who worked at Harvey Nichols in the evening gown department, ironically selling dresses I'd never be able to afford.

Rubbing my forehead, I fought back tears of frustration at the endless rejection I had to face.

Max shot me a look of concern.

I rested the cold pack on my lap. "You want only the best for Nick."

"We all do." He tugged at his scarf and pulled it off.

I watched as he unbuttoned his coat and peeled it open to reveal a T-shirt that showed off his toned abs. His jeans clung to his thighs, showing off their muscular strength. This man looked like he hit the gym frequently.

My consolation prize for a horrible evening was sitting in the back of an SUV with Nick's big brother and savoring this man candy. I mean, even his chiseled bits were chiseled. That five o'clock stubble on his perfect jaw had a hint of grey that gave him a sophisticated edge. This man had playboy written all over him.

Quite literally...

I stared at his T-shirt, which had "Playboy" written across it. "Bit on the nose."

"Excuse me?"

I gestured at his shirt.

He peered down at it. "This is a band from São Paulo. They're called 'Playboy.'"

"Right." I gave him a skeptical look and he returned my cheekiness with a heart-stopping grin.

"They're like Pearl Jam," he added.

"Okay, the name rings a bell. I think Nick has their latest album."

"Because I bought it for him." He paused, staring at me. "How's your...face?"

"Why?"

"You hit that pole pretty hard."

"Does it look bad?"

"No." He didn't sound convincing. "Do you have a spare pair of glasses?"

"No, but I have contact lenses, too."

Late-night shoppers were scurrying along the pavement, all looking like they were having a much better time than me. Even with the sky pouring down on them.

He reached into his pocket. "Let me pay for new glasses."

I reached for his hand to stop him. "No, thank you." I wasn't going to accept cash in the back of a car like a tart.

"Maybe we can come to an arrangement," he said.

"Arrangement?"

"A financial agreement. I'd like to avoid a lawsuit and keep this out of the press."

"What are you talking about? Anyway, we don't go around suing each other here."

"People actually do take legal action in the U.K. all the time."

"How would you know?"

"I'm a lawyer." He turned his head to look at me. "In São Paulo."

"Nick didn't really talk about you."

"We've been mysteriously kept from each other." The way he said it made me think he, too, was feeling stung by Nick's secrecy.

I felt sorry for him. He was clearly finding this charade uncomfortable.

"I forgive you," I said softly.

He dragged his teeth over his bottom lip. "Why?"

"Well, all that was missing was the handcuffs and a nice spanking." I gave him a wicked smile.

He went to say something and seemed to change his mind.

My cheeks flushed. "I'm joking, of course."

He gazed at me intently, his deep brown eyes revealing

conflicting emotions, and then he slid into a heart-stopping smile and held it.

My breath caught in my throat.

I looked away and changed the subject. "Why do you have a bodyguard?"

He exhaled sharply. "Carl's my mum's chauffeur."

"Why does *she* have a bodyguard?"

When he didn't answer right away, I turned to face him. He looked confused, as though I should know the reason.

"I've not met her," I admitted.

"Mum's cautious, that's all."

"She's not famous, is she?"

"Not in your circle."

What the hell did that mean?

"Nick told me that after his dad died, he stopped speaking to his family."

Max shrugged. "My brother acted out for a while, but he's fine now."

"Doesn't seem fine to me."

"Look, if there's any way I can make up for tonight—"

"Maybe you can talk to Nick."

"About what, exactly?"

"Everything seemed fine with us, and then one day he just left. It was sudden. I know I sound like a jilted lover when I say this, but he's making a big mistake with that girl."

"My brother seems to have made up his mind. I'm sure the decision wasn't easy." He mulled over his words. "I hope you can find a way to move on, too."

"I've been living with him for six months. I'm worried about him. Morgan can be manipulative."

"You know her?"

"Only from the Internet."

He frowned. "What does she do?"

"Talks about fashion and gives make-up tutorials, mostly. Companies pay her to promote their products. Morgan's one of the most popular influencers out there. She's even followed by the Kardashians. She's like Taylor Swift, only instead of writing a sad song about her ex she changes her looks."

"Taylor Swift is misunderstood."

I stared at him. "You're a fan?"

"I've had my moments," he said, chuckling.

I reached for my handbag. "I just don't want Nick to become famous for being her ex and not a talented footballer. These things tend to stick."

"That's why you were there tonight?"

I nodded. "To show him photos, proof of the way she treats her men."

"She seemed serious about him from what I could see."

What the hell? He had spent all of ten seconds with her tonight.

He really did just think of me as the jilted lover.

I pulled the envelope out of my handbag. "When I ran into you, I was trying to give this back to Morgan."

"How did you end up with it?"

"It fell out of her purse." If Max was a lawyer, he'd know I was lying.

He took the envelope. "What is it?"

"I never looked inside." I assumed it was an invitation for a fancy event.

"It was good of you to try to return it."

I turned my head, hoping he hadn't noticed the guilty look on my face. "You're in London for Nick's birthday?"

"Yes, I can't believe he's turning twenty-five." Max tucked the envelope into his coat pocket. "I'll give this to him tomorrow. We're having a party—" He bit his lip as though he regretted revealing this bit of information.

"Will Morgan be there?"

"Honestly, I don't know."

"Tell him I said happy birthday."

"What do you like to do for fun, Daisy?"

"You don't have to do this."

"Do what?"

I looked out the window as we pulled up to a terraced house. "We're here."

"Let me see you to the door."

"That's very old-fashioned of you."

"I'm an old-fashioned guy."

"You're Nick's opposite then." As I stepped out, I realized how that sounded. I quickly met Max on the pavement. "That came out wrong."

"Trust me, I was like him once. All fun and foolishness."

"You're not fun now?"

"My clients need a man who appears reliable. Being sensible comes with the territory."

I smiled. "You must do something for entertainment when you aren't at work?"

"I dabble in pleasure."

My heart fluttered in my chest. I scurried on ahead down the pathway to hide the fact I was blushing again.

He joined me at the front door and waited patiently as my trembling hands fumbled for the keys in my handbag. Looking at him was half the problem. This man had me feeling all sorts of things and none of them were acceptable. He could have been my brother-in-law.

And he was so good looking, with a hint of charming, that it was hard to hate him completely. I liked knowing that Nick had a big brother to look out for him. Max would be there when things went wrong.

I pulled out my keys. "Here we are."

"You'll be all right?"

"Of course." I forced a smile. "Oh, Nick left something behind. Should I give it to you?"

"Sure."

I led him into the sparse sitting room and turned to watch his reaction. Max scanned the room as though trying to figure out what kind of life we'd lived here.

Had he visited the month before, Max would have seen how lovely I'd gotten the place. It had been a home. Now it was empty, other than the lone couch in front of us and a stack of boxes in the corner.

"Six months?" His tone sounded incredulous, as though he found it hard to believe I'd lived here with Nick that long.

"We were happy," I whispered.

"I never came here," he admitted. "Nick always met me at my hotel."

This made me feel even worse.

Nick had told me he felt like the black sheep of the family and that was why he kept me out of their way. But there had been something else going on. Maybe he thought I wasn't good enough for them? I knew his dad was the late David Banham, but he'd never made a big deal about it. Nick had always wanted to make it on his own.

"Are those his?" Max pointed to the boxes.

I shook my head. "They're mine."

He gave me a sympathetic look as I bent down to pick up the shoebox Nick had left behind.

I handed it to Max. "This is his."

He gave it a shake. "What's in here?"

"His pet mouse."

Max held it at arm's length. "What the fuck?"

I giggled. "Just joking."

"I'm just going to take a look." He lifted the lid. "Oh, it's Pelé!"

"Yes, his Brazilian toy."

"Pelé is not a toy. He's a figurine. Edson Arantes do Nascimento is the most talented goal scorer in the world."

The Brazilian football player was on a stand, posed at mid-kick with his leg in the air, his foot striking a ball.

"He's your favorite player?" I asked.

"Yes, even though he retired forty years ago, he's still a legend. This is a collector's item. I thought Nick would like it."

"Maybe you should keep it."

"Already have one in my office." Max looked incredulous. "Nick must have forgotten it."

"It was hidden behind a bunch of stuff." I tried to make up a reasonable excuse.

Max's eyes crinkled in a warm smile, as though he knew I was trying to save his feelings. He seemed like a man who could be compassionate…someone who'd be good in a crisis. My life was crumbling and here he was like a knight in shining armor, making sure I got home safely after my hellish night.

Don't kid yourself, he's making sure you're willing to leave here and disappear out of their lives.

"What's that look for, Daisy?" he asked.

"I have to go back to that bar tomorrow," I said. "I need to get my car before it gets a ticket."

He held out his hand. "Give me your keys?"

"Why?"

"I'll have Carl drive your Mini here. He'll drop the keys through the letterbox. Will that work?"

"Yes, thank you." I handed him my keyring.

"Well, Daisy, I should probably go."

I smiled. "Thank you for the lift home."

"Did Nick leave anything else behind?"

"Some clothes—they need washing."

"Let me take them."

"It's fine. I plan on cutting them into thousands of pieces."

His brow furrowed in concern.

"Or perhaps I'll set them on fire in the garden. Hopefully, I won't burn off my eyebrows."

"You have lovely eyebrows. Let's not risk burning them off. Let me take the clothes." Max rested Pelé on the arm of the couch. "Why are you moving out?"

"I have somewhere better to go."

He seemed to know I was avoiding the truth. "It'll work out, Daisy. It always does."

"I know." *Another lie.*

"Is that his laundry?" He pointed to the linen bag in the corner.

"You don't have to…"

Max strolled over and picked it up.

I hurried across the room and grabbed the other end. "Really, it's no problem."

He gave a tug. "It won't be a problem for me either."

I tugged back. "I insist on taking care of it."

Another tug from his end. "No, really."

"It's no bother." Another yank from me.

He pulled harder and the drawstring at the top of the bag loosened, spilling dirty clothes all over him as he staggered backwards into the wall. His face contorted into a mask of horror when he looked down to see a soiled sock stuck to his chest. The rest of the smelly laundry had landed on the hardwood floor.

I stared on, embarrassed. "I'm so sorry."

"Where's that HazMat team when you need them?" He peeled off the sock and threw it down in disgust. "That's going to take years of therapy to get over."

"You're in therapy?"

He laughed. "No, Daisy." He stood up straight and glared down at the offensive pile of clothes. "Maybe burning them in the garden isn't such a bad idea."

"It's all I have left of him."

My words surprised us both. Max's eyes filled with sympathy.

Keeping hold of Nick's unwashed uniforms had been a new low for me.

"You'll find someone special." Max shook his head. "I know that's the wrong thing to say in times like these, but it's true."

"Nick and I never got the chance to talk," I admitted. "He left and didn't give us a chance to work things out."

"Did you try calling him?"

"He's blocked my number."

"Why?"

"I might have drunk-called him."

"Don't worry." Max sighed. "It'll all work out. One day you'll find your happily ever after."

Silence filled the room as his words echoed in my mind like an impossible promise.

"I don't think that someone exists," I mumbled.

"How about I talk with Nick? Get him to call you."

"You'd do that for me?"

"It's a better idea than keeping his laundry here waiting for his sorry ass to pick it up. It might give you some closure. I'll tell you what, I'll take his clothes and you watch over Pelé."

I walked over to the figurine and picked it up. "I can do that."

He knelt and shoved the laundry back into the bag. "I'll be hosing myself down later."

"Thank you for being so nice."

He cinched the drawstring and hoisted the linen bag over his shoulder. "Being called 'nice' is a first," he said, giving me a wink. "That word has never been associated with me."

"Really?"

"No, I'm a criminal defense attorney. I eat people like you for breakfast."

"Innocent people?"

"No, I meant…" He shook off a thought.

Was he referring to me as the enemy because I was being *dealt* with by him, the family lawyer? The man who knew how to make the family's problems go away?

Max seemed to realize his mistake. "What I meant was—"

"It's fine." I gave a thin smile. "I'll show you out."

He followed me down the hallway. "This is difficult for everyone."

"It was lovely to meet you." At least it came off as polite.

"Feeling is mutual. I didn't catch your last name?"

"Whitby." I paused by the front door. "And how is this difficult for you?"

"I meant for all the parties involved."

"I move out tomorrow. Neither you nor Nick will ever see me again."

He followed that up with a nod of gratitude, and I decided asking for his last name was pointless.

With the front door open, I paused on the top step and let him edge by me.

"Max, will you give Nick a message?"

He stopped halfway down the path and turned to face me. "Of course."

"Tell him I hope it all works out with Manchester United."

His expression softened.

"Look out for your brother," I warned.

"Always."

There was still time to save Nick's reputation. Maybe I was just having difficulty moving on, but I couldn't shake this feeling that Morgan was going to be his greatest regret.

"Like you, I just want the best for him," I added.

"I believe that, Daisy."

I waggled Pelé's plastic arm and faked his voice. "Don't go accosting any more young ladies now, Max."

Max smiled at me and then looked down at the figurine in my hand. "Watch over Daisy for me, Pelé."

He turned away from me slowly and then strolled out the gate and over to his waiting car. He threw the dirty washing in the boot.

I returned to the sitting room and placed Pelé back in his box to keep him safe. For some reason, the room seemed even lonelier now.

Plopping down on the couch, I squeezed back tears, trying to come to terms with leaving my home, the place where I had finally felt like I belonged.

There were so many good memories here.

This breakup had happened so fast I'd not had time to process it. Now, with no TV and no Internet, I was left with nothing but my thoughts to torture me. I couldn't eat, couldn't read, couldn't think straight. My body ached as though I were sick. My heart kept cycling through all the stages of loss with no end in sight. Betrayal felt like a living, breathing entity that clung to my soul. This shadow would never lift.

Nick Banham had destroyed me.

Chapter
FOUR

Max

IT WAS EASY TO GET LOST IN SUMMERHOUSE, ONE OF THE largest private homes in London and home to my eccentric mum.

She and David had bought the sprawling Hampstead mansion years ago—thanks to Mum's stellar modeling career and my stepfather's iconic footballer status. The estate had a gym, an outdoor swimming pool, a grand ballroom, and a lush garden with a tennis court. The house was too big for a widow, but Mum seemed happy to remain here. It was where Nick had been raised. The place where all his foibles had formed.

Growing up in the shadow of two icons had clearly been a strain at times. So much so that he had kept his parents' identities a secret—and he'd not even told Daisy, apparently. But he'd been honest with Morgan. Maybe she really was The One for him.

For me, time spent with my stepfather was pretty fantastic for a boy obsessed with football. The man who became my second father had always been kind to me, welcoming me into the family with open arms. David never treated me differently than Nick.

Fond memories of the place washed over me as I joined the hundreds of guests milling around the vast garden. We were surrounded by towering outdoor heaters, which proved the hostess had money to burn—quite literally.

"Who the hell thought a garden party in the middle of winter was a good idea?" I mumbled to myself.

"I did." Nick's voice piped up from behind me.

I pivoted to look at him. "Why?"

"Morgan." He gave me a sheepish grin, admitting he was trying to impress her.

Not surprisingly, he'd dressed down in ripped jeans and a casual sweater—compared to me, who'd followed the formal dress code for *his* soirée. My three-piece suit felt stuffy as hell. Obviously this high-brow event was not only meant to appease Nick, guests and staff bowing down to him to impress his new girl, but to show me off as the eligible eldest son.

Nick looked me up and down. "Playing the part of gangster lawyer?"

I might have represented some shady characters in my time, but that was unfair. Anyway, this was a tailored Savile Row suit. A look he'd adopt after he'd worked through his bad boy phase.

"There are other ways to impress a woman," I chided.

"Morgan will be rubbing shoulders with the rich and famous. Least a boyfriend can do."

"To post on her Instagram?" I said. "Better ask the guests first. This is a private affair."

After a beat he studied me. "You recognize Morgan, then?"

I didn't have the heart to tell him that I only knew about her infamous status from Daisy. "Where did you go last night that was so important?" Having left me on the side of the road with his ex, no less.

"We went home."

I flashed him a wary glance. "How have you been, Nick?"

"Fine."

"How have you *really* been?"

He gave a shrug. "Just wish Dad was alive to see what I'm doing."

"He'd be proud of you. You know that."

"I miss him more every day. I still can't believe he's gone."

I felt that sting, too. "I'm here for you. Don't ever forget that."

"Thank you for coming all this way for me."

"Of course. How's Mum?"

He shook his head. "Same. She refuses to sell this place."

"Her best memories are here."

I could relate.

Aged ten, I'd scored my first goal in this very garden—only later realizing that David had let me because he was seriously that cool. Despite the circumstances of their marriage coming after the scandal of an affair, Mum really had seemed happier with David. My own dad had worked hard to establish his law firm back in São Paulo, building it up from nothing. Sadly, he'd done it all for her. A heartbreaking fact I tried not to think about.

I looked around at the partygoers. "I hate these things," I muttered.

"Want to grab a drink?" asked Nick.

He led me onto the patio where we each snagged a glass of champagne and huddled beneath a heater.

Nick raised his glass to toast a stranger across the lawn and then turned back to me. "So, how have you been?"

"This trip is the break I needed."

"Maybe we can spend some quality time together before you head back."

"I insist." Following his line of sight, I saw Morgan. She

was standing with a circle of women who looked like they'd huddled together to gossip. "Are those Morgan's friends?"

"Yeah."

"Anyone from your team here?"

"No, they're banned after what happened at the last party."

"Do I even want to know?"

He smirked. "Probably not."

"When do you hear about Manchester United?"

"Coach tells me I should find out in about two weeks."

"That's fantastic, Nick. I'll be here to help you celebrate." I studied his reaction. "You still want this, right?"

"More than anything. Only, I can't help but think they just want me because of who my dad was—not because I'm a bloody good player."

"Normal reaction," I assured him. "It could be Imposter Syndrome."

"I bet you don't get that."

"Being an attorney is in my blood." It wasn't strictly true, but he didn't need to see doubt right now. He needed someone strong to lean on. "You Brits are famous for being self-deprecating. It's in your DNA. You apologize for everything. Even if it's not your fault."

He grinned. "Yeah, sorry about that."

I smiled back at him and gave his shoulder a reassuring slap. "Football is not only a passion, it's a business too. Manchester United needs you. They only go after the best players."

"Hope you're right."

He was staring at his girlfriend again.

"How're things with Morgan? She seems…" I wanted to say shallow, but I didn't really know her, except for what I'd seen after an agonizing peek at her social media.

He shook his head in awe. "Look at her, she's gorgeous."

"She's very…"

"Glamorous, right?

"She is."

I waved at a passing waiter and snagged us both another glass of champagne, handing one off to Nick.

"She always has her hair and make-up done before she leaves home." He downed his drink in one. "She's in the public eye so has no choice, really."

My first thought went to Daisy, who didn't have those kinds of resources. But she was naturally pretty. She had an authenticity that was refreshing. A beguiling presence that my thoughts returned to all too easily.

"She's a savvy businesswoman, too." Nick remained focused on Morgan.

Surely there'd be less drama with Daisy, compared to a woman who was high maintenance. Morgan was posting pictures of Nick already and letting the world into their relationship. It felt like a bad idea to be so open.

I turned to face him. "I gave Daisy a lift home yesterday."

"Why?"

"When she ran into me her glasses got broken."

Mentioning to him that she'd gone and bumped into a lamppost afterward seemed bad form—Nick didn't need to know that detail.

His eyes turned dark. "Was she upset I left with Morgan?"

"She's taking it well. She wanted me to give you a message."

He set his empty glass down on a table. "I hadn't spoken with Daisy for weeks, and then she turned up at my party last night and was all weird."

"Weird how?"

"Like she was desperate to get my attention."

"Perhaps if you hadn't blocked her number."

He spun to face me. "Did she tell you that?"

"She's been trying to call you and can't get through."

Nick pulled his phone out of his back pocket and swiped the screen. "She's not blocked. I'll show you." His frown deepened and then he flashed a wary glance over to Morgan.

"She is blocked, then?" I said.

"That's strange. I'll unblock her."

"Give Daisy a call. It won't hurt to check on her."

He gave a reluctant nod. "I don't know why she came to see me last night."

"She's concerned for you."

"Why?"

I glanced over at Morgan. "How well do you know Morgan? I mean, really know her?"

"I'm living with her."

"It's all happening very fast, Nick."

"Max, you don't live here. You can't fly in and start bossing us all around."

"I'm just looking out for you."

He sighed. "What was Daisy's message?"

"She wished you a happy birthday." I rubbed my brow, wondering how much I should say. "And best of luck for getting into Manchester United."

"She needs to move on."

"You're ready for that? I mean, you were living together."

"Yes, of course I'm ready. We're over."

"I glanced at Morgan's Instagram page earlier."

"She has over a million followers." He shook his head. "Amazing."

"Nick, Morgan does seem to have had a lot of boyfriends."

"What the fuck? Did that come from Daisy?"

"No, I just scrolled down Morgan's profile page and there they were."

The comments I'd seen beneath their photos were brutal.

Nick looked pissed off. "Can't you just be happy for me, please?"

It was my turn to sigh. "If you're truly happy that's good enough for me."

"What else did you and Daisy talk about?"

"Nothing, really. You were together for six months. I'm surprised you never introduced us."

"Mum has very high standards," he said. "I didn't need her on my case."

"How do you mean?"

"Daisy works in a shop."

"You can't be serious, Nick!"

"Mum likes Morgan. They're both into fashion."

This was another reason I had to be more involved in his life. He was clearly making questionable decisions. His father had hailed from the north of England, and a more down to earth and easy-going man couldn't have been found. David would have balked at any kind of snobbery from his son.

"Look, Daisy's sweet," Nick admitted. "But she's not as daring and exciting as Morgan."

"She's younger, too."

"Oh, shit, there's Mum."

"It's your party! She arranged it."

He flashed me a wary look. "I don't want her giving me a hard time for wearing jeans."

At least it would take the heat off me.

"When I dropped Daisy off yesterday, she gave me the clothes you left behind. It's just uniforms." *Along with your socks, spawned from hell.* "I put them in the laundry."

"You didn't need to worry about that. I have uniforms at Morgan's."

I frowned at him. "Who's helping Daisy move?"

"Don't know."

"Did she book movers?"

"She can't really afford that."

"Does she have a family member who can help? A brother, or…?"

Nick held my gaze for a long time. "He died."

"Her brother? When?"

"Six months ago."

"Before or after your dad passed?"

"Does it matter?" he snapped.

"She's moving out of the house you both lived in, with no one to help her?"

"I'm sure her aunt will help her out."

I paused the conversation long enough to return Mum's wave. She was in her element, lording over a group of elites and holding court like a true icon of style—a former fashion model that still graced the covers of magazines. A touch of cosmetic surgery here and there had helped maintain her fiery beauty. She'd been hailed as Brazil's Grace Kelly once, and even now her elegance made her the most beautiful woman here.

"Does Daisy have somewhere decent to move to?" I asked.

"I assume so." Nick turned to face me again. "It's unlike you to care about strangers."

"I'm going soft in my old age."

He chuckled. "You're thirty-three."

And looking every year of it… I was burned out from work and only now realizing it. I'd been driven to succeed over the last few years and rarely had time to spend with family. And Mum needed me now, so being here was the best decision I'd made in a while.

"Daisy asked me to return this." I reached into my jacket pocket and pulled out the gold envelope she'd given me.

"It's Morgan's." He gave a nod in her direction. "We can't make the event. It conflicts with her schedule. Morgan has a Vanity Fair photo session instead."

I turned it over in my hand. "What's the invite for?"

We were interrupted as Mum rushed towards us, the crowd parting for her like Moses separating the Red Sea.

"Darling, you're here!" Her Portuguese accent had faded slightly through the years, but the warmth of her demeanor was a constant in our lives.

"You look wonderful, as always." I kissed her left cheek and then the right.

Gillian Banham looked quite regal and glamorous in her silver gown, with her quaffed blonde hair suspended in a sea of hairspray and diamonds shimmering at her throat.

Her cold hands cupped my face. "*Meu lindo garoto. Tão precioso.* You look more like your father each time I see you." She pulled back. "Why didn't you shave? Is this a new look?"

"I'm on vacation," I replied, defending myself.

"I suppose you'll do," she chided. "There's someone here I want you to meet." She took my hand. "Lucia is lovely. Her father owns a newspaper."

"Oh, God," I muttered.

"Sorry?" she asked, glancing over at me.

I smiled. "Oh, good."

She winked. "Help your mother help you, Maximus." She

was the only one who called me that. "Dating a debutant will win you points."

Turning, I offered the envelope back to Nick along with a look that begged for him to save me. Like arranging for a helicopter to arrive and throw down a rope, hoisting me to freedom—our private joke during these kinds of events.

"Keep it," said Nick, refusing the envelope. "You should accept the invite. Might meet someone nice." He mimicked our mother by winking at me.

My face twisted in misery, but I hid my frustration when I turned away from him.

Mum and I merged into a crowd of flowery perfume-drenched debutants who were all pretty in their own way…a reflection of horsey parents and good living.

"This is my son," announced Gillian to the aristocratic circle, as they munched on hors d'oeuvres. "He's the highest paid lawyer in Brazil. He defends rascals."

I cringed and stared at the well-manicured lawn beneath my feet. There came the expected coo of admiration, ironically followed by my internal screaming.

"I've been boasting about how big you are," announced Mum.

With my best poker face, I hid my embarrassment and went with my tried and tested expression of friendly with a dash of nonchalance. Leaning back, I snagged another glass of champagne off a tray and raised it high. "To the British empire!"

Everyone took me seriously and raised their glasses, too.

The thought crossed my mind that if Daisy were here, she'd be the one I'd gravitate to…someone who came across as authentic, genuine. A woman I could approve of my brother dating.

But Daisy was gone from our lives. A rare beauty in a sea of uncertainty, lost to our history—a victim of my brother's upbringing, growing up in the shadow of icons. He'd not seen Daisy's worth because he'd been blinded by superficiality. It made me sad for him. Sad for them both, really.

From behind me, I heard someone faking the sound of spinning chopper blades. I turned to see Nick, who walked by us with a grin, totally enjoying my torment.

Chapter
FIVE

Daisy

YESTERDAY, I'D GOTTEN A TEXT FROM NICK. IT WAS the message I'd been holding out for. He was coming home to help me move. I'd get to see him. Maybe, if he was willing, he'd talk about what went wrong.

Maybe he'll change his mind.

I'd have the chance to share my concerns, which now burned ever brighter. Last night, Morgan had posted an image of them doing shots at a party. With a football match coming up, Nick shouldn't be drinking.

Shivering on the couch, I realized having the electricity turned off the morning before I was to move out was stupid. Not that I'd been thinking clearly lately. Even with my coat on the chill was unbearable.

Six weeks ago, Nick had returned to collect his things. The memory of watching him walk out the door still hurt like hell. Having to leave our home was going to destroy me all over again. My throat tightened at the thought of locking that door and never coming back.

Be brave.

Let him see how calm you are. How strong.

I still couldn't believe that Morgan wasn't just a fling. I loved him with all my heart, and he'd loved me right back—or so I'd believed. He'd certainly made me feel that what we'd had was real.

All our "firsts" had been here. Our first time cooking together. The first time we'd taken a bubble bath together. The first time I'd felt comfortable peeing in front of someone else. Those were just the highlights. We'd experienced more laughter than I'd believed possible.

We'd been happy.

Even with all the grief that wove itself between us—me grieving for my brother and Nick for his dad—we'd fought for days when that crushing sense of loss wasn't so stifling.

I pushed those thoughts away, trying not to make myself feel worse, and rubbed my stomach to soothe the ache.

Looking around, I couldn't fight off the memories. We'd decorated our place with carefully chosen pieces we'd bought from antique stores. A few remained scattered around the house. They reminded me of another time when laughter had rippled through this home.

Nick had gotten too close to me and it had scared him away.

I recalled other days on lazy weekends when we'd curled up on this very sofa together with mugs of piping hot cocoa. We'd watched football, sitting through re-runs of his matches. Nick had shown me the moves he'd made that marked him as a player to watch. Even after the millionth time of seeing him kick a goalie, I'd cooed with pride. His obsession had become mine.

We'd danced in this room like we hadn't had a care in the world. There had been passion-filled, sleepless nights.

I'd not seen this coming. This crushing of my life.

Morgan would never respect his dream like I had. She'd never be willing to sacrifice their time together to allow him to attend games that took him out of town.

I'd find a way to tell him this.

The sound of a truck pulling up out front broke the quiet. Psyching myself up to face Nick, I headed down the hallway. Taking a deep breath to calm myself, I reached for the door handle.

Forcing a bright smile, I yanked open the door.

I'd forgotten how tall Max was. How handsome.

I finally exhaled. "It's you."

"It's me," he said, giving me a dazzling smile.

I peered around his shoulder for Nick.

"I offered to help you move," he said. "Nick told you, right?"

"I thought it was going to be him."

Disappointment squeezed my heart. This had felt like my last chance to save us.

"Will I do?" Max waggled his eyebrows, and then turned and pointed. "I hired a truck."

I motioned for him to come inside. "Thank you for being here. I...don't actually have that much."

Max looked around the living room. "This is it?"

This was it—five cardboard boxes and two suitcases.

He looked concerned. "What's happening to your furniture?"

"Nick is going to collect the rest. I thought he'd be doing that today."

"You're not keeping it?"

"I have no room."

"Where are you moving to?"

"My aunt's place." *For now.*

He nodded. "Ready?"

"Ready as I'll ever be." I tried to sound cheery.

We stepped outside and he directed the movers to come in, and then turned to face me. "Why don't I drive your car so you can relax? Moving can be stressful. Carl will follow us."

"He won't mind?"

"Of course not."

"Tell him I'll be gentle."

"How do you mean?"

"The last time I got close to you he overreacted."

He tipped my chin up. "I can handle you, Daisy."

"I'd like that." I tried to hide my embarrassment.

My stomach felt like it was filling up with butterflies.

Max smiled. "It's the least I can do."

He pivoted and walked toward the truck.

The upbeat movers seemed happily surprised by the lack of items they had to carry out of the place. They stacked the boxes and suitcases into the back of their ginormous truck—so few they looked ridiculous on their own in there.

Within a few minutes, I'd locked up the house and handed over the door keys to Max.

I hesitated on the walkway, looking up at our former home.

My insides turned to jelly as I replayed all the things I could have done to prevent this from happening. Our relationship had always seemed easy, and maybe that was where it had gone wrong. It had felt as natural as breathing, and we'd always felt safe. *I'd* always felt safe.

My feet wanted to carry me back inside and return somehow to that life of happiness. I wanted to wake up from this nightmare.

Max looked at me with concern.

I continued down the pathway, holding my breath until what felt like a tidal wave of loss no longer paralyzed me. With a fake smile, I wrote down my aunt's address and gave it to the truck driver.

"You don't have to stay," I told Max. "The truck is more than enough."

"It's fine."

My voice cracked with emotion. "Nick sent you to make sure I left?"

"I wanted to be here."

"Everyone dreads moving day." I looked at him, surprised. "No one volunteers for this."

He smiled. "Well, it's not like I've had to lift anything."

"There're plenty of other things you could be doing."

"You saved me from having afternoon tea with my mother and her friends. Quite frankly, I owe you."

I relented and led the way over to my Mini Cooper, clicking the doors open.

Before Max got into the car, he looked back at the house. "You were good for Nick, Daisy, no matter what else has happened."

"You really believe that?"

"After his dad died, you were like an anchor in a storm for him."

His words sent regret through me, because this was how I felt, too. Yet nothing could be done about it. It was like watching someone you love drive on the wrong side of the road. Yes, they'd hurt you, but the mistake they were making somehow hurt more.

Max climbed into the driver's seat of my Mini, shaking his head in amusement at how cramped it was as he adjusted the seat back to accommodate his long legs. I sat beside him, pointing out where the indicators were.

With my mind spiraling and being so distracted, I was relieved that he had offered to drive. Had I been alone, I'd have sobbed all the way to Richmond and probably crashed on the way. With Max throwing me reassuring glances, I was able to hold back my emotions and not embarrass myself.

"You don't mind driving on the other side of the road?" I asked, simply trying to make conversation.

Max gave me a sexy smile. "I'm versatile."

This forbidden crush I was developing was making me feel guilty. It was the way his hands gripped the steering wheel, the way he shifted the gears with confidence. Not to mention his gorgeous profile. I suspected he knew I was stealing glances.

Considering Max was used to driving on the right, he was handling the traffic well—like someone who lived here. Yet he lived a million miles away.

"So…you and Nick have the same mum?" I asked.

He nodded. "Yes, her name is Gillian."

"How well do you and Nick get along?'

"The older we get, the easier it gets. I was eight and living in São Paulo when Nick was born."

"That must have been hard. Having your mum here, I mean."

"It is what it is."

I wanted to say that he must have missed her a lot, but I didn't want to bring us both down.

I turned to him. "Did Nick say why he couldn't make it?"

Max threw me a glance. "He has a meeting with a coach from Manchester United."

That actually made me feel a little better. "Oh, he couldn't miss that."

"Thank you for understanding, Daisy."

"I'm keeping my eyes, fingers and toes crossed for him."

Nick's dream was coming true. He'd sacrificed so much along the way, attending every after-school soccer training day. His talent had been spotted young when he'd played in the little leagues—though his famous father had probably helped shine a spotlight on him. Nick's focus on the sport had intensified to an obsession when he'd finally believed in his own talent.

His entire life was football.

As a senior player, he was being offered the chance of a lifetime—to play for Manchester United. The money would be amazing, but that had never been Nick's motivation. It had always been the game. The chance to prove he had what it took to play in the premier leagues. To join the same team that had made his dad an icon.

I'd been there to help Nick get to this point, supporting him any way I could. But now I'd not be able to see him cross the finish line and achieve his dream. That realization stung because it had been my dream, too.

"Want to talk about it?" asked Max.

"I'm fine."

"I get it. I've been there." He saw my look of disbelief. "I used to be geeky in college. I was the student who always got straight A's. I loved hanging out in the library. Always had my head in a book. This, I discovered, wasn't enough to keep her."

"Keep who?"

"The prettiest girl in school."

"What happened?"

"She broke my heart. Ruined me for all other girls."

"There must have been someone else?" My heart stuttered as I waited for his response.

"I run a busy law firm. I'm unable to devote the kind of attention that a serious relationship needs to flourish. But I do date, obviously."

"Obviously."

He laughed at my expression. "You're so cute."

I let my breath out slowly, while trying to hide the way he made me react—I felt all flushed and giddy. He saw me as his brother's ex. That was never going to change.

"Don't worry about Nick and Manchester United," he said. "He's got this."

"He's making it happen."

"Focus on you, Daisy." He reached over and rested his hand on mine.

I bit my lower lip, trying to suppress a wistful sigh and the urge to rest my head back and just stare at him.

He withdrew his hand and the loss of his touch sent a chill over my entire body. I clutched my hands together to warm them.

"Nick told me you work in a shop?"

"Harvey Nichols."

"I bet you're good at your job."

There it was…that hint that a shop girl wasn't good enough for his family.

I shrugged, not wanting him to know that being around fashion made me happy. Or that I had a thing for shop window displays. Or, that in another life, I'd not have left Uni and finished that degree in art and design. My job at Harvey Nichols was to help shoppers find that one special gown, and I allowed myself to live vicariously through them.

Up ahead, the white moving truck pulled up to my aunt's townhouse. We parked behind it. In the wing mirror, I could see that Carl was right behind us. Soon, Max would be in the back of that SUV, driving away from me forever.

My last link to Nick would be gone.

I tried to undo my seatbelt with trembling hands, and

Max reached over and helped me get it unfastened. His fingers lingered on mine in a comforting gesture, as though he knew how difficult this moment was for me.

Aunt Barbara rushed out to greet us, waving at me with enthusiasm. When I climbed out of the car, she hurried over and wrapped her arms around me in a tight hug.

To many, Aunty seemed eccentric, especially due to the way she dressed in bright blouses and flowing skirts—as though she had just arrived from the seventies in all its billowy, flowery glory.

She pivoted to face Max, and gave him a hug, too. "You're a nice strong man, aren't you?" she said.

I tried not to cringe, even as Max returned the hug to appease her.

"He's Nick's brother," I explained.

"Nick couldn't make it?" she asked sourly.

"No, but he sent Max to help instead." I widened my eyes at her so she wouldn't make a scene. "Which is nice."

She looked annoyed, but didn't say anything.

"Max even drove me here," I added.

"There is chivalry left in the world." She gave his arm a squeeze. "Oh, you are firm, aren't you?"

I forced a smile, flinching from embarrassment, but Max looked amused.

"I'm delighted to make your acquaintance. I'm Max Marquis."

It was my first time hearing his last name and it sounded dreamy.

"Barbara Rowling." My aunt's face lit up. "Obviously not related to *that* Rowling or I'd be rich."

It was funny seeing my aunt flustered. It was good to know that Max had this effect on other people and not just me.

"I'll put the kettle on," she said, and then looked at me. "I've put you in the spare room, Daisy. You know the one."

"Thank you—I love that room. But it's only for a while."

"It's company for me," she said.

Barbara directed the movers to carry my belongings up the staircase to the top floor of her two-story house. It wouldn't take them long to finish.

I was relieved my aunt knew better than to ask how I was doing in front of other people. Undoubtedly she could see I was on the verge of tears.

Max and I followed her into the front hallway.

"I have a client here at the moment." She nodded toward a back room. "Okay for me to finish up with them?"

"Yes, of course," I said. "Sorry my timing was off."

"Nonsense," she reassured me. "You are always welcome in my home, Daisy." She looked back at Max with a curious expression and then gave me a bright smile before walking away.

I started up the staircase toward the room that would be mine. At least until I had saved up enough for a deposit to rent a flat.

Max reappeared at my bedroom door. "I think that's it."

"I need to tip them," I said.

"All taken care of." Max sat on the bed beside me.

Following his gaze around the room, I looked at the familiar chintzy wallpaper and old-fashioned curtains. I absolutely loved it.

Max looked concerned. "Are you sure you're going to be fine here?"

"It's my home away from home."

"Where do your parents live?"

"Scotland. They run a bed and breakfast on the Isle of Harris."

They had moved up there to avoid being reminded of the worst day of their lives. They kept busy, hosting tourists in their seaside home. I was glad they weren't around to see how badly I'd messed up my life.

Max reached into his pocket and withdrew my car keys. He set them on the bedside table. "Your aunt seems nice. What does she do?"

"She's a fortune teller."

He blinked in disbelief.

"A high-end one," I added. "She works from home and has an office at Selfridges."

"Does she ever read your tea leaves?"

"She read mine two months ago. Her expression told me everything I didn't want to know."

"That you and Nick…?"

"I'm guessing she saw our breakup."

"She didn't say anything?"

"No, she just brought out the lemon cake. It was like she was trying to sweeten the truth." To think I'd once liked lemon cake, too. "Will you let Nick know where I am?"

"Daisy, I want you to focus on you."

There wasn't much to focus on in my life, not really. I just went to work and then came straight home.

But I nodded anyway.

He leaned forward. "These changes in life, the ones that come at you fast, out of nowhere, sometimes it's the universe sending you in a new direction. Sending you on to something better."

"To someone better than Nick?" There would never be anyone else like him.

"Someone different."

I sighed. "Do you want to stay for tea?"

49

"Thank you, but I have to go."

I tried to swallow the lump in my throat. "Look out for Nick."

"You know I will."

"And…thank you for today."

He rose to leave, and the mattress shifted on my single bed. There was only one pillow—only one was needed.

"It's time to move on," he said softly.

"I'll be fine."

"Yes. Yes, you will."

He headed for the bedroom door.

"Wait!" I leaned over one of the boxes and ripped up the sealing tape. Reaching in, I pulled out a shoebox and opened the lid to show Max what lay inside. "Don't forget Pelé."

Max looked happy to see him. "You keep him. Unless…"

"Unless?"

"He reminds you too much of…"

I glanced down at Pelé. "He reminds me of you."

Max's gaze focused on me, and I saw uncertainty in his eyes.

"I'll keep him in the box," I added quickly.

"Daisy, I mean this in the best kind of way…"

I nodded. "No more turning up at inconvenient times."

His expression softened with relief. "Good. We wouldn't want to have to put a restraining order on you, Miss Whitby."

My face blanched.

"Daisy, that was a joke."

Feeling awkward, I averted my gaze so I wouldn't have to look at him.

He stepped forward and touched my face, forcing me to look up at him as he traced his thumb along my bottom lip. "Take care of yourself, Daisy Whitby."

I peered up at the man too tall to kiss, and stared into his deep brown eyes, letting myself draw strength from his kindness.

He pivoted and hurried out of the room.

I listened to his footsteps as he rushed down the stairs—he obviously couldn't wait to leave. When I heard the sound of the front door closing, I collapsed on my bed and curled into a ball, just longing for this day to be over.

Chapter
SIX

Daisy

THIS WAS PROBABLY AGAINST THE HARVEY NICHOLS staff policy—squishing my nose up against the outside showroom window and leaving a smudge. It was my usual pose when I left work, since I could never resist peering through the window at the beautiful evening gown on display.

Gold braiding and twinkling crystals adorned a fitted bodice, below which hung a delicate, wispy chiffon skirt.

God, how I love that dress.

I let out a sigh and my breath steamed a patch of glass. The gown represented hope. The promise of a life of glamour and excitement—that perhaps, by some miracle, a fairy Godmother would appear and give me the confidence to be more than what I'd always been.

The girl next door who rarely left the house.

My days at work kept me busy helping others...watching their faces light up with happiness when they tried on a dress. But it wasn't all fairy dust and contented customers. Now and again, a snobby client came into the store, one of the stuck-up types. To them, I was the invisible shop girl whose only job was to fetch their size and then help them in and out of it. That's how I'd learned to master a fake smile.

I turned my back on the display window and walked away, finally rising from my daydreaming to notice the sounds of traffic and pedestrians surrounding me, the noise nudging me home so that I could escape.

The Knightsbridge Tube was my usual way back home to Richmond. My mind felt as numb as my hands in the bitter cold, despite my parka and gloves. Once on the Tube, I buried my face in the *Vogue* magazine I'd found discarded in the coffee room, flipping through pages filled with women who looked incredible, having found happiness in a handbag. It reminded me of Morgan's Instagram page.

A moment later, I did myself a favor and deleted the Instagram app off my phone. This was the kindest thing I could do for myself. An act of selfcare that might well save my sanity.

As soon as I made it home, I went straight to my bedroom.

I lay on my single bed, flipping through all the channels on the TV, not really watching anything. I tried not to think about what I could have done to prevent my life from going tits-up.

Competing with someone like Morgan was impossible. She was larger than life, and it hurt like hell knowing that Nick had spent time with her while we'd been together.

It was devastating to realize that my love had never been enough for him.

A knock at the door had me pushing PAUSE on the remote.

Barbara came in and glanced at the TV screen. "How are you, love?"

"Fine."

She looked concerned. "You're in your PJs already?"

"They're comfy."

"Well, you have a visitor." She spoke the words as though offering me hope and encouragement.

"Nick?"

"No, it's that handsome young man who helped you move."

I shot up. "He's here?"

"In the sitting room," she said with a nod. "Do you want me to send him away?"

A rush of excitement made me giddy. "No, I'll be right down."

Maybe Max had come to give me a message from Nick.

Within minutes, I'd dressed in jeans and a T-shirt and had pulled my hair up into a ponytail. Feeling decent enough to face Max, I headed downstairs with my heart racing and my spirits rising.

Max was sitting on the sofa, balancing a small teacup on his knee. His worried stare was fixed on Auntie's new Corgi, who was ensconced right next to him.

He'd removed his coat to tolerate the central heating— Barbara had the place as hot as a furnace.

I let my gaze take in his ripped jeans, stretching tightly over his thighs, and the J. Crew jumper that fit him so well. His thick, raven hair was the kind a girl wouldn't be able to resist running her fingers through. I imagined kissing the stubble on his rugged jaw.

He turned to look at me, a tender expression in his eyes. "Hey, Daisy."

His voice caused a shiver to run down my spine. I walked farther into the room.

"I see you've met Wilma, then," I said.

He glanced at the Corgi. "She's not scary at all."

"I think she likes you."

"How can you tell?"

"You're still alive."

He threw his head back and laughed. His reaction made me crack a smile, too.

"Wilma has that whole staring competition thing going on," said Max, reaching out to scratch her head. "You win, girl."

Wilma wagged her tale and buried her nose in his side as he continued to rub her.

"How are you?" he asked, his tone laced with concern.

"Hanging in there. Is everything okay with Nick?"

He hesitated. "Yes, of course."

"Um…" *Then why are you here?*

He pushed to his feet and set his teacup on the coffee table. "Grab your coat."

"I'm…a little busy right now."

"I need your help with something, Daisy."

My eyes widened in surprise. "What's going on?"

"It's best if I show you."

Within minutes, he'd helped me into my coat and I'd been shuffled out of the house into the cold. Max opened the passenger side door on a flashy silver Tesla.

"Where's your bodyguard?" I asked.

He frowned. "Carl believes I'm at the Waldorf."

"You lied to him?"

"I gave him the day off."

His frown deepened as he studied me. "Thought you and I should have some privacy. Is that okay?"

Instead of answering, I climbed into the front passenger seat, sinking into the cream-colored leather. "Where are we going?"

Max got in and pushed a button. Heat blasted over us. "You're going to approve."

"Why do you need my help?"

"You'll see."

Warmth curled around my bum—the seat was heated. We were driving through London in the lap of luxury, but it would have been easy to look at Max and forget everything. He was that alluring. The smile he gave me when he sensed I was staring his way was so damn sexy. It made my insides curl with pleasure.

My face broke into a grin...

It was turning out to be the best day ever since my life imploded. Right up until Max stopped in front of Sunny's, my optometrist. Deflated, I realized he was just trying to shake off the guilt he felt for breaking my glasses.

"Your aunt told me this is where you got your last pair." He gave me a satisfied smile. "Your prescription will be on record, I imagine."

"You're buying me..." I stated the obvious, shaking my head.

"It's the right thing to do."

"But it's completely unnecessary."

"I insist, Daisy. You were trying to catch up with Nick when I got in your way."

"You left out the harassment bit."

"Carl ushered you aside..."

"Ushered?"

"It's our story and we're sticking to it," he said, giving me a wink.

I let out a sigh.

"This should make us even." He looked at me expectantly, waiting for me to cooperate.

I fought back my disappointment. At least I'd have new glasses.

Inside the store, Max walked along the aisles ahead of me perusing the collection. He lifted a pair of sunglasses off the display case and tried them on, turning to see my reaction. He put them back and continued to move around the store, cheerfully picking up spectacles to examine them.

He found a pair of sunglasses with blacked out frames and put them on. He rocked the look. "Olá!"

"Are you going to get them?"

Max looked surprised as he took them off. "No, we're here for you."

I was still feeling some guilt over the secret crush I had on him—though I would never risk my connection to Nick. Deep down I held on to the hope we would one day reconcile. But Max was charismatic and being with him made my evening bearable.

Glancing over at the shop assistant, I saw I wasn't the only one ogling the cutie studying the display of fashionable eyewear. Max was now over in the designer section, viewing the selection with interest.

I hurried over. "These are very expensive."

Max studied the price tag. "These are okay."

"Those over there are on sale." I pointed toward the other end of the store.

He narrowed his focus on the bargains. "I can't be seen with you if you wear any of those."

"That section is where I got my last pair!"

Max chuckled, then lifted a pair of fancy looking frames off the panel and handed them over. "Try these."

Blinking up at him, I let him ease the new frames on my face, his warm fingers trailing over my cheeks.

He took a step back and studied me. "No."

"Why?" I liked the way they looked.

But I let Max remove them. He put them back and chose another pair, sliding them onto my face. "Look in the mirror."

I turned and studied my reflection, loving how the delicate frames complemented my face and made me look pretty. Max rested his hands on my shoulders and turned me around to face him. His eyes were so easy to fall into, but my gaze dropped to his mouth.

And my surroundings slipped away…

Dazzled by him, I was unable to stop staring, and I felt my cheeks blaze with heat at my failure to tear my gaze away.

A ghost of a smile curled Max's lips. "Beautiful," he said, as though I confounded him.

He stepped closer and reached around to pull out my hair tie, releasing my ponytail. Locks tumbled over my shoulders. Gently, he tucked a loose strand of hair behind my ear, sending a shiver through me.

Looking up at him made me feel protected, as though all he had to do was wrap his arms around me and everything would be all right again.

I heard a sigh, and it was mine, full of wonder as both of us remained suspended in a moment seemingly meant for us.

"Let me know if you need any help!" the shop girl piped up.

She broke the spell and we stepped away from each other self-consciously.

Max threw a nod her way. "I was making sure they go with her hair." He faced me again. "What do you think?"

I spun to look in the mirror and caught my surprised expression—his comment had made my insides feel warm and fuzzy.

"They make your eyes pop." He grinned at me. "Like them?"

"I love them." This was the kind of excitement usually reserved for something a lot bigger than buying glasses. I couldn't deny how much I loved being around Max.

His soul was on fire for life—he was a person willing to embrace happiness and share it.

"I found the one!" he said, and then quickly corrected himself. "The right glasses, I mean." Max took them out of my hands and walked over to the counter. "I'd like to buy these, please, for Daisy Whitby. Her prescription should be on file."

Minutes later, we headed out of the shop after receiving the promise that I could pick them up tomorrow.

Max drove me home and parked outside the house. He sat for a moment, tapping the steering wheel as though he wasn't ready to say goodbye just yet.

"Thank you, Max." I reached for the door handle.

"I have something for you." He reached into his coat pocket and pulled out a folded piece of paper.

I took it from him, and realized it was a check. "What's this for?"

"You helped pay the mortgage."

"This is more than I paid." In fact, it was more money than I could make in years.

"It'll be a nice deposit on a flat when you're ready."

My lips trembled at what this meant; what he really thought of me.

"You want more?" He reached into his coat again.

"No!"

My relationship had a number on it. No, that wasn't it. The shopping trip to buy new glasses had been a ruse. Max had merely waited for me to let down my guard so he could pay me to disappear.

I ripped the check into tiny pieces, throwing it over him

like confetti. It landed in his hair and sprinkled his shoulders and coat.

He didn't blink. "Well, that didn't go as expected."

"I don't want it." I drew in a sharp breath. "I just want Nick to be safe."

Max rolled his eyes. "For God's sake, Daisy. He's fine."

Whipping out my phone, I brought up the Instagram app and Morgan's page, turning the screen so he could see the latest photo she'd posted.

He kept his gaze on me instead. "Daisy, you need to delete Instagram off your phone."

"I did." Okay, that sounded batshit crazy. "Then I went and reinstalled it." *Because someone has to watch out for your brother.*

Max looked down at the photo and flinched. "Whoa, what is that?"

"That's your brother's bum. Morgan had him do a moony out of a limo window."

Max shook his head, his hands scraping his face in exasperation. "That's one for National Geographic."

"Now do you see?" I snapped.

"Can't un-see it."

"This is not funny."

"Don't give Morgan the pleasure of seeing you following her on there." He sounded annoyed. "She'll only taunt you with worse photos."

"Don't you see? She's taunting everyone."

"Daisy, you need to move on," he said.

"I don't think I can."

Max reached into his inner pocket and pulled out a gold envelope. "You probably won't be interested in this, then."

My cheeks burned as I stared at the same envelope I'd pinched from Morgan's purse.

"It's an invitation," he said, passing it to me. "Thought you might like to go."

"Not sure I should." Though curiosity had me wanting to know what event it was for.

"Why not?"

"It's not meant for me."

He looked away. "All you have to do is turn up. Have fun."

Fun?

I'd given up on fun. My fingers traced along the broken edge of the envelope. Reluctantly, I shoved it into my handbag. This was karma reminding me of my wayward behavior at Isobel's.

Getting those new glasses was a sign my connection with Nick's family was over. Max had merely ensured there'd be no hard feelings. It meant I'd be wearing evidence of their pity. They could keep their money.

Max climbed out of the Tesla and it was impossible for me to drag my gaze away from him as he strolled with confidence around the front of the car. He seemed unaffected by our tension-fueled conversation. Whatever chemistry we'd had back at the optometrist had seemingly evaporated into thin air.

My crush on Max had morphed into feelings of doubt and humiliation.

He opened my car door and helped me climb out onto the pavement.

We shared an awkward hug. My face squished against his firm chest in an annoyingly perfect fit as he held me there, as though he were forcing an apology on me.

He suddenly broke away from me and headed around to the other side of his car without looking back. Because I was firmly in the history zone to him.

I stood on the curbside with my heart still racing and watched Max pull into traffic. Remembering the way his cologne made my nipples bead with pleasure caused fury to surge through me.

It turned out that hating Max Marquis was easy. He was an arrogant bastard with a pretty face. His full lips had a magnetic pull that could make you believe all your problems would go away with just one kiss.

I pulled the invitation out of my purse and peeled open the envelope.

The Dare Club
Fun events to bring you closer to a new you.
7 PM
The Waldorf Hotel
Upper Floor Bar
Casual Attire.

Well, this was stupid and so not me.

The event was tomorrow night.

I was not having *anything* to do with this crappy idea. I'd never been the daring sort before and I had no interest in being that kind of girl now. This invite was going in the trash bin.

Max obviously had no idea what he'd given me.

Once inside the house, I paused at the bottom of the staircase. The invite had been addressed to Morgan because she was daring. She was fun. She was everything a man could want in a woman.

You know what…

Morgan wasn't the only one who had an Instagram page. I had one, too. And Nick still followed my account. Posting a snapshot of me at a Dare Club might get his attention. All I needed to do was tweak his curiosity by letting him see I was attending the event, making me look spontaneous—even if I remained on the sidelines.

No daring deeds required.

Chapter
SEVEN

Daisy

RIDING THE LIFT TO THE TOP FLOOR OF THE WALDORF Hotel, I caught a glimpse of my reflection in the walled mirror. I looked pretty in my new glasses. Even if they were the result of Max Marquis' evil meddling—his way of getting me to let my guard down so he could pay me to go away.

Shortly before leaving home, I had changed my outfit for the third time. Now I had on jeans and a white blouse. I'd also added some delicate silver jewelry to round out my casual I-haven't-really-tried look.

I almost bit through my lip at the thought that I would soon be ready to post photos of me dabbling in the spontaneous—or pretending to, anyway.

Stepping out of the lift, I hurried toward the small crowd gathered near the bar. A young man wearing a *Dare Club* T-shirt was talking to a group of people, all eager-looking adventurers. The mood was as ebullient as you'd expect it to be, coming from a bunch of losers like me.

"Hi, there, I'm Ted," he greeted me. "I'm your Dare Club guide."

I gave him a nervous smile. "Daisy."

"We're thrilled you decided to join us."

Join is a strong word.

He looked down at the envelope I was holding out, his expression one of confusion. "You signed up online?"

"I just have this," I said, tucking the envelope back in my handbag.

"What's your last name?"

"Whitby."

Ted glanced at his clipboard. "Yeah, I have you down."

He turned to address the group. "Welcome to my Ted talk! I'm assuming everyone created a Last Will and Testament?"

Ted was a right comedian.

He laughed raucously. "Welcome to the Dare Club! Designed for people who want to challenge themselves and push past their personal boundaries. Previous members have gained the courage to apply for that promotion, or ask for that pay rise—and they've gotten it. There are so many benefits to joining us! We help you stretch yourself beyond what you believe you're capable of achieving. Over the next three weeks, you'll push yourselves to the limit. This is going to be the most fun you've ever experienced. Can I hear a hurrah?!"

"Hurrah," I said weakly and then shot up my arm. "I have a question."

"Sure, Daisy."

"For tonight only, can I watch? If that's all right? See if I like it?"

He looked amused. "Good one. *No.*"

We were each handed a badge. I scribbled my name on mine and stuck it to my chest. I was ignored by Ted as he continued to spout passionately about what the evening would entail. Us facing our fear of the unknown, apparently.

The first dare was imminent.

I tugged on Ted's shirt. "Excuse me. Have you got a brochure about the dare? So we can prepare."

I meant bail.

He gave me a strained smile. "We'll meet up at a designated location, emailed to you a few hours before, and only then inform you of your dare for that day. It prevents members from backing out."

My mouth went dry. "That doesn't seem very...safe."

He turned back to the crowd. "Are we ready for our first dare?"

There was cheering, accompanied by my inner moaning.

"I'm going with *no*," I mumbled.

That earned me a look of disapproval from the group.

"Of course, you're not ready, Daisy," said Ted. "That's the point!"

"It's just that..."

"What do you need?"

"A few more details, perhaps. Like, has anyone died doing whatever it is we are about to be doing? That kind of thing."

Ted's long hard stare of disdain came with a side of impatience. Instead of answering, he addressed the crowd once more. "Follow me!"

He led us down a long hallway with all the charisma of a museum tour guide—not like someone who was leading us into danger. We trailed along behind him like lost sheep and followed him through a door.

No bloody way.

Along a glass wall was what looked like a glass chute *outside* the building. Considering we were hundreds of feet up, it was terrifyingly spectacular. No way was I going down that slide. Anyone stupid enough to try it out would see the sheer drop below them to the pavement as they skidded along. If that thing cracked, you'd fall through to a very squishable end. No one would recognize the parts of you that were left.

And I was wearing my new glasses. The most expensive ones I'd ever owned.

We handed over our handbags to Ted's assistant, who brightly told us she'd return them when we joined her at the other end. I kept my phone and tucked it into my shirt pocket.

I watched in horror as members of my group got in a queue, ready to climb into the glass tube that jutted away from the building. The first volunteer, a young woman with the name Debbie written on her badge, made her way through the small space. She sat down on a blue mat that had been provided for this debacle, seemingly enjoying the anticipation.

She shot down and out of view at a million miles an hour.

Suddenly I couldn't get my legs to move.

One by one, my fellow adventurers ducked into the glass tube and moved out onto the edge, plopping onto the mats and zooming out of view.

I was the last to go.

Ted turned to me. "You're up, Daisy."

"Where does that lead?" I pointed at it with the fear it deserved.

"Five floors down."

"But...why?"

This was why my life had stalled out. Morgan had been able to lure away my one true love because she was the spontaneous type. The come-hang-with-me-and-we'll-have-fun type.

This was something she'd do.

The proof was in my handbag. That envelope had been meant for her, someone who would never turn down a dare. Had I been less cautious and more open to taking bigger risks, maybe Nick wouldn't have gotten bored with our relationship.

"Daisy, it's perfectly safe," whispered Ted. "You could sue us if the glass broke and you fell to your sudden death."

"Funny."

"You have nothing to lose and everything to gain," he coaxed.

"What could I possibly gain?"

"Why are you here?"

To win him back.

In a daze, I leaned over to avoid bumping my head on the low ceiling and climbed into the glass square. The drop below was only slightly more distracting than the glass structure that disappeared around the corner of the building. What was I willing to do to win Nick back?

It was easy imagining how Morgan would react to an adventure like this—she'd glide majestically forward without hesitation, looking like a goddess with her golden locks flying—doing it all for her adoring fans who were ready to applaud her bravery. She'd film her glamorous risk-taking adventure and showcase it to the world. Her antics would be posted all over social media.

I sat on the mat and tried to get comfortable—as comfortable as you can be when seeing your life flash before your eyes. I lifted my iPhone and pressed the LIVE button on Instagram.

I spoke into the camera. "I'm currently thousands of feet in the air, ready to take on gravity." I felt like a reporter providing moment by moment feedback of a dangerous mission. "I'm going down a death slide!"

"It's called the fun slide, Daisy!" Ted interjected from behind me.

Ignoring that, I went to kick off and then froze—live on the air—my face reflecting terror. Instead of showcasing my bravery, I was caught mid-panic and unmovable.

The mat slipped forward with me on it and a scream tore from me as I shot down the chute with my ass sliding over the glass bottom at warp speed. Horrified, I slid left until my butt was now on the outer wall of the glass. My balance righted itself as I bounced awkwardly toward the other side of the chute, moving swiftly back and forth as I raced along like an Olympian bobsledder going for gold.

I rounded a bend and saw the end of the slide approaching. There, standing a little ways back, were my cohorts—all of them wearing shocked expressions as I flew toward them like a bat out of hell.

I shot out of the end of the tube, my legs trying to slow my projectile speed as I stumbled forward unable to slow down. Then I saw a blur…a man moving forward to catch me.

I fell into his arms with force.

He staggered backwards and crashed to the ground with me landing on top of him, straddling him like a pony.

I stared down into the face of Max Marquis.

I finally overcame my mortification enough to speak. "It's you."

He smiled. "Your glasses still look nice."

My lips came crashing down on his with the sole purpose of letting him know I was forever in his debt for saving me… for simply existing in the world.

He nipped my lower lip, his tongue darting into my mouth, his hand reaching around to the back of my neck to pull me closer as we forgot time and place…forgot that we hated each other…and that we had an audience.

Finally, he broke away.

"Daisy," he whispered.

I sat up quickly, realizing what I'd done.

Chapter
EIGHT

Daisy

S ITTING ASTRIDE MAX WITH MY FACE ON FIRE, I LET out a shaky breath. "You...saved me."

Max managed a grin. "Right up until you knocked me into tomorrow."

I climbed off him and leapt to my feet, vaguely aware of the applause coming from my teammates.

Max stood up and gave a charming bow to the cheering crowd, acknowledging his act of chivalry.

You kissed him.

You actually kissed Nick's brother.

Have you lost your mind?

"Sure you're okay?"

He stretched as though realigning his spine. "I don't think there's any permanent damage."

He wasn't mentioning the kiss. Not now, not ever, hopefully. The embarrassing mistake I'd made in front of everyone was running through my mind on repeat.

I covered my flushed cheeks with my hands.

Max reached out to pull my hands away from my face. "I'm just glad you're not hurt."

His touch sent a shiver through me.

As though rising from a trance, I almost began jumping up and down with happiness at the realization that I'd completed the first dare. Somehow, I'd done the unthinkable. I'd risked my life for one moment of bravery.

Seeing my elated expression, Max gave my shoulder a friendly pat. "Well done."

All he was doing was standing there, being Max, and I was bewitched.

He brushed off his trousers. "That actually looked like fun."

I beamed at him. "It was amazing."

Everyone was still buzzing from the rush. The daring few who had risked life and limb to partake in this ridiculous scheme were laughing, adrenaline spiking their veins like the people you see coming off a rollercoaster.

My thoughts cleared enough for me to ask Max how he had come to be at the hotel.

"I'm staying here." He ran a hand through his tousled hair. "I set up my office at the Waldorf when I'm in town. Thought I'd grab a drink at the bar."

Thinking back, I seemed to recall he'd mentioned staying here before. It was an amazing coincidence.

Ted walked over and handed me my phone. It had slipped out of my grasp during the bumpy landing. I stopped the recording and then tucked it into my back pocket.

"That was quite some performance, Daisy," he said, grinning.

I tried not to feel self-conscious. "Thank you for the near-death experience, Ted."

"Plenty more of that to come. We'll send out an email with tomorrow's meet-up location." He slapped his hands to get everyone's attention. "Let's all have a drink together."

Ted's assistant approached me to return my handbag.

I noticed that Max was staring at me intently, tilting his head as though he were intrigued. Maybe he was trying to work out what his brother saw in me. Or maybe he was trying to look into my soul. That's what it felt like when Max Marquis' focus was solely on you.

He knows. He knows you're falling for him.

"I have to go now." I pivoted and hurried toward the lift.

Ted called after me, "You don't want to stay for a drink?"

With a wave and a shake of my head I hurried out.

Summoning the lift, I waited for the doors to open, my heart racing with a swirl of emotions. I'd kissed him. That alone had me reeling. Making eye contact with Max now was impossible.

A hand rested on my shoulder. I knew that touch, that presence.

"At least let me escort you out," said Max, his voice husky. "I won't take no for an answer."

With a quick nod, I stepped into the lift.

Max followed me in and stood watching me, as though he wanted to make sure I was really okay.

I couldn't stand the embarrassment any longer. "I'm sorry I kissed you."

He did that thing with his lips...that curling of the mouth that ended in a devastating expression of joy. "Really?"

"Yes, it won't happen again. I was just so glad to be alive."

"That'll do it."

"Do what?"

"Inspire you to be spontaneous." He lowered his sights on me. "Daisy?"

"Yes," I said breathlessly.

"Are you going to do the honors or shall I?"

"Excuse me?"

He leaned over and pressed the DOWN button.

I let out a sigh. "You know that gold envelope you gave me yesterday?"

"Yes."

"It was for membership to a Dare Club. That's what this was all about."

Max's expression was inscrutable.

"Did you know about it?" I asked.

He smiled. "I must admit that I love seeing you in those glasses."

"You have a lovely taste." I gulped. "I meant you *have* lovely taste. In things. Like glasses. And hotels. This place is so nice."

"Daisy," he said softly, his tone seductive. He moved closer until he was towering over me.

I felt an electric charge in the air, a crackle of volatile chemistry between us.

He reached out with both hands and yanked the front of my coat closed, the tug nudging my breasts together and causing my nipples to bead in pleasure.

"You lost a button on your shirt," he explained.

"Sorry?"

"I was pulling your coat closed to cover your shirt."

Looking down, I saw where my bra was peeking through a gap in my shirt. I let out a long moan of mortification; it sounded erotic.

Max stepped back and leaned against the wall. He whipped out his phone, now seeming to ignore me.

I pulled mine out of my back pocket and swiped over to Instagram. I raised it closer to my face to better see the screen.

Max hurried toward me and crushed my body against the wall. "Don't."

"Don't what?"

His eyes narrowed. "Don't take my photo. I don't want Nick to see it."

I cringed inwardly. "Of course not."

His intense brown gaze met mine. "Daisy, what I meant was…"

"Why would I want a photo of you?" I asked, his closeness making me shudder.

Our breathing was in sync, our eyes still locked on each other. His minty breath tickled my face. The pressure of him leaning against me made me feel alive.

"I was seeing if Nick watched it," I finally admitted.

He flinched. "Watched what?"

"I recorded my adventure."

"Right."

I gave him a polite smile and showed him my screen. "See? Me sliding down the glass chute."

The angle of the recording hid the fact that I had crash landed into Max.

I squinted at the number of "likes" my video had racked up. "Wait. That can't be right."

"What's wrong?"

My gaze snapped to his. "It's got two thousand hits already."

He turned my phone around so he could see the screen again. "Are you okay with this?"

My eyes widened with a sudden realization. "Nick will see it!"

Max's jaw tensed. "He doesn't deserve you."

Silence filled the space between us as I replayed his words. It was the kind of moment you wished you could rewind so you knew you hadn't misheard it.

Max read a text on his phone. "Carl's at the curb, ready to drive you home."

"I'm fine with the Tube—"

"Under no circumstances. I'd drive you myself, but I have a conference call scheduled with my firm."

"Oh, I wouldn't want you to drive me." I lied because the feelings I had were so intense, they scared me. I didn't want him to see I had a silly crush.

Our eyes met as the panic in my words weighed heavily in the small space between us.

"Then I won't drive you," he said flatly.

I gave him a weak smile. "Thank you again for the soft landing up there."

His expression softened and he broke into a grin. "The pleasure was all mine."

I wasn't imagining it, was I? The sparks that sizzled when we were close…the undeniable chemistry between us.

The doors to the lift opened.

"I'll walk you to the car." He gestured for me to go first.

"Such a gentleman." I headed out to the lobby.

He caught up and rested his hand lightly on the small of my back. "Guilty as charged."

His touch sent a shiver of delight through me, his accent making me delirious.

We exited through the front door of the hotel and strolled out into the chilly evening air. Self-conscious about the lost button, I tugged my coat tighter.

Max rested a hand on my arm. "*Até logo, doce Margarida.*"

"I feel the same way."

His brow furrowed. "That was, 'Goodbye, sweet Daisy.'"

"I know." I gave him a *silly you* look.

He chuckled, and then his lips pressed together as though

he were trying to prevent more words from spilling out of his perfect mouth.

We reached the curb where the SUV was parked. Before I thought better of it, I rose onto my toes and planted a light kiss on his cheek to thank him, brushing my lips across the stubble there just to see how it might feel. He smelled so damn good I didn't want to pull back.

His lips were now lingering close to mine.

I heard Carl open the back door of the SUV. "Everything all right, sir?" he asked.

Max jolted back. "Of course. Miss Whitby is ready to go home now, please."

I lowered my head and climbed into the back of the car.

Max leaned down to peer at me. "Let me know how the next one goes?"

"Next one?"

"Your next dare."

Oh. I'd already forgotten about that.

He cupped my face with his hand. "You're going to get through this, I promise."

"The dares?"

"No, that's not what I meant."

I wanted this moment to linger, but he pulled his hand back and gave Carl a nod. "Get her home safely."

"I will, sir," said Carl.

Max offered me a business card. "If you need anything, call me."

I took it, a bit bewildered that he was willing to stay in touch with me after I'd nearly killed him tonight.

Max shut the car door.

I could still feel the buzz of chemistry shimmering between us.

He strolled back into the hotel, his broad shoulders and distinguished height inspiring respectful nods from those around him.

I threw one last glance his way as the car pulled into traffic. My fingers traced my lips, trying to soothe their burning desire. I was feeling the same sort of adrenaline rush I'd experienced when I'd slid down the glass chute.

Though certain I'd never call him, I tucked his card into my handbag.

Reaching inside my coat, I caressed that vulnerable spot where the button should be.

Chapter
NINE

Max

THIS WASN'T UNUSUAL FOR ME...SPENDING ANOTHER evening alone, eating a bowl of spaghetti I'd ordered up from room service and sipping a chilled can of Miller Lite with my laptop open, trying to tackle an endless amount of work emails.

I'd attack the minibar later. Eat the caffeine infused crap in there to keep me awake late into the night. For now, I was numbing myself to do what had to be done.

I'd promised Dad I'd take care of the firm. He'd sacrificed so much for it, and near the end of his life I'd believed it had helped to hear I would continue *his* work. See his legacy honored by his only son.

Day after day, week after week—the years rushing by, one after another, as I put my head down and thrived on winning in court. Those wins were the reason my father had become addicted to this profession.

We defended those on the fringe of society. The kind of men you would never want to get on the wrong side of—the politicians, the businessmen, and the wealthy ones who had everything to lose. Our high-paying clients relied on us to do the impossible.

This passionate dedication to the job was what had separated my parents—too many late nights and weekends spent in the office saving other people's lives.

I was my father's son, destined for the same future. Though I'd not be ruining my marriage because I would always be inaccessible—it was the easy way to prevent a divorce. The key to avoiding loneliness was to keep busy, obsessing over the fine print of the law, the legality that terrified others.

On the table my phone lit up with my office number. I picked it up and pressed it to my ear.

"Olá, Maximus." Gylda's bright voice was a welcome sound from home.

"Practice your English," I teased.

My secretary cursed in Portuguese. "How are the family?"

"Great!" I told her.

Things were going well enough.

Gylda had worked for my father for decades. After his death, she'd stayed on to work for me. She was a competent and kind woman who liked to bore me with photos of her grandchildren. Secretly, I adored her.

She proceeded to share news of a potential client. "Maria Alves is distraught, Max," Gylda said, compassion in her tone. "Her brother's been arrested. He was protesting in front of the embassy, denouncing political corruption. She's in a state of panic."

"Not an unusual reaction when being threatened by the law," I reassured her. "Put the client's sister through."

"I'm afraid it's a waste of your time. Miss Alves is looking for a civil rights attorney. She's asking about pro bono."

I let out a sigh of frustration. "Well, then, we're the wrong firm for her."

"I've told her, but she's very insistent. Your reputation precedes you."

"Can you advise her, please?"

"I'm in it."

"You mean, 'I'm on it.'"

She huffed at my correction and put me on hold.

While waiting for her to speak with Maria Alves, I took another swig of beer and checked to see if I had missed any other calls while I'd had my phone silenced.

Gylda came back on the line. "She's begging, sir. She wants to talk with you."

I rubbed my forehead. "Find her a good civil rights attorney."

"I will do my best."

I had a bad feeling in my gut, turning away someone in need, but this was not the sort of work I did. It certainly wasn't what our firm was known for. I felt confident that Gylda would deal with the woman fairly and compassionately.

She hung up and I clung to the comfort I'd felt having that brief contact with home...the only place I'd ever belonged. I enjoyed London, but my heart was in São Paulo.

I needed to refocus.

It would be a lot less difficult if my mind didn't keep circling back to Daisy. That kiss had touched more than my lips. It had awoken a longing inside me for something more—though a relationship was something I had no time for...even if I couldn't fight the compulsion to keep checking my phone.

It would have been so easy to steal another kiss from her outside The Waldorf.

No, I can't think about that.

Family first. Nick was my priority. If he hadn't gone out with Morgan tonight, I'd be pushing work aside and hanging out with him.

I couldn't help wondering, though, what Daisy would be

like in bed. A sweet and eager lover? I imagined her back arching beneath me as I took her hard and fast, my hands buried in her hair as she moaned loudly, her way of asking me to thrust my cock deeper inside her.

Great, and now I had a hard on.

Shut. This. Down.

I took a swig of beer, blinking to clear my vision so I could refocus on reading the emails on my laptop—only this time processing what I was seeing. My latest court case had been postponed by the judge.

I stared at the screen, realizing that my schedule had just opened up. I could even consider staying another week in London.

Just don't think about it.

Don't think about her.

Not kissing Daisy last night had been the right decision. I was so damn good at being sensible. But still, my mind kept circling back to thoughts of the way Daisy's eyes had brightened when she saw me. Her easygoing nature was a pleasure to be around. I admired her sweet disposition and her natural beauty. She'd captured my attention in a devastating way. Whenever I was around her she made me feel...happy.

Nick was an idiot.

There, I rest my case.

I looked down at my smartphone and saw Daisy's number lighting up my screen. Conflicting emotions warred within me. An hour ago I'd made the wise decision never to see her again.

I let out a deep breath and pressed the phone to my ear. "Yes?"

"Max?"

At the sound of Daisy's voice, warmth saturated my body

like I'd just had a personal hit of bliss. She was fast becoming my drug of choice.

Push her away.

"It's late," I said.

"It's only nine o'clock. You gave me your card."

"I did?" *I did.*

I climbed off the bed and began pacing the room. "Everything all right?" I should pretend not to care. I glanced back at my laptop at the emails stacking up.

Fuck the emails. This was more fun.

She was more fun.

My heart stuttered with the realization that my father would have ignored her call had this been my mother. He'd have worked late into the night despite her needing him. Those kinds of choices had devastated his existence. He could have hired someone to do half his workload. His ego, his arrogance, his blind determination had taken him down and his marriage with it.

I'm no different.

Nor will I ever be.

Daisy piped up, "Are you still there?"

"Yes."

"I'm on top of The Shard."

"The tallest building in London?"

"Yes. It's super high. Very windy."

"You're with the Dare Cub?" I brushed my fingers through my hair. "What have they got you doing this time?"

"This one's scarier than the first dare. The one with the glass chute."

"Like I could forget."

"Yeah...right."

"Next time, land on my face."

"Excuse me?"

"I said, next time give it some space."

"Oh, I thought you said something else." She paused. "This one seems harder."

Did she have to say it with a husky tone? I felt my cock twinge in response to her subconscious tease.

I squeezed the bridge of my nose with my thumb and forefinger. "I suppose they're making them incrementally more challenging—"

"That's not why I'm calling, though. Ted says no invitations went out. All the sign-ups were online."

My gut tightened with uncertainty.

"Max, I'm trying to figure out who the invite came from. I showed it to Ted, and he has no idea."

From my window, I could see the The Shard, a beautiful structure of monstrous height. The skyscraper dwarfed the buildings surrounding it.

My mouth went dry and I was hit with an attack of vertigo. "Really?"

"Nick asked you to give me that invite, right? Do you think he was trying to send me a message?"

"Daisy, does it matter? You're having fun, aren't you?"

What the hell did they have her doing up there?

She let out a wistful sigh. "I was thinking maybe Nick is leaving things open with me. Maybe he wants to see if I can be more spontaneous."

I felt a wave of pity for this beautiful girl. My brother was still wielding his spell over her. "What's the dare, Daisy?"

The line was muffled as she called out to someone. "Sorry, Max. I have to go."

"What have they got you doing?"

"We're going over."

"Over what?"

"The top of the building." She huffed out a nervous breath. "Sorry to have bothered you. I won't call you again. I know it's awkward. I didn't mean it to be."

The call dropped and I heard only silence.

Chapter
TEN

Max

I STARED AT THE SKYSCRAPER WITH A FEELING OF DREAD, my throat constricting.

Going over it?

What the hell did that mean? Studying the silhouette of The Shard, I realized that whatever they had her doing was quite possibly illegal. No city would grant permission for anything that hazardous to their clients or the pedestrians below. There'd been no initial indication of the organizers leaning toward criminality. It had seemed more like trivial fun...the get-out-of-your-comfort-zone kind, not the get-yourself-killed kind.

The last dare had been in a controlled environment with the glass chute being constructed for this exact purpose in a well-respected hotel. It had been open to the public and proven safe for over two years. It was in the Waldorf Astoria, for God's sake—the best hotel in London.

What Daisy was suggesting was that they'd rigged something at the top of the building and were going rogue.

As the blood chilled in my veins, I pulled on my coat and headed out. Different scenarios kept flashing through my mind and none of them were good. Within a minute, I'd hailed a taxi and was heading through commuter traffic toward that towering skyscraper.

If anything happened to her, I'd be to blame. I'd encouraged Daisy, and I'd even found the whole idea amusing.

After hopping out of the taxi, I bolted into the foyer.

I navigated through the milling crowd and eventually arrived at the glass lift. Once inside, I was alarmed to see that it jutted outside the building. Rising fast, the view of the city was spectacular, if not alarming. I experienced a momentary sense of weightlessness as we arrived at the top floor at lightning speed.

I exited the lift and the chatter of a crowd drew me in the right direction. The members of the Dare Club I'd seen last night were all here. Over in the corner, Ted was helping Daisy pull on a red jumpsuit. He interacted with her in a flirty, confident way, which spiked a protective reaction in me. I'd be quite happy to see her make a smooth transition back to singlehood and find happiness again. But if I wasn't careful, batting off wayward suitors who could hurt her all over again could turn into a full-time profession.

Daisy disappeared through an emergency exit. I followed the others up a staircase to the roof.

A blustery gale whipped at my coat and disheveled my hair as soon as I stepped outside. I immediately felt chilled to the center of my bones.

We were impossibly high. The noise from the city was drowned out by the sheer force of the winds. It was hard to deny the iconic tower's spectacular positioning. The tallest building in the city provided a clear panoramic view of London.

Clearly, I wasn't the only one in awe of the scenery. People were gathered at the far end of the roof and they, too, were staring out as though hypnotized by this incomparable vantage point.

Daisy's cheeks were flushed from the cold and she fought to keep her hair out of her eyes. She looked windswept and vulnerable, biting her bottom lip nervously, her eyes filled with terror—yet her beauty was startling in the moonlight.

I stood transfixed, unable to drag my gaze away from her angelic presence. Even in a situation like this, her enduring sweetness was revealed. It was the way she smiled at her new friends to comfort them. The way she seemed to rally her courage to go through with the dare.

Holy fuck!

They were going to be dangled over the edge of a ninety-five story skyscraper.

Ted's team was attaching people to an overhead wire safety system.

The first volunteer stepped forward, a young man who looked as nervous as hell, understandably. After a slight hesitation, he placed his feet on the edge of the building and leaned precariously forward, the rope loosening behind him until he was horizontal with the ground.

Insanity.

Daisy, too, was secured to the wire. Slowly and with trepidation, she stepped toward the chrome edge as Ted guided her forward.

Sidling up to share the same view, I looked over the edge and sucked in a breath of panic.

Shit.

Feeling an attack of vertigo coming on, I spun around so I wouldn't have to look.

Snapping my gaze back to Daisy, I realized she'd seen me.

She stared at me with an inquisitive expression and surprise in her eyes.

Straightening my back, I tried not to look fazed, as though being this high up wasn't an issue—as though this latest dare wasn't anything to be worried about.

I glared at Ted as he strolled by me.

"Oh, look, it's the hot Brazilian." He was obviously peeved I was here, which proved that he planned to hit on Daisy at some point.

"I'm checking on Daisy." I made it sound matter-of-fact, like if he wanted to get to her he had to go through me first.

"You're her ex-boyfriend's brother, right?"

"I'm her friend."

"Want to join her?"

"That's not why I'm here."

"Scared?"

"Hardly. I've faced riskier situations."

"Great, we'll get you set up." Ted called over to Daisy. "Your *friend* wants to join you. You okay with that?"

Daisy beamed with happiness. "I'd love it!"

I turned my head to stare at the security rail. "Is that even safe?" I asked in a low voice only Ted could hear.

"We've had the fire department give us their stamp of approval. Shall I tell Daisy you're reluctant to join her?"

My jaw flexed at his arrogance. "Are you going over?"

"Already have. I never ask members to do anything I'm not up for." Ted slanted a sly eye at me.

Within minutes, I'd signed a waiver I would usually spend a great deal more time examining. Then I slipped on a red jumpsuit, relieved that no one could hear my inside voice screaming like a little girl.

Questioning my life choices, I soon found myself strapped

to a wire connected to a harness secured around my torso. In my muddled mind, I couldn't figure out if I was trying to impress Daisy or not lose face in front of Ted and his staff. Both, I suppose.

Those emails waiting for me on my laptop back in that cozy hotel room now seemed particularly inviting. That unfinished beer was calling my name.

This was the most ludicrous idea I'd ever agreed to in my life.

If I went ahead with this, I'd be suspended over a thousand feet in the air and facing off with death. I only had myself to blame.

Even more alarming was the way Daisy stood on the edge, staring at me as though I was her hero.

I couldn't let her down.

I let out a shaky breath, pretending this was business as usual, and took my place beside Daisy. She flashed me a questioning look.

"Not staying in this hotel, too, are you?" she asked cheekily.

"No. Couldn't let you have *all* the fun."

She broke into a grin and her eyes lit up. For a split second I almost forgot I was about to flirt with death.

Daisy reached out and threaded her fingers through mine. "We'll go together."

"Go? We're only leaning forward."

"That's what I meant."

"It's good to be specific." I squeezed her hand tightly.

I felt the loosening of the winch behind my back as I leaned forward, the jaw-dropping view made the people on the street below us look like swarming ants.

Fucking hell.

"I'm actually doing it," said Daisy breathlessly.

Sweat snaked down my back. I winced when it reached my butt crack. "What are we meant to be achieving again?"

"It's meant to make us braver for those important life decisions."

The winch loosened again.

"Jesus e todos os anjos, por favor me ajudem!"

"What did you say?" she asked.

"This is fun."

"Somehow, I don't think that's what you said." Her voice sounded shaky.

I wondered if she had her eyes closed.

My thighs trembled and my feet had gone numb. A bird flew by my face, its wings too close to my nose. "Jesus Christ!"

Daisy giggled.

I glared at her. "It wasn't funny."

I took a deep breath and settled into the moment as my adrenaline rush peaked. My heart was pounding against my chest as though it was trying to escape, reminding me what mortality felt like. It was quite stimulating, if you didn't mind an internal organ beating you up from the inside.

"I need to pee," whispered Daisy.

"Don't put that thought in my head."

"It would be very bad for those people below."

She smiled at me.

"Why are you looking at me like that?" I snapped.

"You're already spontaneous. I want to be that way, too."

We are reckless. This is irrational and idiotic.

I could only imagine the headline in the *Folha de São Paulo Newspaper*: "Crazy Lawyer Takes Last Dare of His Life."

"I won't let you fall," Daisy whispered.

"How do you propose to stop me?" I blurted out.

"I won't let go."

My gaze met hers, and I studied her trusting blue eyes, suddenly entering a dream-like sense of Zen.

My brain struggled to process the stress I was putting myself through. Every worry now seeming insignificant, all that counted was surviving.

My mind grew still.

Everything became clear. What was most important to me was connected to the woman squeezing my hand and showing me comfort.

I drew on her bravery.

Everything else paled—my work, the effort to succeed and grow wealthier. Now, here, being with someone who was so real felt like everything I needed. All the superficialities were stripped away.

My life was being wasted…

No, that wasn't right. Fear was doing crazy things to me. I had a good life. A great job. A happy existence that didn't need to be analyzed or questioned. I didn't need to change what was working fine.

Just get through this and get on with things…

We were finally winched back up to the ledge and unhooked. I stood in the middle of the roof and fought an urge to kiss the ground, adrenaline still pumping though my veins. I was no longer chilled. Instead, my body was heated like a furnace, an after-effect of this terror-drenched mistake.

Trying to look unfazed, I strolled toward Daisy, wanting to see if she was coping with the shock.

She stepped forward and wrapped her arms around me. "We did it!"

Conflicting emotions caused me to shudder against her. Hugging Daisy, I surrendered to her warmth, leaning low and burying my face in her silky brown locks, inhaling her delicate scent, a soft, flowery fragrance that brought with it the kind of comfort I couldn't remember having experienced before.

Tying to compartmentalize, I reassured myself that showing her kindness, since she'd been starved of it for so long, was a good thing.

Who am I kidding? I needed this hug as much as she seemed to, which was a bit mortifying. Because I had never needed anyone. My body went rigid with this realization.

She pulled back and studied me. "I'm sorry. I didn't mean to make you uncomfortable."

"Never."

"Was it really Nick that gave you the envelope? You can tell me."

Rising out of a trance, I reached out to stroke her cheek, ready to open up about its origin...

Ted interrupted us. "I took photos, Daisy."

She looked at him and blinked as though trying to process what he was saying.

"Your Instagram page is going to light up. You'll break the Internet." He threw in a wink.

My gut tightened in annoyance.

Ted looked at me with a triumphant smile, knowing he'd interrupted something special between us.

I gave a nod. "I think posting a photo of this is a great idea."

"Max, you were going to tell me something?" she said.

Somewhere in the middle of all of this madness, I had started to fall for the girl with the broken heart.

"I should go," I whispered.

"You came here to check on me?"

"Of course not. I was in the area."

Her smile broadened, the brightness reaching her eyes,

sending out a wave of loving energy that hit me with unexpected force.

I wanted to taste her lips, get to know her completely. I wanted to have her in every conceivable way. Fall back into that embrace…the one that made me feel whole.

All of this was impossible.

She would always hold Nick in her heart. The only way to undo this spell I was under would be to do the unthinkable.

Walk away.

Otherwise, these moments that had thrust us together would lead to more heartbreak. We could never be. I didn't belong in this city—could never live here. London was her home. She'd never want to leave.

What I had hated about the way Nick had treated her, I now saw in my own actions.

We were both bad for Daisy.

"Be careful." I threw that in as a warning to Ted as much as to her.

He rolled his eyes as he walked away to begin a conversation with the others. As he threw looks of contempt at me over his shoulder, I kept thinking of other ways I could piss him off.

I hadn't been quite this immature since college—another good reason not to see Daisy again.

I tried to let her down gently. "Maybe being part of this club isn't such a good idea. I don't like you being placed in this kind of danger." I shook my head. "It's a mistake."

Daisy tugged on my sleeve. "It really is helping, though."

"Promise me you'll stop this debacle."

"Didn't facing your fear of heights help?"

"I don't need this." I blinked at her with an attitude. "I don't need any of this idiocy. And, quite frankly, neither do you."

"Of course you don't." Her eyes narrowed with a cute expression.

"Not sure we can trust Ted."

"He's fine." She leaned forward. "You know he's gay, right?"

"He is?" I sounded more relieved than I should have. "I mean, he is." I gave a nod as though I knew this. "Promise me you'll not do anything like this again?" I said forcefully. "It's reckless. Not to mention it messes with your head."

She gave a nod to acknowledge she wouldn't, which meant I'd no longer have to worry about her...or even think about her after this. Now leaving her here didn't feel quite so wrong.

I let out a deep breath.

Stay.

There's something unique about her and that's what's scaring you.

"Daisy, I'm flying back to São Paulo soon. So this is goodbye." She didn't need to know the details.

"Oh?"

"Let me drive you home."

"We're all going for drinks afterwards," she said. "But thank you."

I gave her a kind smile. "You'll be okay, right? With everything?"

"Of course." She stepped forward. "Do you feel it?"

"Um...not sure what you mean?"

She whispered, "I feel changed...somehow braver."

"Braver?"

"Yes, facing off with—" She glanced toward the edge of the roof.

No, it wasn't the same experience for me. I wasn't

questioning the status of my relationships. I wasn't questioning my career choice. Or doubting my father's wishes. Or being the good son. Wasn't going to see my life going any other way.

This was how it had always been...

Second guessing myself had never been an issue for me. Though with Daisy, that trait felt threatened.

If I stayed and we became more than friends, she became mine, what kind of life would she have? Married to a man like my father, Daisy would be as miserable as my mother had been. At some point, she'd see no reason to stay. The pattern would be repeated. I'd be left as heartbroken and alone as my father had been.

She seemed to sense my reticence. "I'm not going to see you ever again, am I?"

"No, Daisy, I'm afraid not."

"Max..."

I was already walking away, trying to suppress feelings of regret for leaving her. Whatever this was, staying and marking out a future with her would be as reckless as stepping off that ledge.

I wasn't that kind of man.

I was a third generation Marquis.

Chapter
ELEVEN

NOW AND AGAIN, A TALENT COMES ALONG WHO astounds a nation. A person who has the potential to excel beyond the ordinary. Nick was that man. Football was in his DNA. His father had him playing as soon as he could walk. Major league coaches had kept him in their sights.

He was not only my brother, he was my hero, too. I loved this sport as only a Brazilian could—it ran through my blood.

During my visits, there was nothing I liked better than sitting in the stadium seats and watching Nick train.

Leaning forward with my elbows on my knees, I was riveted by his ability to run in different directions with the ball in full control. His balance and coordination were enviable. This would always be the highlight of our time together...the hours dissolving as we talked football, forgetting all too easily everything else in life.

After practice, Nick joined me up in the first row. We sat side by side watching a little league team playing on the field while we spent quality time together. The referee shouted instructions to the young players and they fell into line.

Ten minutes ago, Nick had been surrounded by those kids

while he signed autographs. To them, he'd already made it. He was a poster on their walls and a player they could aspire to be like. The fact he was watching them play would leave an indelible mark. This side of Nick made up for his foibles.

"Manchester United will be lucky to have you," I told him. "You're not only a good player, you'll be kind to your fans."

Nick wiped sweat from his brow with a towel. "I just need to focus on the game."

I gave him a nudge. "You remind me of your dad."

He threw his head back and laughed. "I wish."

"You focus on what's important."

He sat up. "You always did *see* me."

"I'm your brother."

"You know what Dad was like. The bar was set so fucking high."

"That's what made him an icon." I shook my head. "But don't let all of that go to your head."

"Like he did?"

"He came from humble beginnings. Your background is different."

"You mean privileged?"

"Privilege only gets you so far. You're proving you deserve to be here."

"What do you think Mum saw in him?"

"Your dad? I'm guessing his thighs."

"Shut up. I mean, he was obsessed with football."

"She's independent. Always has been."

"Like you, Max. Even down to the killer good looks." He flashed me a devilish grin.

Nick always made me smile. "Football is a sexy sport."

"You don't hate him for stealing your mum away from your dad?"

"I was very young." *Seven, but I remember everything.*

Enough years had gone by for me to see it from Mum's perspective. My dad had been a hard man to love. Our family had placed second to his passion for winning cases most lawyers wouldn't take on. Mum had looked for love, and she'd found it in Nick's dad—along with adventure, too, apparently.

A visit to England with her sister twenty-six years ago had changed our lives irrevocably. During a game at Wembley Stadium, Nick's father had spotted her in the crowd. At half-time, he'd given her his number. The fact she was married hadn't put him off. Then again, she'd been named one of Brazil's most beautiful women. Most men had a hard time looking away from her beauty.

I changed the subject. "Everything okay at home?"

"Yeah, seems that way. Though I've not kept up with the family saga."

"What saga?"

"You know what Mum's like. Continues her social climbing. She's joined some elite group that donates to the Royal Heritage. They meet once a week. I think she's checking out the families to find you a potential wife."

I leaned back, trying not to think of her scheming. "She just wants us to be happy."

"Define happy."

"Well, you are, aren't you?"

He scraped his fingers through his hair. "Trying to be."

"You moved in with Morgan?"

"Yeah, she has a penthouse. It'll do until I sell my house and we buy something together. You should come stay with us. No more booking into hotels, okay?"

"I don't mind it, but why the change of heart? You never had me over to your house when Daisy was there."

He shrugged. "I should have. The place is just so small."

"London is expensive."

"I'm twenty-five. And you know what that means."

"Access to your trust fund." He'd never been short of money, though.

"I love the house in Bermondsey, but there are too many memories there. With Dad… you know. And Daisy and I living there."

"Mum bought me my first place, too." The mansion in São Paulo had a breathtaking view of the city. Just thinking of it made me homesick.

"Maybe I'll visit you in the summer." He glanced at me. "If you don't mind?"

"I'd love that."

"The salary from MU is pretty decent, too."

We were talking a multi-million dollar deal within the premier league. Not too shabby for someone his age.

"Is Morgan financially stable?" I asked.

"Yeah, she's paid by sponsors. She doesn't care what people think of her. She'll try anything once."

"An extrovert, then."

"She matches my sense of fun." He turned to look at me. "How's things in São Paulo?"

"Firm's doing great." I let out a wary breath, trying to find the words to tell him I had seen Daisy yesterday. Revealing her escapades might rekindle his interest in her. The fact she was willing to hang off The Shard would probably blow his mind.

Nick sprung to his feet. "Goal!"

My attention shot to the kid on the field who'd scored. His teammates were jumping up and down around him with joy. I pushed to my feet to praise him with a standing ovation. When the nine-year-old saw Nick applauding from the stands he almost fell over.

Nick took his seat again. "I need to get into Manchester United like I need to breathe."

"You'll make it."

"None of this would be bearable if you weren't here."

My chest constricted. "I love spending time with you."

"You're the best intermediary to have around when Mum nags me."

"She's on my case, too."

"Anyone back in São Paulo?" Nick eyed me with interest. "Yeah, I can see there's someone." He broke into a grin. "Do I know you or what?"

"I...well...she's a friend."

Daisy. He'd picked up on my uncanny fascination with his ex. We were never seeing each other again so it was fine. It would just complicate the issue to mention it. It should never have happened really—me allowing this affection for a woman we were all meant to be avoiding.

And forgetting.

"She must be a special friend, then." He buried his face in his hands. "Oh, my God, I almost forgot to tell you. Daisy posted something wild on Instagram."

"A video?"

He nodded. "Recorded at the Waldorf—a video of her literally flying through a glass chute at a hundred miles an hour." He chuckled. "Totally out of character for her."

"Maybe she's trying to come out of her shell?"

"It's like she's had a personality transplant."

I leaned back to study his reaction. "She can be adventurous."

"I had no idea."

I rested my hand on his back to add weight to my words. "Nick, Daisy is still in love with you."

He leaned forward. "She needs to get on with her life."

"I believe she's trying."

"She needs to meet someone new."

"How would you feel about that?"

His narrowed gaze held mine. "I'd be fine with it. Why are we still talking about this?"

"She's part of your past. That's important to me."

He blew out a sigh infused with frustration. "I knew her brother, Liam. We were at university together. I liked him. We had a lot of stuff in common, you know. He was heavily into winter sports, an expert skier, and for a while there he was headed to the Olympics. That guy could stick to a black run like Spiderman."

Nausea welled in my throat. "What happened?"

Nick looked uncomfortable. "He died in a plane crash."

A shiver slithered down my spine. Daisy had never mentioned it.

"It changed her," said Nick. "Apparently, she was a fun-loving girl in college, but after Liam's death she turned into someone who always plays it safe."

"Were you and Daisy friends at first?"

He looked thoughtful. "I suppose we were. I met her at her brother's funeral. At the reception afterward she got blind drunk—completely wasted. A few of us picked her up and brought her back to the house. We didn't want her family seeing her in that state."

"Your house in Bermondsey?"

"Yeah, I watched over her until she was sober. Stayed awake all night in a chair while she slept. When she finally woke up, she was still unsteady so I helped her into the shower." He raised his hand defensively. "I didn't take advantage."

"I know you would never do that."

"Then, not two weeks later, my dad died…" He shook his head. "We were a right pair, me and Daisy. Grieving together. That was what we had in common. We both knew how the other one felt. After Dad died, I didn't want to be alone, so I asked her to stay at my house."

"Nick," I said with sympathy.

He gave me a sad smile. "Our relationship was built on a foundation of grief."

"I should have visited more."

"You were there for me."

"Not enough."

"Don't get me wrong, I love Daisy. I owed it to her brother to watch over her. Help her get over his death. She was fun and innocent in a cute way. I just feel like something changed inside me. Like I started to love her like a brother. I believed a clean break was best for both of us."

"Maybe it was the pressure you were under?"

He looked at me. "People change, right? Our mum fell out of love with your dad. You just wake up and feel differently one day."

"What is it about Morgan you prefer over Daisy?"

"I was playing it safe with Daisy. Morgan is exciting."

"Wasn't your life exciting enough?"

"I need to explore another side of me. Anyway, I think Morgan improves my game."

"How?"

"She makes me forget myself. She's all-consuming. Like I can't think straight when I'm around her because she's unfathomable."

I wasn't' sure that was a good thing.

"How long have you been with Morgan?" I studied him carefully.

"Three months."

I sat up straight. "You were cheating on Daisy?"

"She really has gotten under your skin, bro." He looked concerned. "You're not still in contact with her, are you?"

I gave a shrug. "There's no reason to be."

I felt a dull ache of longing for all the times I'd stood in her presence and felt like a different man.

Nick had failed to notice my melancholy tone.

He inhaled sharply. "At the end we were living together like roommates."

"I didn't know," I whispered.

"You're way overdue for a steady relationship, Max."

"I'm fine. I just want to see you both happy."

"Morgan and I are happy in our own way."

I was talking about him and Daisy, but I didn't correct his thinking.

"You're coming over tomorrow, right?"

I gave a wry smile. "When I'm here, Mum just tells me my itinerary. Obligingly, I turn up."

"Did she spill my news?" At my look of confusion, he added, "You're going to want to sit down for this."

I flinched. "I am sitting down."

An uneasy feeling settled in my gut, but my forced smile hid my reaction. I knew what came next—the news no one was ready for.

Chapter
TWELVE

Daisy

THIS ONE WAS PERSONAL. NO SLIDING DOWN GLASS chutes. No hanging off buildings. This dare was about going after what you wanted with all your heart and making that dream a reality.

Earlier today, Ted had delivered his motivational speech in the Kings Head Pub in Kings Cross to us members of the Dare Club. The place had also been packed with regulars—a typical atmosphere for a Tuesday lunch crowd.

"Tonight, there will be no second guessing," he'd told us. "No turning back. No backing out."

In that very moment, I'd decided what this new dare meant to me.

Chasing my heart was all I had left—even if it made my stomach twist into knots, even if it made me question my worthiness.

Don't think about Max.

Don't.

Anyway, he was back in São Paulo. Not to mention the fact that every time he saw me he was only thinking about damage control. Hoping for there to be something more between us was wishful thinking. That same naivety had kept me from seeing my relationship with Nick was about to implode.

But I was becoming a new person, someone I could be proud of.

Driving out of London and all the way to Hampstead had taken a full hour. I'd watched the city give way to the countryside, blasting Billie Eilish out of the speakers, a proper soundtrack for the Shakespearian drama my life had become.

The dare plan: gatecrash the cocktail party at Nick's family home. This newfound confidence had me all revved up and ready to do what had to be done to turn my life around. This dare felt different, because it was so personal.

There'd been no official announcement in the press yet, but after tonight the world would know Nick's name. This event was being thrown by his family to celebrate him being accepted into Manchester United. What other reason could there be?

I was happy for him. I really was.

Thoughts of Max had eased the strain of my breakup. I really should have taken his advice and deleted that app permanently off my phone.

As though I'd not endured enough torture, I'd watched the video of Morgan shopping in Harrods for a dress to wear to the event, shop assistants fussing around her as she tried on different styles. Then she had asked her fans to vote for their favorite.

Oh, the suspense…

Would it be the elegant Badgley Mischka that showed off her long legs? Or the flowing pink chiffon that hid her Maleficent side?

We'd all just have to wait and see…

I, too, had bought a brand new outfit—a Marks and

Spencer flowing black skirt and a white blouse with flouncy sleeves. Perfect for a cocktail party. I'd spent time on my makeup, too, adding some blush to disguise my pallor from lack of sleep, and applying soft pink lipstick to round out my I-kind-of-tried-but-didn't-have-to ensemble.

I styled my hair so it tumbled down my shoulders in shiny waves. Nick had always loved it when I wore my hair down. Though doubt had settled amongst my happy memories like weeds in a flower garden, creeping in unseen, strangling what was once beautiful and sacred. I'd never seen our breakup coming.

Tonight, I'd get to meet his family. I wasn't sure how I felt about that.

Though I knew if I were caught, Nick would bail me out—as long as I didn't act like the crazy ex-girlfriend, he'd see the funny side. He'd see I wanted the best for him.

My GPS led me all the way to a brass gate entryway. Beyond, a vast estate. I stared through the car window.

This can't be it.

At the end of the long, gravel driveway loomed an intimidating manor of grey granite that was surrounded by sculpted hedges. Sixteenth century lancet-style windows added to its Gothic splendor. A bunch of rich snooty types lived here, no doubt.

The gate swung open.

My heart rate took off at a thundering pace.

A guest arriving ahead of me pulled up in her Rolls Royce to the front door where she was met by a valet. The woman climbed out of her flashy car and showed off her glamorous gown.

Shit.

I was underdressed.

Another woman in a billowing dress was being escorted into the manor by a guy in a snazzy tuxedo. I recognized several of Nick's friends exiting a long limousine, each wearing a tux. From their laughter I could tell they'd had a few drinks on the way.

I ducked down in my front seat, not wanting them to see me and give Nick the heads-up I was here. I didn't want to be escorted out by a stranger before I'd gotten to speak with him.

Before I realized what was happening, a valet had ushered me out of my car. I watched him drive my Mini Cooper around a corner.

Following the crowd through the impressive front door, I tried not to gawp at the elegant foyer. It reminded me of a *Vanity Fair* spread with its green drapes and marble flooring.

Maybe they'd rented the place for the evening? This made the most sense as no way had Nick ever lived here.

Had he?

A middle-aged waiter hurried toward me. "Are you going to just stand there?"

I realized he was talking to me.

"We need help with the hors d'oeuvres." He gestured with a crook of his head for me to follow.

My gaze snapped over to a waitress holding a tray, offering wine to the newly arrived. She was wearing a white blouse and black skirt. I had dressed the same as the frickin' staff!

I inhaled sharply at the vision at the end of the foyer.

He was here.

Max was chatting with an older couple. He'd told me he was flying back to São Paulo, but he hadn't mentioned when exactly. His way of shaking me off, no doubt.

His tuxedo enhanced his already generous shoulders, fitting him so well he looked like royalty. His dark hair looked tousled, like he'd run his fingers through it in a moment of rebellion. And those eyes, *God*, those brown irises glimmered with good humor as they greeted those around him. Guests were just as enamored with him as I was, it seemed. They surrounded him, fawning over the man who stood out in the crowd; the brother of the star of evening.

Max was annoyingly gorgeous. The kind of distraction I didn't have time for. If he saw me, he'd tell me to leave. Stepping back, I hid behind an enormous vase.

Oh, fuckadoo.

Max was walking in my direction.

I turned quickly and burst through a door, following a waiter down a long corridor teeming with staff—all of them dressed like me in black and white.

My humiliation was complete.

It wasn't my fault. The last thing I'd been expecting was an über-posh event.

The staff swarmed around me, some carrying trays of food, others returning with empty glasses, everyone scurrying around looking busy. It was organized chaos in the kitchen as chefs prepared the food, shouting orders and sending dishes out on trays.

Two fingers clicked in my face. "I need you with it," said a waiter.

"I...um..."

"This place may be filled with football royalty," he snapped. "But you need to do your job." He handed me a plate of hors d'oeuvres.

This wasn't exactly the plan but being undercover as a waitress might be a great way to sneak around unseen. I improvised, heading out into the party and offering food to the party-goers, all the while scanning the room for Nick. It was kind of nice to nosy around and get a glimpse of Nick's secret world.

Inside an empty sitting room, I took a few minutes to strategize. As soon as I saw Nick, I'd grab his attention and have him follow me to somewhere more private. We'd talk, clear the air, and I'd get the precious minutes I needed to make him see sense.

My jaw slackened.

There, hanging on the far wall, was a portrait that had apparently been taken a few years ago. David Banham stood beside his beautiful wife, Nick's mum. Two proud looking parents posed with their children, Nick and Max.

This *was* their home.

Nick had grown up here.

The realization made me tremble with unease.

I'd never been good enough to be introduced to any of these people.

They'd had the money to throw at me. They'd used their authority to make me go away quietly.

Yeah, not so much.

I was the hero here and one day they'd come to see that.

I walked over to the tall glass window and stared out at the beautiful people having fun in the elaborate garden. Even their laughter sounded posh. The people out there knew Nick better than I did. It was the kind of crowd Morgan would feel at home in. The glamorous types.

I'd gone from loving my outfit to feeling frumpy.

I didn't belong.

Never would.

Fresh air beckoned as I stepped out onto a stone patio. I rested the tray on the linen-covered table.

"What do we have here?" A middle-aged man was

pointing at a table strewn with a selection of delicious edibles. "Recommend anything?" He offered me a warm smile.

"I think that's salmon." I gave a shrug of doubt. "They have a nice white wine over there that will pair well."

"Oh, lovely," he answered in a crisp accent.

Realizing he was waiting for me to pour him a glass, I got on with it, sloshing the contents of an oversized carafe of white wine into a large glass and handing it over.

He looked amused. "Thank you, my dear."

Then I recognized him—this man was the son of the owner of Manchester United. His say would influence Nick's career.

"I want you to know," I began. "Nick Banham is not only a brilliant player but a good person, too."

"I appreciate that," he said.

"He'll give his all. You'll have someone who'll make you proud. Football's in his blood, but more importantly, he'd be a team player and he'd also be good to the fans."

He held out his hand. "And you are?"

Oh, right.

"No one important. Just someone who cares deeply for him."

He headed off and disappeared into the crowd.

Peering beyond the throng of party-goers, my eyes adjusted to the dark, making out the seemingly endless amount of land that belonged to the estate. The curtain was drawn back on who Nick really was—a man who'd lived a privileged life.

I'd never really known him.

Yet my heart reacted the same way it always had when I saw him across the lawn, as though forgetting the pain he'd put me through.

Nick was pulling Morgan down a garden pathway. The

sight of them together sent an arrow into my heart, lodging there, causing my chest to constrict with a sudden pain. I bit my bottom lip and put a hand over my heart as though I could soothe away the agony.

Turn back.

But I couldn't.

Blinking into the darkness, I hurried along beside a fence that surrounded a tennis court. Inhaling deep breaths to calm myself, I followed along after them, trying to convince myself that what I was doing made sense. I'd have to wait for Nick to be alone before I confronted him. All I had to do was not lose sight of them.

The lights dimmed and the grass became uneven, so I paused to take off my high heels. The sounds from the party grew fainter, the laughter now cut off by the high hedges. This place seemed to go on forever. I continued down the blue and white tiled steps.

The ground suddenly felt unsteady beneath my bare feet.

Oh, God.

I was standing on a beige tarp, the material stretching across a swimming pool. Water seeped around my feet, turning my toes into icicles. I turned back, but slipped on the unstable cover, not making any headway.

I was stuck, balancing precariously in the center of a plastic tarp that barely supported my weight, with rushing water meeting my calves and drenching my hem.

"Help!"

"Daisy?" It was Nick.

"You've got to be joking!" That was Morgan.

Now that I was closer, I could see she'd gone with the gown from Badgley Mischka. A good choice.

She looked stunning.

In contrast, I'd gone with a more modest look—that of Nick Banham's jilted ex-girlfriend, dressed as staff with a dash of crazy.

Lights blared on and I squinted at the gathering crowd that had come to see me—the girl floundering in the center of the pool who wished she could walk on water.

Chapter
THIRTEEN

Daisy

"Daisy?" Nick called out. "What are you doing?"

"How embarrassing," Morgan muttered loud enough for me to hear.

Ignoring her, and the gathering crowd filled with posh outfits and judgy faces, I kept my focus on Nick as I fought to keep my balance.

"Hi." I was holding my shoes in my left hand, so I waved at Nick with the other.

"What is that girl doing?" asked an elegant-looking woman. She was staring at me with a harried expression.

"Oh, hello, you must be Nick's mum?" I said. "It's nice to meet you."

Her brows knitted together as she swapped a wary glance with Nick.

Tonight's big "Dare" wasn't going so well. This share-your-true-feelings-and-be-your-authentic-self moment felt like my worst idea ever. Doubt crept in like the water around my ankles.

But I forced myself to finish what I'd started. "Nick, there's something I need to tell you."

"Daisy, don't," he said, his face twisted with worry.

"This is what best friends do," I said breathlessly, trying to ignore the squelching around my feet. "I know we're over. I respect that decision—"

"Daisy!" Max drew my attention toward him.

"Oh, hello," I said brightly. "Fancy seeing you here."

"Oh, God," said Mrs. Banham, moving closer to Nick.

Her embroidered silver high-slit dress shimmered beautifully under the lights.

What must I look like to her?

"Don't move," ordered Max.

Each time I saw him he took my breath away. His eyes were kind, but his sophistication was enough to make anyone feel inferior. Holding Max's intense gaze almost made me forget this disaster.

Almost.

I'd been brave enough to come here—I wasn't going to let my resolve weaken now. Not with Nick's full attention on me.

"This is your family home?" I asked him.

His shoulders slumped as he realized that now I knew the truth. He'd never brought me here. Never introduced me to his family. Never admitted to the world we were *a thing*.

"It's very nice," I added. "You grew up here?"

He gave an unsteady nod.

I raised my hand to reassure him. "Nick, I need to tell you the truth about..."

Her.

Morgan's narrowed hate-filled gaze locked onto me—morphing into something tangible, something that seeped inside and weaved vitriol around my soul.

This woman had ruined my life and she was about to decimate Nick's—because that was what she did. The trail of evidence was devastating. Morgan was a Tasmanian devil whirling around and wielding destruction.

Only for Nick it hadn't happened *yet.*

"Daisy, can you take a step toward me?" Max stood on the edge of the pool gesturing to me.

"I have to say it," I answered in a rush.

"Daisy, they're engaged," Max said quietly. "This is their party."

My gaze snapped to Nick for confirmation.

No…I can't be too late…

I blinked through my tears, only now seeing the ostentatious diamond ring shining like a constellation on Morgan's finger.

Max reached out to me again. "Grab my hand."

"Careful, Max, you'll fall in!" his mum snapped.

I tried to move toward the edge, but the tarp sank deeper with a jolt, the shock of the cold water too much for me to handle. My throat tightened and I let out a panicked wail as the cover gave way.

I plunged underwater…

My screams were muffled as I flapped my arms and legs, managing to break the surface, gasping and filling my lungs with air. I frantically started swimming toward the edge of the pool, with the plastic tarp bobbing beneath me.

A strong hand wrapped around my wrist and lifted me up and out, pulling me farther away from the side of the pool. The chill was paralyzing, making each breath I drew painful. I clutched my arms across my chest, refusing to look at the staring people and their gawps of horror. I couldn't help but notice before looking away that Max's mother had slapped her hands over her mouth…and Nick and Morgan had scurried away.

Max shrugged off his jacket and wrapped it around my shoulders. "Come on, let's get you dried off."

"I'm sorry." My teeth were chattering and my body was shaking. I couldn't move…couldn't think straight.

Max lifted me into his arms, grasping me tightly to his chest, and carried me away from the pool. Water dripped off me, soaking his chest.

"I'm getting you wet." I cupped my face in my hands.

"Relax, Daisy," he said. "I've got you."

Feeling humiliated and disgraced, I glanced back at his family and friends…their expressions of pity and confusion would forever be seared into my mind.

Max carried me into the house, up a winding staircase and along an endless hallway. He walked into a bedroom and then straight through into a bathroom en suite. It had the kind of tile a girl could drip on without worrying about the damage.

Max stood in front of me and towel-dried my hair, peeking through my damp locks to give me sympathetic smiles.

I realized I had lost my high-heeled pumps in the pool.

"We have to get you out of your clothes." He turned his back and faced the door. "Put this on." He pointed to a bathrobe. "I'll step out."

He left the room.

Shaking from the cold, I pulled at the catch of my skirt and slipped out of it, then peeled off my blouse. I took off my underwear and threw all of the sopping wet clothes into the sink. Drying myself off with a plush towel, my thoughts returned to Max's announcement.

They're engaged.

I'd gone out in a glorious burst of humiliation. The memory of seeing Nick walking away hand-in-hand with his bride-to-be was scorched into my brain.

I heard a knock at the door.

"Are you decent?" asked Max.

I quickly pulled on the robe. "Yes."

He came in. "That's better." Max threw me a smile I didn't deserve. "Let's find something you can borrow."

He took my hand and led me out into the hallway.

"I'll never live this down," I muttered.

"Nonsense."

"I ruined his engagement party."

Max nudged open another door. "In you go."

"I'm so embarrassed."

"My brother has done far worse," he mumbled, closing the bedroom door behind us.

I'd lived with a man I hardly knew. A man who had never really loved me. Trying not to think about it, I looked around at the elegant room's burgundy wallpaper and furniture plucked out of a Harrod's catalogue. A mahogany dresser complemented the enormous canopied four-poster bed.

I tried to shake off my sense of disorientation. "This is your mum's room?"

"We'll find something of hers that will fit."

"She won't mind?"

"It's like Selfridges in here." Inside the spacious walk-in closet he rummaged through her clothes, all neatly arranged on velvet-covered hangers.

Some of the outfits still had tags on them.

"We're spoiled for choice." Max plucked out a satin gown to show me. "Check out her shoes."

I stepped back, feeling uncomfortable with taking anything that belonged to her. Max was just being kind. No doubt wanting me dressed and out of here.

Sensing my unease, Max put back the satin gown and

said, "She'll be fine with you borrowing her things. She has a generous nature."

I walked over and sat on the edge of the bed, unable to make eye contact with him. I'd made the worst mistake of my life by coming here.

Max sat beside me. "Feel all right?"

"My high heels are at the bottom of your mum's pool. As long as I live, I don't think I'll be able to top this humiliating experience." Though, lately, I'd had a lot of embarrassing moments to choose from.

He patted my hand. "People tend to forget these things."

"Not *those* kinds of things." I suppose it didn't matter now—I was hardly going to be invited back.

He shrugged. "Most people are only into themselves."

"You don't believe that?"

"I'm afraid I do."

"But you're not like that."

He nudged me with his shoulder. "Some people make you want to know them better."

I wasn't falling for that. He'd told me before that he was leaving for São Paulo. He'd been the one to offer me money so I would go away.

The silence stretched on between us.

He reached over and pushed a lock of wet hair out of my face.

"Your mum must hate me."

"She doesn't know you."

We both knew after tonight she'd be glad to get rid of me.

"Do you need a drink?" He chuckled. "Other than pool water?"

Chlorine was in my hair and my skin was coated with it. My sopping wet clothes were taking up space in his bathroom. I was a mess.

Then I saw his shirt and jacket.

"I'm so sorry." I pointed to his chest.

"Anything to get out of this tux, Daisy. You gave me an excuse to change." He paused and cleared his throat. "I'm sorry about Nick."

"I didn't know." I shook my head. "I should never have come here. I wasn't even dressed up enough."

"You looked pretty."

"I looked like a member of your staff!"

He cringed. "You did a bit."

"At least you're honest."

"My worst flaw."

"I failed him." My lip trembled. "I let your brother down."

Max wrapped his arm around me. "You can't use yourself as a buffer so that the people around you have a better life than you."

"I'd do anything to stop him from getting hurt."

He stared at me. "Were you spying on them?"

"No! This was one of my dares."

His eyes widened in realization and then he flinched.

"Obviously not the bit where I mistook a pool for the ground."

He leaned back to peer at me with intense brown eyes, biting his lip as though to prevent himself from laughing. "Feeling better?"

"Yes, thank you," I fibbed.

"Let's go back."

"What?"

"Why not?" He gestured towards the closet. "Find something you can dance in."

I jumped as someone knocked on the door.

A female voice followed the sound. "Are you in there, Max?"

He got to his feet and strolled over to the door, opening it slightly. "Hey, Mum."

"Is she in there with you, in my room?" she said. "That girl?"

"Yes." Max glanced back at me with a smile.

She lowered her voice to a whisper. "Do you think that's wise? Considering."

"Considering…?"

"Seriously?" she hissed.

Max slid out to join her in the hallway and closed the door behind him. I heard their footsteps moving away.

The scent of a familiar cologne wafted up around my face. I was wrapped in Max's robe and it felt fluffy and warm, so luxurious. Dipping my head, I sniffed the collar and was enveloped in his dreamy essence. This was like being engulfed in a Max hug—the kind you leaned into, never wanting it to end…

Pushing to my feet, I strolled over to the walk-in closet and peered in at the shoe cabinet in the center. I would feel dreadful borrowing any of his mum's things. I knew she wouldn't want me to.

I heard the sound of murmuring voices in the hall. I headed over to the bedroom door and pressed my ear against it, eavesdropping on their conversation.

"Daisy's a sweet girl," said Max. "Give her some time and she'll settle down."

"She can't stay!"

"Keep your voice down, Mum."

"She just can't."

"What's the harm?"

"Think of your brother. It's his party."

He let out a frustrated sigh. "She's been through enough."

"No one forced her into that pool."

"It was a mistake. She didn't know it was a swimming pool. She fell in."

"What if she sues?"

"Don't be ridiculous. She's worried about Nick. That's what this is about."

"She's only worried about getting him back," his mum said, and then sighed. "You're going to have to change. Your tuxedo is wet."

I turned and headed back into the bathroom. Still wearing the oversized robe, I tried another door on the other side of the room. Mercifully, it opened to an empty hallway. Hurrying down the spiral staircase, I ignored the disapproving stares of a few guests and a handful of staff lingering nearby and made my getaway through the foyer and out into the chilly evening air.

Barefoot and looking as straggly as a drowned rat, I rushed toward the valet. "I need my car."

After enduring his amused smirk, I waited—hopping from one frozen foot to the other—for what felt like an eternity before he drove my Mini Cooper around to the front of the house.

I climbed in feeling relieved, and quickly headed off down the driveway.

Maybe this dare had really been about getting an answer. Even if it wasn't the one I'd hoped for.

I sent out a silent prayer that I'd never see any of those people again. Of course, after the way I'd behaved tonight I had a virtual guarantee.

I hadn't wanted to see the disappointment in Max's eyes…couldn't bear to hear him say goodbye with an air of disdain. Even if I deserved it.

Mercifully, the gate swung open right away and let my Mini escape out onto the poorly lit lane. I leaned forward to better see the glow of my headlights on the dark road.

The only comfort I felt came from the heat blasting out of the vents and from being enveloped in a snuggly bathrobe that smelled like *him*...Max Marquis.

Chapter
FOURTEEN

Max

THERE ARE NO SUCH THINGS AS GHOSTS.

With this in mind, I strolled through the abandoned house renowned as one of the most haunted mansions in London. A strange way to spend a Friday evening, walking in my highly polished brogues down deserted hallways that had scuffed floors and paint flaking off their walls. This run-down Victorian residence was a faded beauty, but it had clearly not been forgotten. Apparently, the Dare Club directors had rented the property for their crazy escapades.

What was meant to be a hot spot for ghost hunters was conveniently situated next to Highgate cemetery. Tours would no doubt go from one location to the other, with tourists hoping to catch a glimpse of the afterlife in a shadowy figure that could be anything, really. Nevertheless, their photos would go viral as alleged proof that once we've shed our body our spirits live on for an eternity.

What a load of bollocks—as the English would say.

Somewhere within these rooms, Daisy had hunkered down for a night of being haunted to fulfill the demands of her next dare. I was surprised she was still in the club after the dumpster fire of last Tuesday when she'd almost drowned in my mother's pool.

Daisy had posted this place on her Instagram page, surreptitiously leading me here with that photo of the red door belonging to the house at 7 Makepeace Avenue.

I carried with me her freshly dry-cleaned skirt and blouse and her high-heeled pumps—retrieved from the bottom of the swimming pool. It was my peace offering and a pretty good excuse to see her again, the thought of which caused my heart to start behaving like a jackhammer.

No, I'm just reacting to this environment, I told myself. *It's the possible threat of discarnate spirits that's creeping me out.*

I walked around a corner and saw a blur of movement. I let out a high-pitched scream, shattering the quiet.

It was Daisy, looking up at me in shock.

I leaned against the wall to recover, raising my hand to let her know I needed a second to remember how to breathe.

"Max?"

"Hey." I straightened and tried to pretend I hadn't just screamed like a girl.

She'd dressed for the occasion in jeans and an oversized sweater. Her coat rested on a blanket in the corner. There was something earthy about the way her hair was pulled casually back in a ponytail. With no makeup, she looked bewitchingly natural. It took my mind off the fact I'd almost been spooked to death.

"Are you just going to stand there staring at me?" she said. "What are you doing here?"

"I was in the neighborhood."

She didn't look convinced. "How did you know I'd be here?"

Instead of answering her question, I held up the dry-cleaning bag and the shoebox. "I have these for you."

I could have left them with her aunt. I hoped she'd not see through my ruse and mention it. When it came to her, I was crap at faking I didn't care.

She recognized her clothes. "Keep them."

"I was going to burn them but was scared I'd scorch off my eyebrows." I followed that up with a smile.

She stared at me suspiciously. "Have you come to warn me not to turn up at one of your events again?" She wagged a finger. "You've wasted your time. I'm over the Banhams."

"I'm a Marquis."

"I meant your entire family."

"I'm here to make sure you're not too traumatized."

"I've been through worse."

"Really, what?"

"I'm kind of busy."

I looked around. "Ghost hunting?"

"No, the whole point is waiting for them to come to you." She crossed her arms over her chest and raised her chin. "I've never been more ready."

"Okay, well, I'll just leave these over here." I hung the dry-cleaning on an old picture hook and set the shoebox down on the floor beneath it. I glanced around with disapproval. "This place is pretty rundown, Daisy. I don't think you should stay."

"You don't get to tell me what I can or cannot do."

"You don't want my advice anymore?"

"No, because you're nothing to me." She inhaled sharply.

It was a bald-faced lie—the one we'd been telling each other since we'd first met.

I scratched the back of my head as I tried to ignore her beauty, her compelling eyes tracing my every move.

Stepping forward to grip her chin and plant a fierce

kiss on her pouty lips would undoubtedly be too aggressive. I wanted to press my mouth against her neck and nibble my way tenderly up to her ear, but that couldn't happen either. Not now, not ever.

This unbearable desire I felt to drag her into my arms and crush her to my body was my cue to leave.

"I thought that after last Tuesday you'd never want to see me again," she said softly.

"You left the house without saying goodbye."

"I was going to send your bathrobe back."

I shook my head in frustration. "Are you alone?"

She placed her fisted hands on her hips. "Yes."

"Stupid idea," I muttered. "Anyone could wander in here."

"I'm locked in."

"Daisy, I walked in through the front door."

Her pouty mouth turned up at the corners. I could plant a kiss right there on the side...

She was infuriating.

I pointed to her blanket in the corner. "Let me carry your things out."

"I'm not leaving."

"Staying here all night is not a good idea."

"I brought a picnic basket. Might as well make the most of it."

I sighed.

Fading sunlight filtered in through the fogged windows and shimmered over her delicate features. I'd never been able to look at her without being drawn to her presence. I wanted to know her intimately.

"It'll be dark soon. Let me give you a lift home."

"I'm having fun." She pointed to a flask by the basket. "Want a cuppa?"

She stubbornly returned to her tartan blanket and sat down on it, crossing her legs into a yoga pose and getting comfortable. She reached for a packet of biscuits and offered me one.

"I don't have time."

She gave me a cute smile and shook the packet insistently.

With a huff of annoyance, I stepped forward and accepted the biscuit, taking a quick bite. The taste of sugary cream melted over my tongue, mixing with the chocolate. If the English were good at something, it was baking biscuits.

"You're not scared to be here all night?" I asked between bites.

"No, not really. I brought something to read."

I sat beside her, thinking this was damn uncomfortable.

On the rug next to her lay a copy of *Where The Crawdads Sing* by Delia Owens.

"How's the book?"

She followed my gaze. "Wonderful so far."

The books in my To Be Read pile were also victims of my demanding job.

I looked around at the peeling paint and the dusty floor. The dimness was unsettling. The torch next to her picnic basket better have good batteries.

I resigned to sit awhile. "You don't strike me as someone who believes in ghosts."

"My aunt's a clairvoyant."

"That's right." I resisted the urge to roll my eyes.

A rustling down the hallway drew my attention.

"I've heard other strange noises." She watched my reaction. "The trick is to ignore them."

The small hairs on my forearms prickled. I scooted closer to her on the rug, shuddering at the thought of seeing anything that resembled a ghost.

I shook my head. "These dares really do push you to do questionable things."

"They make you vulnerable," she admitted. "They call it total exposure."

"Funny."

"After what happened Tuesday night I almost quit. Then I thought, what do I have to lose? Might as well keep going."

Her adventurous spirit was inspiring.

In another universe we might have evolved into more than friends. Developed the kind of trust that's coveted by those willing to give love a go.

I admired her flawless complexion. The weight of my stare must have made her self-conscious, because she looked away, revealing a profile that could have made a master like Vermeer weep.

She broke the quiet. "Do you like being a defense attorney?"

"Like is a strong word."

"Because you defend criminals?"

"Innocent until proven guilty."

"I heard you can get away with anything if you have a good lawyer."

"I defend the law."

"Have you ever defended someone you knew was guilty?"

"You can't ask me that, Daisy."

"But I just did."

"Everyone deserves a trial."

"I imagine you could win over any jury with your charisma."

"You find me charismatic?" I teased.

She blushed a little. "Let's just say..."

"Yes...?"

"You're ridiculously hot. Like, embarrassingly good looking."

"Why is it embarrassing?"

"Because women wonder what it would be like to…"

"To…?"

"You know."

"Enlighten me." It was fun to see her squirm.

"You're easy on the eyes."

I laughed. "So are you. You're very pretty."

Her coyness was adorable.

She cleared her throat and changed the subject. "Are you looking forward to going back to work?"

"Are you fishing to find out when I leave?"

"Might be."

"I've managed to get another week in London." I let out a weary sigh. "My work is pretty draining so it's a welcome change."

"That's not good."

"I didn't always want to be a criminal defender," I admitted.

"What did you want to be?"

I shook my head, unsure whether to share this detail about my life.

"Max?"

"I wanted to be a civil rights attorney."

My thoughts wandered back to that call from a woman named Maria. She'd searched me out to take on her brother's case and I'd not even spoken with her. I'd had my secretary handle it. I could have dug around and found out more details about the case but there'd been no point, really.

"Why aren't you, then?" asked Daisy.

"Life had other plans for me."

"What changed?"

I drew in a deep breath. "My father owned a law firm. I was expected to join it."

Another sound down the hallway drew my attention. "Are you sure we're alone?"

"Yes. I looked around when I first got here." Daisy placed her hand on mine. "My aunt says it's the ghosts from our past we need to be wary of."

"I suppose that's true."

"The ghosts from your past influenced your decision."

"How do you mean?"

"Well, when your mum came to live here, you were left to fend for yourself. You had your dad but it wasn't the same. You leaned on him. He took care of you the best he could. But he was working a lot, I imagine. You felt you owed it to him to join his firm."

Now I was the one being exposed over a truth I'd managed to suppress.

I shook my head. "Let's talk about you."

"There's not a lot to say."

"Do you enjoy your job?"

"Kind of. My dream was to design high-end shop windows. The ones in the finest stores in London."

"And especially the ones for Christmas?"

She nodded. "I wanted to create something unique. Something that stands out and can be seen by many…something artsy, but also for retail. I didn't just want to work inside the store."

"How do you get that kind of job?"

"You get a degree in art and design."

Yet she'd dropped out of university sometime soon after her brother's death, I gathered. Continuing her education had been too difficult. Daisy had been too grief-stricken to continue.

"You can go back to Uni," I said.

"Maybe one day." She shook her head as though clearing her thoughts. "After last Tuesday night I feel like I have some closure."

"How so?"

"I did what I set out to do. I warned Nick about Morgan. Now it's over. I've done my bit."

"Right." I hoped she was really ready to move on.

"What about you?"

"Me?"

"Yes. What's holding you back, Max?"

"It's a long story."

She shrugged. "I'm not going anywhere."

"I wanted to follow in the footsteps of lawyers like Martin Luther King…"

A pained expression came over her face as she listened to me explain, as if she felt my regret and sensed the yearning of a soul unable to fulfill its purpose.

"Why not become a civil rights attorney now?"

"I run my father's firm."

"But he passed away," she said softly. "Maybe it's time to fulfill your dream."

"Life doesn't work like that."

"Why not?"

"I made a choice." My chest felt crushed with the pressure of knowing such a thing wasn't possible, not really. My staff and clients back in São Paulo depended on me.

Daisy rested her hand on mine again, her touch warm and gentle.

I turned my hand over to grasp hers. "I don't usually talk about it."

Being with her was easy, opening up to her cathartic. This was fine, we could hang out awhile before it got too late and I had to leave.

"You genuinely care for people," she said, her expression sincere.

"You deserve all the praise, Daisy."

"Why?"

I'd been waiting to break the news to her…

"He made it. Nick's been offered a place with Manchester United."

Her shoulders relaxed and her eyes closed in a way that proved she'd always wanted the best for him. She gave a nod and we shared a moment of gladness for him. Even though Nick was the ultimate asshole at times, my brother was essentially a good man and he'd worked hard for this. He'd dedicated his life to football, and it had all been worth it.

"You got him there," I whispered. "When his dad died you were there for him."

She smiled and her gaze met mine. We let the special moment linger, feeling mutual respect and understanding for how we'd both influenced him in our own ways, sacrificing our time and energy to support him.

Reaching out, I brushed a strand of hair behind her ear, my fingers lingering against her cheek, feeling her soft skin beneath my touch, the warmth of her blush.

A rustling sound reached our ears—we'd both heard it.

"Do you think it's a ghost?" she asked softly.

"Maybe it's someone checking on you."

"Ted told me he wouldn't return until the morning." She paused. "Maybe it's a ghost who needs me to guide them into the light."

I pushed to my feet. "Or into hell."

"Aunt Barbara told me what to say to the ghosts, if I saw any."

I shot her a skeptical look. "Ghosts don't exist, Daisy."

She rose and stood beside me. "Then what was that noise?"

Chapter
FIFTEEN

Daisy

BEFORE TURNING THE CORNER, MAX GAVE ME A WINK to reassure me he'd be fine. I didn't actually believe someone was in here with us, but I'd definitely heard something.

He had no idea how sexy his cute grin looked, but with that one gesture of reassurance, he'd made my toes curl and my heart flip-flop. He was still here, after he could have made an excuse to leave.

I felt a twinge of regret at the thought that he would soon disappear out of my life and I would not have the chance to get to know him better. He'd been kind to me at Nick's party. I shouldn't have run out on him like that at the Hampstead estate. I'd just been so mortified that all I'd wanted was to place as much distance as possible between me and that manor.

Max took my hand and pulled me closer, leading me down the hallway. At his warm touch, my limbs went weak and I almost forgot what we were up to. *Ghost hunting—that's right. Checking out the spirits, guiding them into the light.*

I couldn't think of another person I'd rather go ghost chasing with.

All Max had to do was walk into the room or arch a brow or breathe for heaven's sake.

We stopped just outside one of the rooms.

"Let me go first," he said, shaking me out of my daydreams.

"Don't you want me to instead? I'm more qualified to deal with ghosts."

"No," he said incredulously. "That's not how this works."

It made me smile.

"Stay here." He disappeared inside the dark room.

This was the stuff horror films were made of…the couple splitting up, one left alone while the other goes off bravely exploring the mystery. Each one had a fifty-fifty chance of dying first.

"Max," I called out.

Silence.

"Max, are you okay?"

A shuffling sound reached my ears.

I hurried after him through the door and slammed right into a firm chest, knocking the air out of my lungs. Max's strong arms reached around my waist and lifted me off the floor. He pressed me against the wall and leaned his body against mine. I inhaled sharply and wrapped my legs around his middle, hooking my fingers behind his neck.

His lips lingered dangerously close to mine. "I want you off the floor," he said huskily.

"Why?"

"It was a ghost," he said. "But it's gone."

"You saw it?" I was panting.

"It floated off."

I studied him. "It was a rat, wasn't it?"

He relented with a look that said *yes*.

"How big?"

"The size of a double-decker bus."

I squealed and buried my face in his neck, cringing. Immediately, my senses were stimulated by the familiar scent of the sexy Alpha male who'd protected me. Being this close to Max Marquis made my head spin.

"Are you okay?" he said.

I nodded.

"You shouldn't be here. Not alone, anyway."

"I'm not alone."

"I can't stay, Daisy."

"I know."

"And I can't kiss you. You understand why, right?"

I understood nothing at the moment because he'd pushed his pelvis against me. I felt his erection nudging between my thighs and there was no moving away. I felt suspended in bliss, lulled by the erotic sensations coursing through my body, thrumming my clit.

Max's eyes fell to my lips.

I could feel him growing harder.

When he dragged his teeth across his bottom lip it was dangerously inviting…and proof that he was fighting an urge to do more.

"I need to make sure you're safe." A flash of desire sparked in his eyes.

I stared at his beautiful mouth.

"I've never felt safer," I said softly.

He was speaking now, saying something in Portuguese, his words hypnotic.

Max leaned in to kiss me and then stopped himself.

I pulled back to see his look of confusion.

He peered into my eyes as though searching for the words to appease me.

"Can I kiss you goodbye, Daisy?" he whispered.

I let out a wistful sigh, which he knew meant *yes*. His mouth captured mine greedily, persuading me to relent. Our tongues lashed passionately, our moans of desire colliding as the world fell away.

We could have been anywhere.

I'd never been kissed like this...not by any man. It was like nothing I'd ever experienced, this fierce heat that shook me to my core, promising eternal happiness, a life lived in the sun—the kind of affection that could erase a past filled with sadness, replacing it with hope.

He pulled away and studied my face, nearly gasping. "God, your kiss intoxicates me!"

I'd never felt more alive.

Max's warm breath touched my face. "To taste you..."

The thought of him going down on me caused me to shiver. I wouldn't say no to anything he asked of me. My heart had been shocked back to life...it was beating again, feeling again. I'd planned on being alone tonight—I'd been trying to think of anything except Max. Now, thoughts of him consumed me, stealing my very breath.

He rested his forehead against mine. "This place is not right for...a first time."

To think he'd even gone there in his mind, just like I had. Imagining what it would be like to make love.

Max eased away from the wall and let me stand, but I felt the strength of his arms around me, pulling me toward him. My face nuzzled against his chest and I inhaled the scent of the man who always seemed out of reach. Even now, I was trying to fathom how we'd come to this moment. All those times I'd sensed our chemistry.

I hadn't imagined it. There had been something between

us from that first moment when we'd crashed into each other outside that bar.

Being with Max was the healing I needed—a knight in shining armor delivering me to a place where I could start again, I could build trust again.

"I'm a better person for knowing you," I whispered.

"I wish I could be more to you, Daisy."

Max was trying to let me down gently—a kind gesture for a girl who'd already had her heart torn in two. I stood on my toes and kissed his cheek to show my gratitude.

"Let me drive you home," he said.

"If I leave, I'll break my dare."

He looked conflicted.

"I'm going to see this through, Max. I have to stay until morning. I've already pushed myself beyond what I thought possible and I won't stop until I can see myself in a new light."

My gaze held his defiantly for a long moment.

Then he sighed and brought my wrist to his mouth, kissing it, his eyes closing as his lips brushed my skin.

"That rat is probably still in the building," he said.

"Pretty sure I can run faster than a rat—even a big one."

Smiling, he led me out of the room and down the hall, back to the place where I'd set myself up for the evening.

Max sat down on the blanket and leaned against the wall. I curled up beside him and rested my head on his lap. His fingers trailed through my hair, sending shivers of delight through my body.

I would let him do me this one last favor, guarding me. And I wouldn't fall asleep. I didn't want to waste one second of my last few hours with him.

Chapter
SIXTEEN

Daisy

I OPENED MY EYES AND LOOKED OUT THE CAR WINDOW. We'd arrived at my aunt's home.

Max turned off the engine and unclipped his seatbelt before turning to face me.

I gave him a sleepy smile. "Thank you."

"Hopefully, I made your night bearable."

It was the best night of my life, Max.

Despite my best efforts, I had fallen asleep. But he'd been with me, in the solitude of that old house, and I'd known what it was like to feel safe.

Instead of saying this I went with, "It was totally different to how it could have gone."

"It's fun being your dare buddy."

"Three down," I said. "Three to go."

"What's your next dare?"

"They don't tell us until a few hours before."

"I wouldn't like that."

I shrugged. "It doesn't give me as much time to worry or back out."

"Are you working today?"

"No, would you like to come in?" The words were out before I could stop them. Realizing how forward that sounded, I added, "I can make pancakes. My aunt's out of town visiting my cousin—and she took Wilma."

He grinned at that bit of news, reaching over to play with a strand of my hair, his fingers trailing through one of my brunette locks. It was easy to become lulled by the way he touched me, easy to yearn for his affection.

I saw that familiar look flit across his face—his confliction lingered.

This was goodbye.

"Last night..." he said softly.

I nodded, knowing what he meant to say. "It was lovely. The best goodbye a girl could ask for."

Well, not the best goodbye, since nothing happened besides that kiss—but it was as dreamy as I'd imagined it would be. I could close my eyes and relive the feeling, the scrape of his five o'clock shadow marking my face, his lips hungrily devouring mine...

He let out a sigh. "Being more to each other would be complicated, Daisy."

I just had to let that sink in and become my reality. A part of me was sensing a connection to Max that had my entire body aching for him, my soul longing for more.

Even though he'd stayed up for most of the night he still looked perfect, his hair ruffled, that stubble adding ruggedness to his chiseled jaw.

"I'll see you inside." He reached into the back of the car for my dry cleaning and shoes.

I took them from him, but I didn't want to look at the outfit covered in plastic. I'd worn it and bared my soul to a man I no longer loved.

Then again, I'd been wearing it when Max had carried me away from the pool in his arms. What I felt for Max was very different. It was like my soul was linked to him in some inconceivable way.

These futile thoughts carried no resolution.

We made it to the doorstep and I eased the key in the lock, psyching myself up to look at him one last time. If I was going to tell Max that I'd developed feelings for him, now was the time. Though when I went to speak my throat tightened with uneasiness. I didn't want my last interaction with him to be me embarrassing myself one more time.

He leaned forward and kissed my forehead. "*Seria fácil te amar*, Daisy."

"What did you say?"

"Goodbye." He pivoted and strolled down the pathway towards his car.

He was leaving and I was letting him. There was no other choice.

I nudged open the door and stepped inside.

I hung my dry cleaning on the hallway coat rack and set the shoebox down on the attached bench. Then I leaned against the wall to catch my breath, my mind reeling as I tried to decide what to do next. Letting him walk away felt wrong— it felt like a piece of me was already missing. He'd healed my heart a little. Made me forget the sadness that had brought me to my knees. I'd lost so much, and Max had appeared each time I'd needed him to as though he'd been heaven sent.

Go after him.

Tell him how you feel.

I flew out the front door and bolted into the street.

I stopped when I saw the Ford Escort parked in the same space where Max's car had been. How could I have not told him the truth when I'd had the chance? I'd been so daring lately, right up until it mattered.

Head bowed, I went back inside.

Tracing my fingertips over my lips, I recalled once more the way he'd kissed me the night before. The desire and meaning it held for us could never be conveyed with mere words.

Max Marquis' kisses were a love letter to the soul...*my soul.*

When the doorbell rang, I spun round and pulled open the door.

Max was standing there. "Is the offer still on? For pancakes, I mean?"

"Sorry, kitchen's closed."

His lips quirked up and he rolled his eyes.

Grabbing his hand, I pulled him inside and we stumbled back into the house, laughing.

He shoved the door closed behind him. Cupping my face with his hands, he leaned down and kissed me hard, crushing his lips to mine with a fierce passion that suddenly turned tender and loving.

He eased back a little. "This is what you want?"

I took a deep breath. "Yes...oh, yes."

Stay forever.

We moved together, me tugging his coat off and him working on mine. We reached the staircase and he sank onto the lower step and pulled me onto his lap. Straddling him, I crushed my lips to his again, wrapped in his warm embrace.

"Daisy," he whispered. "If I stay, we're going to do more. We're going to have sex, the mind-blowing kind. The kind that will change everything between us. Do you want that?"

"Yes, I want that. I want you."

In response to his words and his touch, I felt my breasts swell, my sex was wet and ready, my clit throbbing as I rubbed against the bulge of his cock. This felt natural, inevitable, a coming together that we could no longer fight.

He buried his fingers in my hair and nipped my ear. "Bedroom?"

"Yes."

I climbed off him and we raced up the stairs. I took his hand and led him down the hall to my room. We burst through the doorway and were back in each other's arms again, stripping each other's clothes off and flinging our shoes, not caring where they landed.

"Do you have a condom?" he asked.

"I'm on the pill," I said breathlessly.

Max fell to his knees before me and tugged at my panties, pulling them down and then glancing up as though to read my expression.

With my hands on the back of his head, I pulled him forward between my thighs to answer his unspoken question. He let out a lust-filled moan as his tongue darted between my folds.

I inhaled sharply at the pleasure, moving my legs farther apart.

His hands reached around to hold my butt, pulling me closer to his face. This felt forbidden, and at the same time it was as though we'd always been destined to be together like this.

My head fell back, fingers scrunching in his hair, as he continued to masterfully lash me with his tongue as I pleaded for him not to stop. He reached up and cupped my breasts, catching my nipples between his fingers, squeezing rhythmically.

He eased my left thigh over his right shoulder, exposing

more of me, and I shuddered through the shock of an even more intense arousal, my hips rocking against him.

I'd had a crush on this man since I'd first met him. He had transitioned me away from heartache—and now we moved together with the ease of two people who'd always been destined to meet and become more.

"You're beautiful." He eased my leg down and stood up. Covering my mouth with his, he kissed me forcefully, sharing my own taste with me, his tongue tangling with mine, his teeth catching my lower lip in his and biting it playfully.

My fingers curled around the rim of his boxer shorts and I tugged them down, allowing his erection to spring free. I wrapped my palm around him and stroked his length, swooning as his cock hardened even more, becoming firmer.

Max was speaking in Portuguese again; his words timed perfectly with gentle pecks and laps of his tongue along my shoulder and collarbone, then up my neck to my earlobe.

He suddenly pulled back, lowering his gaze. "We have to slow down."

"Why?" My breathing was ragged.

"Because I care about you." He squeezed his eyes shut.

"I want it all, Max. Give me all of it."

He walked over to the chair his jeans had landed on and pulled out his phone, setting it on the bedside table. "Let's have some music."

I was too nervous to offer any requests, too excited with what was happening.

Harry Styles' voice rose into the air, singing the romantic lyrics to "Falling."

Somehow, Max knew this was what I needed, a dreamy backdrop to ease us into making love.

Max nudged me back onto the bed and quickly climbed

on top of me, lifting my wrists above my head and pinning them there.

"You like this?" he asked, his voice husky.

"I've never..." *Been taken like this before.*

"But you like it?"

"God, yes."

"I want to know everything you like." He dipped his head and dragged his lips along my breast, biting my nipple and sending a shockwave of pleasure down between my thighs.

Max moved down to my feet. "Our first time needs to be special, Daisy."

"It's already special."

His lips curled at the edges and then he drew my big toe into his mouth and sucked, watching me, working along my other toes slowly. He kissed my ankle and worked his way up my leg, sending an erotic shiver through me. Again, his mouth found my sex, ravishing it as though addicted.

My body responded to his every touch, alight with each sensation.

He lay on top of me and eased my thighs apart, maneuvering himself between my legs. He raised my left arm to trace kisses along it, and then planted another kiss beneath my armpit, his tenderness sensual and carnal as he worked his way back up to my face. He kissed me passionately, his teeth nipping my lower lip, his tongue warring with mine, driving me wild with its fury.

Using his thumb, he traced circles on my clit, causing me to shudder beneath his touch, rising closer to that moment of bliss.

"Not yet," he teased. "I want to feel you around me when I come."

Max rose over me and used an elbow to support himself

as his right hand directed his cock toward my sex. I arched up as he pushed in deep, dragging my fingernails along his back, the pulsing pleasure building inside me as he slowly eased in and out.

My muscles clenched tightly around his cock as he increased the pace. I was so aroused I couldn't stop moaning.

"I imagined seeing you like this," he said. "Seeing how you'd respond to me..."

"Max..."

"Harder?"

"Yes, fuck me hard."

Our movements became more frenzied, me with my legs wrapped around him as he thrust into me deeper and faster, taking me higher.

The pleasure turned blinding as my orgasm captured me, causing my hips to pump against him furiously as I screamed his name. Max stilled as he came inside me... his groan silenced as he pressed his mouth to mine.

We clung to each other, our hearts pounding, our gasps and sighs filling the room.

We fit perfectly together. All that had happened in my past no longer mattered—the only moment I wanted to stay in was now.

Chapter
SEVENTEEN

Max

I WIPED CONDENSATION OFF THE MIRROR AND STARED AT my reflection.

What's happening to me?

Daisy was merely in the next room and I missed her. *Craved her.*

A glance at my watch showed that we'd slept until noon.

Before that, we'd made love and it had been romantic and tender and passionate and everything in between. We'd rolled around on the sheets on that impossibly small bed, not caring about the world outside her room.

I'd become obsessed with pleasing her, hearing her moan, seeing her come again and again. Afterward, we'd cuddled and she had fallen asleep in my arms with me loving every second of our time together.

When I searched my feelings, I found no regret. Just a deep longing to climb back into bed with her.

She could be awake now. I hated the thought of her mind spinning with uncertainty about our future. Our chemistry was undeniable. Pressing a fingertip to my temple, I tried to think past the doubt that rose up out of the muddle of responsibilities.

I'd rather die a slow death than hurt her.

I'd wrapped one of her towels around my waist. I looked ridiculous in it, really, and it barely covered my generous assets. I couldn't help the devilish smile that crossed my face as I ruminated over the way she'd responded to my lovemaking. The way she'd moved, reacting to my touch, the way she'd shuddered when she'd come with me buried deep inside her. We fit together spectacularly. Fucking her was like finding Nirvana. The taste of her was addictive; *she* was addictive.

Rubbing my face with my hands, I tried to get my thoughts under control…thinking carefully about how my life might be if Daisy was no longer a part of it. A slither of regret slid down my spine in a visceral response to the thought of losing her.

She was never mine to lose.

This bathroom was small. Too small, really. I didn't like the idea of this being Daisy's permanent home. Her aunt adored her, but still… This space carved out for Daisy was too damn claustrophobic.

My brother had made a colossal mistake in leaving her—I knew this deep down in my soul. Squeezing my eyes shut, I tried to push these thoughts of her out of my mind—the girl in the other room, waiting for me to step up and be a gentleman.

I was worse than Nick.

Here I was preparing to walk out of her life forever after I was meant to be the one saving her. If I stayed, things would get way too complicated. This thing between us was never meant to happen. Yet I didn't want to say goodbye.

The choice isn't mine to make.

I headed out of the bathroom and paused in the doorway. If I looked at her, I'd find myself wanting her again. Some of my clothes were flung over an armchair and some were strewn across the carpet next to her bra and panties. It was a mocking reminder of what it looks like to lose control.

I finally allowed myself to take in the morning beauty of Daisy, who was now sitting up in bed, greeting me with an uneasy smile. Her hair was tousled and I was also responsible for her post-fucked glow. Her questioning eyes melted my heart all over again.

It was easy to walk toward her, like I was doing now. To kneel on the side of the bed, feeling it dip as I pressed my lips to her forehead, my smile moving against her soft skin, grazing her cheek and then moving over her soft, pliant mouth. The kiss deepened, our tongues dancing playfully.

I managed to pull back a little. "Good morning."

She raised her hand to cup my face. "I thought I'd dreamt you."

"Not this time," I said, grinning. "I'm the real thing."

"And you're still here."

"Daisy…"

"I know." She let out a sharp breath. "This is how a Brazilian says goodbye."

She made me smile again.

"I kind of like it," Daisy said, giving me a wink. "I might move there."

I leaned back in surprise. "Would you?"

"I'd have to go by boat."

I shook my head and laughed at her. "Boat it is."

"You're leaving me very happy."

Her words caused my chest to tighten, and I got off the bed to stand beside it. "I only want what's best for you, Daisy."

"What's best for me is for you to climb back in bed."

She grabbed my hand and pulled me forward. I sank down next to her on the mattress and my lips met her cheek again, sliding across to her mouth where my moan was silenced. Her scent filled my senses, her perfume so alluring that all I could do was press my mouth to her neck, her temple.

I settled into a peaceful stillness, enjoying the feel of her, drawing her closer, hating even that small distance between us, as though I were fighting against time and its insistence that we were over before we began.

This was our slow and painful goodbye.

And we both knew it.

The way we'd met had made things impossible for us from the start...all those complications crowding us, those unspoken rules of my family, tearing us apart from the beginning.

There was too much history between us and none of it was ours to cherish. It was destined to be hidden away in the confines of our hearts.

Her fingers trailed through my hair. "This morning was something we both needed. Don't feel guilty."

"I don't." I pushed away my melancholy thoughts.

She was right, of course. Her wisdom eased my doubts.

"What are you doing today?" I asked.

This way I'd have a complete picture of her day. I'd be able to imagine where she was at any given moment. It would soothe the hurt a little, or so I told myself.

"I'm going to visit Covent Garden's Quinto Bookshop," she said brightly. "My aunt's birthday is coming up soon. She collects old books. I always find her something special in there."

"Sounds like fun." *Like heaven on earth.*

"It's a treasure trove for booklovers." She beamed with happiness.

There'd be nothing more incredible than spending the day with her both in and out of bookshops. We could grab a bite to eat afterwards, and maybe, if she was up for it, see a show in the West End later in the evening. Ending up right back here in her bed and rolling between the sheets. Though the bed was cramped, what went on beneath the covers made up for it.

Of course, I could take her back to my hotel. We could order room service. We could shut out the world and never leave…

I'd flown thousands of miles to spend time with Nick, but as he was caught up with Morgan, I was guilt free. He'd kept me at arm's length during this visit and I didn't care, because my time had been spent hanging out with Daisy.

"What time are you heading out?" I said. "I can give you a lift to Covent Garden, if you like."

"Thank you, but I'll be fine," she said. "How about you?"

"Well, I was supposed to be taking my mum to church."

"Oh no! I'm sorry."

"It's all right. Anyway, she's always trying to nudge me into the confessional. I'm a backsliding Catholic." I laughed. "Whenever I approach a priest, I see terror in his eyes."

"You're not that bad, are you?"

"No, he just assumes I'm a bad boy because I'm thirty-three and not married. I'm half convinced that's why my mother parades me around after the service to introduce me to potential…"

I'd said too much.

Daisy 's hand rested on my forearm. "Whoever she is, she'll be a very lucky young lady to have you." She grinned. "I mean, you took me to church this morning. I'm a convert. Love isn't so scary anymore." She realized what she'd just said and closed her eyes in embarrassment.

Reaching up, I pushed a strand of hair out of her face and tucked it behind her ear, my hand lingering for a beat too long.

In prolonging these intimate moments, I suppose I was trying to convince myself that being with her for the rest of my life was possible.

"I feel the same way, Daisy. I want you to know that."

"Thank you again for last night," she whispered. "For keeping me company in that old house."

"It was my pleasure."

"Might go back there tonight," she said, grinning. "It's a lucky place for me."

"Even with that rat running around?"

"Nothing scares me anymore."

"You don't need to take on these dares, Daisy. You're perfect the way you are." My fingertips trailed up and down the silky skin of her arm.

She responded to my touch, her eyelids heavy, her breathing shallow.

I pushed up from the bed and strolled over to the chair.

Grinning, I whipped off the towel to reveal my nakedness. She pressed her hand to her lips in mock shock, but she didn't look away. She watched me dress, her eyebrows raised in playful curiosity. This could have been what every morning was like for us. Heading out for breakfast in some café and whiling the day away.

I buttoned my shirt and pulled on my trousers. Finally, when I was fully dressed, I went to give her one last kiss goodbye.

My feet paused at the foot of the bed. If I kissed her again I wouldn't leave.

I looked down at her. "Want me to bring you anything?"

"No, thank you." Her hair spilled over the pillow like silk and she'd raised her arms above her head unconsciously languishing in an erotic pose, a nipple peeking above the sheet.

I wanted to bury my hands in those beautiful locks and lavish her body with kisses.

This was how I would remember her. Just like this.

I headed for the door, then paused and rested my forehead against it as I felt the pull of her stare. The pulse of our connection ever present.

She should have been The One.

"I wish I'd met you before him," I said, my voice deep and full of anguish.

This longing I felt to stay with her was all-consuming.

I forced myself to open the bedroom door, willed myself to walk down the stairs and out of the house.

Later, when I entered my hotel room and collapsed on the bed, I couldn't remember climbing into my car and driving across town.

I stared up at the ceiling with my stomach in knots, the loneliness suffocating me.

I lay there knowing I'd done the right thing by walking away. As the hours ticked by, I tried to think of anything or anyone but Daisy.

Chapter
EIGHTEEN

Daisy

O NCE THROUGH THE DOORS OF THE QUINTO Bookshop, the heady scent of ancient paper woos you, keeping you entranced amongst the tomes.

This is what I needed, to immerse myself in this antiquated refuge for book lovers, keeping busy so I didn't think about the way Max made me feel, knowing that our short burst of happiness was over. I didn't want to mull over how his kisses felt like life itself. Or how incredible it was to lie naked beside him.

Or that I'd let him leave this morning when I should have grabbed his ankles and refused to let him go. Okay, that would only have scared him away faster...

Think about the books.

Remember why you're here.

Taking my time, I searched their well-stocked shelves for an exceptional collector's item that would be a perfect gift for Aunt Barbara. I had no doubt there was a first edition here waiting to be discovered, then cherished by her forever.

Tracing the spines with delicate fingers, I moved along a line of hardbacks. My heart skipped a beat when I found one she'd adore, an original copy of *The Tale of Peter Rabbit* by Beatrix Potter. Perfectly preserved with a colored drawing of Peter Rabbit on the cover.

When I opened the hardback and saw it had been printed in 1901, I knew it would be expensive. Still, my aunt had opened her doors to me and made me feel at home. I wanted to splurge a little on her birthday.

After peeling open the first page, I sucked in my shock at the price. "Bloody hell!"

The book cost a thousand pounds.

Self-consciously, I threw a cheeky smile over at the young man behind the counter. He gave me a knowing look back. Beside him sat an antique till that gave the place character. That was what I loved about this shop, its quaintness. Its prices, not so much.

I slid the book back and said, "As if."

From behind a bookshelf, another customer coughed loudly, hinting that my outburst had bothered them.

Okay, Mr. Quiet Police. But a thousand pounds is too much for a book. For me, anyway.

Continuing my search, I found a hardback second edition of *Harry Potter.* Its condition looked flawless. My heart stopped when I saw the swirl of a signature on the first page— it had been signed by J. K. Rowling.

"Oh, my God!" Barbara would love this one.

"Shush," came the chastisement from the same man behind the bookcase.

I poked out my tongue in the stranger's direction.

The price of the Harry Potter novel was more within my range. I'd read that second editions could also be collector's items if they were in mint condition.

While paying for it, I shared with the shopkeeper how

much I loved this place and how I'd always been able to find that one book I didn't know I needed.

"Keep the noise down," came a gruff male voice from the back of the store.

Then Annoying Bookcase Man stepped out into the aisle.

He was tall and shockingly handsome. He had the kind of face that made me stare because he looked exactly like...Max.

I forgot how to breathe.

Max was dressed casually in ripped jeans and a jumper, and he looked especially sexy in his leather jacket. He was also wearing a panty-melting smile.

My body responded to him like we were back in my bedroom, like his kisses were again running along my skin, his touch firm and masterful, causing time to stand still.

He rose to his full height. "Bookshops are like libraries, young lady," he chastised, pointing to the *"Please Be Quiet— People are Reading"* sign above the counter.

I loudly crinkled the paper bag I was holding.

He looked amused and held out his hand. "Max."

What?

"I'm Max," he repeated as though I didn't know.

"Daisy...?" I made it sound like a question.

This was weird. Like green cupcakes weird. Like, you don't mind eating them because they're delicious, but all the while you're thinking *what the fuck.*

I could be odd myself but right now Max had literally lost it.

"What did you get?" He nodded toward the bag in my hands.

"Harry Potter. It's for my aunt's birthday." I'd already told him my plans this morning.

Right, which was how he knew I'd be here.

My insides did a flip as he leaned forward to say something. He whispered, "This is where you tell me to fuck off."

"Why?"

"I'm clearly flirting with you." He winked.

I glanced over at the man behind the till who was watching us.

I snapped my gaze back to Max as it dawned on me what this was all about. "What's a nice guy like you doing in a place like this?"

Max's eyelid twitched. "That doesn't work, Daisy." Then he stunned me into silence with a devilish smile. "Try again."

My hand pressed to my chest. "I didn't think that you…"

"Want to help me pick out a book?" he asked. "I'm buying a gift for my secretary back in São Paulo. She's sixty. She's like a mother to me and I always bring her back something special. You seem to have great taste."

It was like we were meeting for the first time. And to prove it, his eyes lit up with happiness and amusement, as though hinting he wanted this to be a new beginning.

A moment to cherish just for us.

I looked at him as though seeing him for the first time, admiring his extraordinary features, staring into his deep brown eyes and getting lost in this heady attraction. Max was like that first breath of fresh air you drew into your lungs on a crisp winter morning. Or that bit of luck you prayed for with a heart full of faith.

This felt like an impossible dream might be coming true at last, a chance at something profound that had always seemed out of reach. I struggled to believe it was real…Max and I together.

"Tell me about your secretary?" I said softly. "So I know her taste in books."

"Her name is Gylda." Max thought on it. "She loves the classics."

"Really?" I said. "Me, too."

"I didn't know," he said, but then quickly corrected himself. "How could I? Considering we've only just met."

I gave him a quirky smile and had him follow me around the bookshelf that he'd been lurking behind. Together we searched for the perfect book for Gylda.

Max was thrilled when we discovered the collection of compendiums on John William Waterhouse's paintings. With his secretary's love of Shakespeare, the cover with its elegant portrayal of Ophelia would be perfect for her.

We got in the checkout queue and I looked up at him. "What happens now?"

Max tilted his head, smiling. "What would you like to happen?"

Chapter
NINETEEN

Daisy

M Y HEART STUTTERED AT THE THOUGHT OF spending more time with Max. Not as my ex's big brother, who was always looking out for me, but as someone who could be my friend without my past getting in the way this time.

We left the store with our purchases and headed to Max's sports car. Even though our futures were uncertain, our chemistry held us together with the promise of being more...more than friends, perhaps.

All I knew was that my heart had begun to heal the moment I'd bumped into him outside Isobel's. Our paths had crossed on so many occasions since, and each time my faith in people had been restored just a little bit more.

Max drove us to Soho.

By some miracle he found parking outside a flower shop.

He led me to the front door of a restaurant called Buteco, telling me this was a favorite hangout where expats of Brazil got to spend precious time together while sharing a delicious meal that reminded them of home.

"This place has a modest setting," said Max. "But amongst

the understated décor is a family run business with authentic cooking that will blow you away."

It was easy to see how its hospitality eased the homesick. The owner, Pedro, made us feel so welcome.

He served plate after plate of delicious Brazilian food for me to taste. From the Acarajé, a black-eyed pea ball fried in palm oil and stuffed with shrimp, to a sampling of Moqueca de Camarão, a shrimp stew cooked in coconut milk. It made my mouth water and as soon as I'd finished the food on my plate, I wanted more.

For dessert, we were served coconut truffles.

Max reached for a truffle and fed it to me, looking pleased with my reaction to the delicious explosion of pleasure on my taste buds. Being with him, sharing this food and getting to know more about his culture, it evaporated my problems and made me feel nurtured.

Max made me feel nurtured.

Leaning back, I felt so stuffed I wasn't sure I'd be able to walk out of the place. I rested my hands on my tummy like a pregnant woman, trying to ease the discomfort of having eaten one too many truffles.

"I'm glad you enjoyed it." Max looked so happy. "I love seeing you eat."

I reached over and rested my hand on his. "Thank you for bringing me here."

His expression changed to uncertainty at my touch. Doubt crept in and I withdrew my hand. But Max quickly grabbed my wrist and pulled me closer toward him. He leaned forward and kissed my wrist. "*Minha linda.*"

"I hope you didn't just call me your fat princess?" I tapped my stomach.

"Ha, not even close."

"Are you going to tell me what you said?"

"If you are what you eat, then you look like a coconut truffle. Thought I might lose a hand there for a minute."

"You ate half of them."

"Not as many as you, apparently."

"You fed them to me."

"Only because I love your mouth."

I drew in a sharp breath. "I love your mouth, too."

He rolled his eyes playfully.

"That's it." I rested my napkin on the table as our plates were cleared. "I'm moving to Brazil."

"My devious plan worked," he said with a laugh.

Max thanked Pedro for the incredible meal. They chatted in both English and Portuguese with the warmth of old friends.

When Pedro returned to the kitchen, Max whispered, "He says you're very pretty."

"For a girl who looks like a truffle."

"I hope I didn't scare you back at the bookshop?" he asked, his tone amused.

"It was the best kind of surprise."

"You were happy to see me, then?"

I gave him a look that told him he'd just asked me a ridiculous question. Seeing him again had made my day. It had made my life, actually. Even if all this was fleeting.

He sensed my reticence. "I can't stay away from you, Daisy."

I swallowed hard, my heartbeat racing at the thought that things might work out between us. Maybe we could find a way to be together.

"I'm strong," I said softly. "You know that."

"Yes, I know."

The words had come out wrong, so I tried again. "I know you're going back to Brazil soon."

He looked up at the ceiling and groaned. "Let's talk about something else."

"You'll miss our food."

"What food?"

"When you go back home. You'll miss our beans on toast."

"Do not talk to me about English food."

"What! We have the best food! Bangers and Mash... Toad in the Hole."

"No, thank you." He raised his hands in defense. "And don't get me started on Spotted Dick."

I giggled. "You really have to taste my spotted dick."

He chuckled loudly. "And I thought you liked me."

"Well, I know what you love to eat." My hand slapped to my mouth. "Oh, my God, I didn't just say that."

"Yeah, I think you did."

"You're a bad influence."

"I'm just here for the entertainment."

"That's not fair."

"To be honest, I love getting to know the real you."

"How do you mean?"

"You're *my* version of Daisy." Max bit his lip. "I see who you are and I'm..."

"You're what?"

He sat back. "I'm compelled to spend more time with you. Is that something you'd like?"

I smiled at him, taking a moment to replay his words, letting them sink in.

"What do you like to do for a pastime?" he asked.

"I've been pretty busy lately," I confessed. "With work and..."

"And?"

I shrugged. I was boring compared to him. "How about you?"

"I surf." He let out a sigh of happiness. "Fernando de Noronha is off Brazil's northeast coast. It's a national marine park and ecological sanctuary. The beaches are perfect. Feeling the sand between your toes…there's nothing like it. You get to swim with dolphins and turtles, and you might even see sharks, if you're lucky."

"I don't call seeing a shark lucky."

"They're beautiful."

"It sounds like paradise. I'd love to go."

"Visitors are restricted, but if you know a local who can grant you access…" He arched a brow. "How about you? What's your all time favorite place outside of London?"

"I've never left England."

He looked shocked. "That's ridiculous, Daisy. Are you serious?"

"I just don't…fly."

"But…there are so many beautiful countries to see. Would you visit me in Brazil?"

I hesitated, his question hanging in the air between us.

I finally exhaled. "You come to London frequently, right?"

"Daisy, I work six days a week at my law firm. I come back once every few months."

A cold dread closed around my heart at the thought of not seeing him. I would miss him terribly. I couldn't see a way round it. "Flying is impossible for me."

"You're scared of flying?" He shook his head. "You need to get over that."

"I've come to terms with it."

"With what? Your inability to fly?"

Dragging my bag onto my lap, I reached in and opened my purse, rummaging around for cash.

"Is it the cost?" he asked.

"No."

Max waved a hand. "I've got this."

I need fresh air.

"I want to pay." With a trembling hand, I threw several twenty-pound notes on the table.

Max snatched them up and pushed to his feet. He shoved the money back into my handbag. "This is my treat."

My chair squeaked as I pushed it back. "I'm sorry. I have to go."

He looked confused. "Did I say something to offend you?"

I rushed for the door and stepped outside, sucking in cold air, trying to calm my breathing, glancing left and right to get my bearings.

I needed to get home...needed to push that haunting memory away.

Max's strong arm pulled me back, crushing me against his firm chest.

"Take a breath."

I gave a nod that I was calmer.

He spun me around to face him and gripped my shoulders. "What just happened in there?"

"I'm never going to see you again after you go back to Brazil. And it's my fault."

Max yanked me against his chest in a bear hug. He was too strong for me to pull away from. This was only delaying the agony—parting from him now would hurt so much worse than before.

"I've upset you." He pressed his lips to the top of my head. "You have to tell me why, Daisy."

"Can you take me home?"

"Of course." He led me back to his car, glancing at me with concern as he opened the passenger door. "Please talk to me about what's bothering you."

I climbed into the front seat. "There's nothing to talk about."

We drove across town in silence, the familiar landmarks proving we were heading in the right direction. Embarrassment over my outburst caused my cheeks to burn. This fear was embedded so deep within my soul that I knew nothing could be done about it.

I wanted to reach out to him, but didn't...and I wanted to apologize for ruining our lunch, but my anxiety continued creeping and crawling throughout my body, causing my muscles to tighten and my throat to constrict, making it hard to breathe normally.

Max pulled the car up to my aunt's house. When I went to unclip my seatbelt, his hand grabbed my wrist. "Wait."

"I should go."

I heard a *click* and realized he had locked the car's doors.

He turned to face me. "Consider yourself my prisoner. You're not going anywhere until you tell me what happened back there."

"Please, let me go."

His hand slipped from mine and he leaned back with a sigh. "Trust me, Daisy. Give me that much, please."

Tears stung my eyes and I felt those familiar feelings of guilt return with a vengeance.

"Talk to me, Daisy." He reached over and squeezed my hand. "I promise I'll understand."

I let out a shaky breath.

Get out of the car.

Forget this.

"We've come this far, you and me," he said quietly. "Despite the odds."

A tremor ran through me. I'd carried this tragic event around for so long it had come to define me.

"Does it have something to do with your brother, Liam?" he coaxed.

"I can't…" I shook my head. "I'm ashamed."

"Why?"

I swallowed the lump in my throat.

"Liam was scheduled for a flight to Bavaria," I said, my voice trembling. "He was a member of the ski team and he was flying out there for winter training with his teammates. They all met up at our place first. Whoever was meant to be taking them to the airport was running late, and Liam and his friends were panicking because they thought they'd miss their flight." My throat tightened as I relived the nightmare that had ruined our lives. "I offered to drive them."

Max let out a long breath as he tried to piece together the rest of my story.

"Traffic was heavy," I continued. "With seconds to spare I got them to the airport."

"Safely?" he asked, revealing that he'd guessed at some other horror.

I gave a nod. "I told Liam to grab his gear from the boot. I didn't even hug him goodbye because he had to hurry and get through customs. I helped rush them along. He and his mates ran into the airport with big smiles on their faces because they'd made it there on time." I paused, swallowing hard. "I helped them catch their plane."

"Oh, Daisy." Max studied my face, reading my thoughts.

"He made it to his flight because of me."

"You can't blame yourself."

"They tried to make an emergency landing over Stuttgart. They had engine trouble."

He lifted my hand to his mouth and kissed it gently.

"If only they had missed that flight," I said, my voice breaking.

"It wasn't your fault."

"How could it not be? All those lives lost because I insisted on doing them a favor."

"I'm sorry, Daisy. Truly, I am."

"Liam's instructor told me he was a fine sportsman. He was destined for the Olympics." I wiped my runny nose with the back of my hand.

Max reached over and retrieved a tissue from the glove box. "Here you are."

I dabbed my face with it, sniffing, as more tears sprang from my eyes and trickled down my cheeks.

"His coach should have been more considerate of your grief," said Max.

"I believe their friend was meant to be late, and I interfered with fate."

Max gathered me into a hug. After a moment, I pulled away. "I'll never forgive myself."

"You have nothing to forgive yourself for."

"I replay that morning over and over. It's like an out-of-body experience where I'm shouting at myself not to speak up...not to offer them a lift."

"Have you considered that maybe you were meant to take them, Daisy?"

I shook my head. "What do you mean?"

"Maybe you were meant to see your brother happy as he headed off to do what he loved. It wasn't about the awards to him, it was the sport itself. It was about the camaraderie with his teammates."

"Aunty says Liam's forever happy now, that he's skiing all over heaven."

"You're aunt's as mad as a hatter."

I burst out laughing. "Aren't you supposed to agree with her for my sake?"

"Well, I know this much—he wouldn't want you to be sad. He certainly wouldn't want you to take the blame."

"I know you're right, but I can't shake it." The trauma I still felt was stifling.

I was afraid Max wouldn't want to see me again. I'd been too emotional, and now he knew how damaged I was inside.

I reached for the door handle. "Thank you for lunch."

"You have to go back to university," he said flatly. "Promise me you'll consider it."

"I will," I said to appease him.

"There's something I've been meaning to do," he said. "I just never get around to doing it."

I looked back at him, fingers curling around the door handle, ready for him to release me from the car.

He narrowed his gaze on me. "I want to see more of... London."

"I thought you spent your summers here while you were growing up."

"Yes, but I haven't allowed myself to be a tourist in years."

"What sort of things do you want to see?"

"All of it."

"Even taking a double-decker bus ride? That kind of thing?"

"That would be a fun place to start." He gave me a questioning smile. "Want to be my guide?"

Chapter
TWENTY

Max

I COULDN'T BELIEVE DAISY HAD NEVER VISITED THE Victoria and Albert Museum before.

Together, we strolled along the hallways and huddled close in the vast showrooms awed by the variety of the art and fashion—and even the architecture of the building itself. It was easy to get lost in the place.

Before coming here, we'd acted like tourists, having taken a tour on a double-decker bus around the city, and then getting off at the stop outside this museum.

After her tearful confession of self-imposed guilt earlier, I was glad to be the one to make her feel better.

She'd lit up with joy the moment she'd realized we were stopping at the museum. It housed some of the most incredible sculptures. One could see a brilliant snapshot of Great Britain within its formidable walls, but other objects from all over the world were showcased here as well—from rare manuscripts to a showroom full of glamorous wedding dresses.

"It's impossible to see everything in one day," I told her. "There are well over two million treasures here spanning five thousand years. We'll have to come back again. Just you and me."

She brightened at that. "To be honest, you didn't strike me as the type of person who would want to visit the Victoria and Albert Museum."

"I have a soft spot for Prince Albert." I rolled my eyes. "No, not because of that, Daisy Whitby," I chastised her with a grin. "For what Albert did for the United Kingdom. Advancing social issues, his passion for the working class, that kind of thing."

"It's the most common type of male piercing, apparently."

"Hey, focus." I snapped my fingers in front of her face.

We both laughed, drawing amused stares from the other tourists.

We continued on until we reached the jewelry collection, lingering before a glass case with a collection of rare objects. The one that caught Daisy's attention was an eye miniature from the early nineteenth century.

"This seems to be a common theme around the world," she said.

"Doesn't surprise me," I said. "They are the gateway to the soul."

She rose onto her toes so she could stare right into my eyes.

"What are you doing?"

"Looking into your soul."

"Careful, you might not like what you see."

She wagged a finger in front of my face. "You can't fool me, Max. I see who you really are."

I grabbed her fingers and squeezed them gently. Perhaps she really could see the real me. It felt like a revelation.

Daisy filled the vacuum within me, making it easier for my feelings to find their freedom. I had never really allowed myself to love a woman before. With her, I could see it happening.

We stopped at the entrance to another exhibit. "I have to cover your eyes for this next one."

"It's not horrific, is it?" She sounded nervous.

"Trust me?" I stood behind her and put my hands over her eyes. "Walk forward."

She giggled, finding this mysterious adventure funny.

Once we were inside the exhibit, I eased my fingers off her face. "Open your eyes."

She glanced back at me, smiling, and then turned to face the glass window shop displays. The one before us had been created by Liberty's.

Within the small space directly ahead of us was a mannequin dressed in a green taffeta gown. It was holding up a book and was surrounded by many more that were artfully positioned here and there. Liberty had created a glamorous shop window with a colorful collection of romance novels. The museum plaque stated this one was called "*The love of reading captured in a moment of time.*"

Daisy let out a gasp filled with awe.

"I want the rest of today to be about you."

She seemed dazed. "What?"

"Go look." I nudged her forward.

She hurried over and peered through the glass window, mesmerized by the display. She started to press her nose against the window, but then seemed to think better of it.

"Does it inspire you?" I asked.

"Tremendously! Thank you so much, Max." She fell back against me as my arms closed around her.

"I can't stop looking at it," I said. "It's the spectrum of colors and the unique way the display conveys its meaning."

"When I was little," she said, excitement in her tone, "we went Christmas shopping, me and my mum, and all I wanted to do was peer into the shop windows. They really can be magical."

I released her and tilted her chin up, staring intently into her eyes. "When you're drawn to something like this you have to listen to your heart."

"It isn't easy to join the design teams. There's a lot of competition."

"You have to believe in yourself."

She looked away. "After Liam died, nothing seemed to matter."

"Your dream matters now more than ever," I said softly.

She gazed up at me. "If you reconsider your career, I will too."

That made me smile. "I'd sit in on my dad's court cases… always in awe at how he tore apart the prosecution's case."

"How old were you?"

"I was a teenager."

"And here you are now," she said. "A top lawyer."

"I've never taken three weeks off before." I gave a shrug. "There was never a reason."

"Thank you so much for today. It's been special."

"I don't want this day to end, Daisy."

"What would you like to do?"

"How about we go back to the hotel for dinner?"

"I'm still full from lunch."

I smiled suggestively. "Go back for a drink, then?"

"I have a fun idea."

She wouldn't tell me what it was, though. She kept her secret from the time we left the museum, all the way back to the Waldorf Hotel.

We snuggled in the backseat of the taxi grateful for the warmth.

When we arrived at the Waldorf, she guided me to the lift with mischief in her step, and punched the UP button. I was amused by her enthusiasm, the way she kept glancing back at me with a cheeky grin.

We arrived at the hotel's top floor bar.

Ahead of us was that long glass chute that went down several floors.

"I'll go first," she said.

After receiving a nod from a member of the staff, Daisy climbed into the entrance of the chute and sat on the blue mat. Her confidence made my heart soar. She looked back at me and grinned, then shot down the chute, screaming and laughing as she disappeared from view.

I climbed in behind her, waiting for the staff member to give me the go ahead. Below me was a sheer breathtaking drop and to my left was a wall of glass. The view was spectacular.

I hesitated before pushing off, realizing the profoundness of this moment.

This act represented me risking everything to go after what I wanted—the person waiting for me at the end of this dare. I had to change my life to get to a place where I could find fulfillment.

I shot down the chute, zooming around the corner with my heart racing, my throat tight, adrenaline surging through my veins, sparking an uncommon joy inside me as the world whooshed by.

The end came up fast, but I slowed just enough to avoid doing a "Daisy"—coming to a halt and using the momentum to stand.

Daisy ran forward and fell into my arms. We laughed hysterically at ourselves. It was ridiculous and yet liberating.

Feeling high from our mutual rush, we jumped on the lift and virtually tripped over each other to get to my hotel room. I fumbled for my door key impatiently.

Finally, we made it inside...

I immediately nudged Daisy back against the wall, pressing my body against hers and kissing her passionately.

I yanked off her coat and then my fingers found the zipper of her jeans, tugging them off her hips and pulling them down. She stepped out of them, her fingers trailing through my hair. Neither of us could stand not touching the other.

With perspiration misting my forehead, I unzipped my jeans and hopped out of them. Neither of us cared about the rest of our clothes.

I cupped her face in my hands. "You're a part of me now, Daisy."

She sealed her lips to mine, fighting to get closer.

I ripped off her panties, needing to be inside her, lifting her up so that she could wrap her legs around me.

I entered her in one thrust, feeling her wet warmth envelope my cock, hearing her moan loudly as she tugged at my hair, both of us captured in a feverish embrace.

Hearing our ragged breathing—and the erotic sounds of our bodies banging against the wall as I took her—only aroused me more.

I wanted to give her everything, every last part of me.

I was consumed with need whenever I was around Daisy, starved even when she was with me, even with me buried deep inside her, her hands around my neck as we clung to each other.

She climaxed with a thready cry, her body trembling against mine.

When it was over, I rested my forehead against hers and whispered, "Daisy Whitby, I love everything about you."

"You don't have to say that," she whispered back.

"But I can show it," I said, lifting her up in my arms and carrying her over to the bed. "I can show you how I feel."

Chapter
TWENTY-ONE

Daisy

MY LIFE WAS PERFECT.

Max and I had indulged in a whirlwind romance over the last four days. I'd been having the best sex of my life with the best man I'd ever met—a man who treated me with dignity, who occupied my every thought.

Today, though, things had taken a weird twist with one of those moments you wished wasn't happening.

Dare Club members had been invited to a large warehouse in Soho, in the arts and fashion district. It was all very exciting right up until I was sitting in a flimsy chair in front of a round mirror with a makeup artist going to town on my face.

This was humiliating. "What am I meant to be, exactly?"

Ted rolled his eyes in that condescending way I'd come to love. "Take a wild guess, Daisy."

Wiggling my nose, I tried to lose the red bauble. "You're lucky I don't have a clown phobia."

"Get over yourself. This is a charity event for sick children," he said. "It's about making them laugh."

"They'll laugh, all right."

"It's a theme. Your job is to walk down the runway like

a model showing off your pretty dress and make those kids scream with delight."

"This isn't a dare, it's a punishment."

"Why so serious?" He pulled his mouth wider.

I glared at him. "You'll miss me when I'm gone."

"Correction, you'll miss me." Ted held out his hand for my phone, a twinkle of amusement lighting up his eyes.

"No need. Thank you, though." In fact, if I saw anyone taking a photo of me, I'd take a running dive and land on top of them.

I stared at my ridiculous reflection in the mirror and muttered, "I've never done anything like this!"

Ted folded his arms across his chest. "That's the point. We have you doing something completely out of the ordinary. Something you'd not normally do. It'll be daring for you to walk out on that stage and have people staring at you."

I'd always hated being the center of attention—even when I wasn't dressed up like this.

"You're on in fifteen minutes. The others are practicing their walk. Go join them."

With my nose scrunched up I said, "It's basically putting one foot in front of the other."

"Daisy, it's not as easy as it looks."

"Were you a model once?" I spun round to get a better look at him.

He grinned at me. "There's more to me than just my pretty face."

"I totally agree, Ted." I widened my eyes at him. "Even though I will never forgive you for this, you've changed my life. I'd never have done any of these daring things if it hadn't been for you."

"Oh, stop. You know I love the lot of you." He ambled off.

At least I wasn't the only one being humiliated within an inch of my life—the others were all dressed up like me.

After a few minutes, I was also provided with a large purple wig and clumpy clown shoes. The wig was itchy and the shoes were so large I was dangerously close to tripping.

Around ten very tall, very slim models wandered behind my seat. Watching them in the mirror's reflection, I felt a pinch of betrayal.

Wait a minute…

They'd clearly had a more talented makeup artist because they all looked sexy as hell in their clown get-ups. I looked like the kind of clown you'd see in horror films. I'd end up scaring the children, for heaven's sake.

But at least no one would recognize me.

The blue satin gown I'd been given to wear was elegant, though, and fit my curves perfectly, so there was that.

The student fashion designer showing off her new collection knew how to complement a figure. If I hadn't looked like Joaquin Phoenix in *The Joker*, I might actually have been able to have some fun.

This *was* for charity after all, and focusing on that fact helped a bit. No one would see me anyway. We were tucked away in a warehouse in the middle of the day.

Slipping off the chair, I tried to walk elegantly and not stand out, but I wobbled instead. The others made it look easy. I looked like I had a stick up my bum.

And I needed to pee.

Halfway down a long hallway, I peeked behind a thick curtain.

The auditorium was filled with guests who were finding their seats. The stage led to a long runway—the one I'd be stumbling down.

These dares were meant to challenge us, but this one was torture—I'd be putting myself out there and making myself vulnerable in the worst kind of way.

I inhaled sharply.

Oh, no.

Morgan Hawtry sat in the front row, surrounded by women I assumed were her girlfriends. They looked as pristine and pretty as was humanly possible, all dressed in designer jeans, flowing shirts and a copious amount of jewelry, with bags that cost a fortune, no doubt.

My eyes locked with hers.

I pulled back and let the curtain fall closed as I hid behind it. There was no way I could go out there and parade in front of her looking like this. The evening had just gotten considerably worse.

There was still time to make a run for it.

I let out a protracted moan; there was no choice but to go through with it for the sake of those poor children, at least. The thought of seeing their faces brighten gave me courage.

This isn't about you. Do the right thing and put on a smile. Make it look like you want to be here.

With my pep talk over and with big, clumsy feet, I wobbled into the loo.

I looked in the closest mirror and reassured myself. Even I didn't recognize me in this curly wig, red painted mouth, dark eye shadow and red bauble nose. I looked like a freak in a nightmare.

I'd be haunting my own dreams.

Scurrying out, I headed back to the waiting area.

"Daisy Whitby?" It was a familiar voice.

She was right behind me. I felt her glare scorching my back.

"I thought that was you," said Morgan, her tone mocking.

I didn't want to turn around, didn't want to talk with her. And I really didn't want to see her smug face taking pleasure in my humiliation.

This was *her* world of high-fashion and glamour, with beautiful people and their posh dresses and overly priced handbags. I'd stepped into hell and she was the Queen of Flames.

Morgan caught up with me. "Are you in this?"

I turned to face her. "This is a charity event."

She looked aghast. "You can't go out there looking like…"

"I'm part of a club that's helping out today," I said in my defense.

She looked me up and down. "Whose idea was it to include you?"

How Nick could find Morgan more appealing than me was a mystery. Yes, she was pretty, but she wasn't kind…or thoughtful…or even someone you could trust. It didn't make sense.

She stepped closer. "Are you going to apologize?"

"For what?"

"You crashed our engagement party."

Her words stung, but I didn't let it show. "I had no idea it was that kind of party."

"Nice little stunt you pulled in the pool."

"So nice of you to notice," I said sarcastically. And then I sighed. "Nick is all yours now."

"That's right. He dumped your sorry ass."

"Because he was cheating on me with you." I glared at her. "I'm no threat, Morgan."

"Really? I'm beginning to think you are. First, you stalked us at…what was that place called?"

"Isobel's Bar?"

"Glad you admit it," she snapped. "Then you turn up at his home at a private event. Now you're here."

I inhaled sharply. "You should believe me when I say I've moved on."

"Well, I don't. And this disguise doesn't fool anyone."

"I'm a Dare Club member. Doing this, being here, is all part of a challenge—not to mention it's for charity."

She studied me with narrowed eyes.

"Please don't hurt him, Morgan," I said softly. "Nick has a brilliant future ahead of him."

"What are you talking about?"

"I know he got into Manchester United. I'm happy for him."

"He got in despite you."

I stared past her shoulder. "I have to go."

"Back to your boring life."

"Actually, I've met someone special," I said. "We're out together virtually every night."

"Is he here?"

"No. I didn't even know I was going to be here until an hour ago. I certainly didn't know you would be here."

Max wanted to be the one to tell Nick about us. Respecting that decision, I bit my tongue.

She shook her head. "You were so desperate to become interesting that you joined a club."

"Funny thing is, Morgan, I have you to thank for it."

"How?"

I rested my hands on my hips. "The invitation to the Dare Club is why I'm here. It's been life changing. I've been having all sorts of adventures, all for free."

"What Dare Club?"

"I'm just saying thank you."

"What are you talking about?"

I rolled my eyes, certain that she knew exactly what I meant.

"The invite inside the gold envelope."

She looked puzzled. "The one that dropped out of my bag at Isobel's?"

"Yes, the one I found and returned to you." My smile resembled a cringe.

Morgan looked thoughtful. "The only thing I received in a gold envelope was an invite to the opening of Bar Ibiza in Soho."

"No," I said. "It was for the Dare Club."

"I have no idea what you're talking about," she said, sounding exasperated. "I would have torn that up. I don't need to belong to some infantile club to be interesting."

I swallowed hard.

Max had handed that envelope back to me.

It didn't make any sense.

I thought back to my first time at the Waldorf, where I'd tried to hand Ted the invite as proof I had signed up. He'd looked back at me with confusion because all the members had signed up online.

Yet the invitation had fit inside the envelope.

Ted called to me. "We're ready to go, Daisy!"

I stared at Morgan's retreating back. She was already wandering off in her elegant heels with her phone in hand—ready to film the show.

What reason would Max have had to give me that invite? The truth caused me to wobble sideways and hit my back against the wall.

"Steady," said Ted. "It's only a fashion show."

Chapter
TWENTY-TWO

Max

I snapped my phone to my ear. "Daisy?"

Whenever I heard her voice, a sense of wellbeing saturated my body and a rush of blood went to my head. I'd be seeing her soon.

I stepped back from the lift and stood in the hall, not wanting the call to drop.

"Max," she said. Her voice was shaky.

"Is everything all right?"

"I need to ask you something…"

"Where are you?"

"Soho. I'm with the Dare Club. It's my second to last challenge. We're doing a charity fashion event."

"Sounds safe enough." *This time.*

I'd be happy when the last one was over and this debacle was behind her.

"I need to see you."

"Can you join me for dinner at the Waldorf?"

"Yes."

"Wear something pretty."

"I'm having a problem getting my makeup off. It's waterproof."

"We'll get a private table. Or we can eat in my room. See how you feel when you get here. I bet you look beautiful."

"I look ridiculous."

"Don't change a thing. Come as you are."

"It's not what you think…" Her voice wavered in and out and the phone lost its connection.

"Still there?" I walked over to the window. The bright moon bathed the clouds in silvery light. London wasn't such a bad city after all.

"Max, I have something to ask you."

"Want to tell me what it is?"

The line went dead.

I punched her number, but it went straight to voicemail.

Riding the lift down, I tucked my phone into my jacket pocket, relieved she'd soon be with me again. I'd never missed anyone like I missed Daisy—and I never before had made so much effort to spend time with a woman. She was the breath of fresh air I hadn't known I needed. I was ready for a deeper level of commitment.

First though, I needed to face the tricky issue of Daisy being my brother's ex-girlfriend. His loss was certainly my gain. However, healing the rift he had with Daisy was going to take some fenagling with my family.

Which was why I'd invited Mum to join me and Daisy for dinner.

There was Gillian, as punctual as always, dressed elegantly in a cream pant suit, waving enthusiastically at me from the foyer. As she approached, I was enveloped in a cloud of expensive perfume. Her big beautiful smile drew attention from everyone in the vicinity.

I greeted her with a smile. "Thank you for being here, Mum."

"Of course, darling." She kissed me on both cheeks. "I wish you would stay with me at home."

"I know. Next time, perhaps." Because Daisy would be with me and she and Mum would have time to get to know each other.

"You look wonderful, Max. What have you been doing?"

"I've been doing things that make me happy."

"That pleases me a great deal." She slid her arm through mine. "Have you heard from your brother?"

"I get a text now and then." He seemed to be in a good place. So many great opportunities were happening for Nick and he deserved it all.

Mum tugged my arm. "You're about to get a lot happier."

"I am?"

"Oh, yes."

I frowned at her. "What are you up to?"

"I know what's best for my son."

"Which son?" I smirked. "Your favorite?"

"You both are...you know that."

I loved teasing her. The years had softened hurt feelings that could have torn us apart. I may have been my father's son, but I'd inherited her forgiving nature.

We arrived at the hotel's restaurant. Having stayed here on numerous occasions, I knew the staff well. Being surrounded by familiar friendly faces was a perk.

I greeted the concierge warmly. "Hey, Jacob, how are you? I'm sure you remember my mother. Could we have a private table, please, if possible?"

"Yes, sir," he said respectfully. "How are you, ma'am?"

They shook hands, greeting each other like old friends.

"I've already booked the table," said Gillian.

The Homage Restaurant was designed to resemble a cozy

and unpretentious café. Still, the place was as grand as you'd expect from the Waldorf.

I leaned toward Mum. "I've invited a friend to join us for dinner. She's on her way."

She fixed a curious gaze on me. "Who?"

"Someone special."

"Not a colleague, then?"

"No, not in London, Mum."

"I thought perhaps you had a friend visiting London."

"It's a woman."

She hesitated. "Why didn't you tell me?"

"I'm telling you now."

"I went to all this trouble to pull off the impossible and you try to sabotage it."

"What are you talking about?"

"That's fine," she said, waving a hand in the air. "A little jealousy might inspire Cresilla to say *yes* when you invite her out."

"Who the hell is Cresilla?"

"Have you ever heard of the Turnip Toffs?"

"Um…no." *What the fuck.*

"Thank goodness you have me, Max." She patted my arm. "The future Queen of England just so happens to be the Queen Bee of a prestigious and very elite group of people."

"Turnip Toffs?"

"Yes."

"Princess Camilla?"

"No, silly, Kate Middleton."

"She's Kate Windsor now. And Prince Charles is next in line, as king, right?"

"Keep your voice down."

"Why? Can we still be beheaded for saying these things?"

"Stop it. I can't take you anywhere." She lowered her voice. "The Turnip Toffs are so called because of their collective ownership of most of the English countryside. These wealthy people are Earls, Countesses, Duchesses—"

"We're wealthy, too." *Not that I cared because I earned a stellar salary.*

"We're talking about prestige. About integrating with the Royal Family. We're talking hunting parties on the weekends and dinners with the elite. Fine dining at Buckingham Palace. The goal is to match you with someone who is in the top tier of the Turnip Collective."

Running my fingers through my hair in frustration, I wondered if now was a good time to tell her I'd never be a willing participant in anyone's vegetable clan. Deep down she knew I'd rather be surfing, or eating a casual meal in a small café with sand between my toes. Or watching the sun set after a day on the beach...with Daisy. I wanted to share all of those experiences with her.

"Cresilla will elevate you to the highest echelons."

"Maybe I can meet her during my next visit?"

"I've invited Cresilla Cranbury and her wonderful parents to dinner. We'll have a lovely evening and get to know each other."

"You're going to have to uninvite them."

"They're sitting over there—"

My gaze shot to a table nearby where an attractive middle-aged couple sat with their pretty blonde daughter. They gave us a friendly wave, smiling, and then swapped a look of approval with Cresilla. Clearly, I'd received passing marks in the "looks" department. A bunch of baby turnips was already on the agenda.

I glanced at the emergency exit.

But I knew it was too late for an escape.

I returned their wave, muttering with clenched teeth, "You need to warn me."

"We're not going into battle, Maximus. This is social mingling of the highest order."

I plastered on a fake smile. "You have to let me live my life."

"Your life is all about work. You need other interests."

"You encouraged me to join the firm."

"I didn't expect you to become a workaholic."

"Lives are literally in my hands."

"That's lovely, dear. Keep smiling."

"I have to make a call."

"It'll look strange if we don't join them right away."

My fingers tapped off a quick text to Daisy: "Homage Restaurant."

Cresilla had been dragged into this debacle as well, it seemed. She was as much a victim of her parents' meddling as I was.

Introductions were made: Gregory and Clementine were Cresilla's parents and they lived in Norfolk on a farm. They were the tweed and Chanel wearing kind, inclined to sit up straight and offer everyone haughty glances.

"So how did you all meet?" I held a chair out for my mother to sit in.

"We host a function for the National Heritage," explained Clementine. "Your mother made a donation to the last event."

"She can be generous like that." I narrowed my eyes on Mum and took the seat next to Cresilla. "It's a pleasure to meet you," I said, shaking her hand.

She blushed. "I hear you're the big brother of Nick Banham."

"Ah, yes. He's the talented one." I reached for my napkin.

The one who stole the spotlight—for which I was always grateful.

"And you're an attorney?" asked Gregory.

"Yes, I live and work in São Paulo."

"Is it terribly hot there?" asked Cresilla.

"Well, as we're all running around naked, we don't really feel the heat. Those Brazilian jungles are quite something."

My attempt at humor was met with weak laughter.

Pain shot into my side where Mum's elbow was currently being pressed.

Our waiter interjected with the timing of a guru who knows just what to say. He took our orders. Wine was summoned and tasted and agreed upon. I checked my watch. We'd only been here ten minutes.

"How often do you visit London?" asked Cresilla.

It would be easy to become enamored by her beauty, but beyond that I sensed an underlying coldness, a level of self-control that was undoubtedly due to a finishing school where they stripped students of all personality.

I feigned interest. "I visit London every few months."

"And what do you do, Cresilla?" Mum asked.

"I help Mummy out with her charity events."

"Oh, that's divine." My mother had cranked up her aristocratic accent.

I took several gulps of wine, receiving a look of disapproval from Gregory. I took another sip for medicinal purposes, hoping to dull the ache of boredom until Daisy arrived.

I'd have to make some excuse and leave with her. I'd apologize to my mother later. Maybe take her to lunch at her favorite bistro. Or buy her some flowers. Then block her phone number for a week.

"I assume you're a football fan?" asked Gregory.

"Yes, we're all fans," I said. "Nick will be playing for Manchester United this season."

"We heard," said Gregory. "You must be proud."

"We're thrilled for him," I said.

"We're all very sporty, too," said Cresilla. "We love to ski in the winter. Do you ski?"

"I hate the cold." I shivered dramatically.

Pain shot into my leg as something sharp connected with my shin. I gave Mum a wide-eyed crazy smile and she withdrew the heel of her Louboutin from what felt like my ankle bone.

"Oh, my goodness," said Clementine, glancing over my shoulder.

"She looks...familiar," said Mum, staring in the same direction.

Turning in my seat, I took in the girl at the concierge desk. She was wearing a purple wig and clown makeup.

The girl seemed to be making a beeline towards us.

"Oh, my God," muttered Clementine.

Daisy, why are you dressed like a clown?

"Hi." She widened her eyes at me. "I didn't know there would be others..."

"You look...lovely," I said, gesturing to her dress.

"Who is she?" Gregory muttered, and then motioned frantically to our waiter.

I pushed to my feet. "Daisy, this is definitely a new look for you..."

"I did try to warn you," she said, glancing at Cresilla.

Daisy's gaze swung back to me. She could see we wouldn't be eating alone tonight. A stunning blonde would be joining us.

Her confused look made my gut wrench in discomfort. I

wished I'd texted her with a warning. Still, Daisy looked cute in an artsy just-out-of-Notting-Hill kind of way.

"You remember Daisy, Mum."

"How could I forget," sneered Gillian.

The concierge approached Daisy. "Excuse me, miss?"

I waved a hand. "I know her, it's fine."

He sidled up to me. "Sir, this is most unusual."

"I tried to wash it off," explained Daisy. "I thought it would be just us having dinner, Max. You and me. Privately. In your hotel room."

Cresilla sucked in a dramatic breath. "Call security."

"What is she talking about?" asked Clementine, in a scandalized tone.

"People are looking at us," snapped Cresilla.

"This is my friend, Daisy." I glared at Cresilla. "I invited her."

Daisy turned to me with a hurt look. I hadn't introduced her as my girlfriend.

"Join us," I insisted.

She pivoted, hurrying toward the restaurant's exit.

Gillian had invested an enormous amount of time and money into the Turnip Toff investment—all on my behalf.

Still, my loyalty lay with Daisy.

I flew after her, following the confused stares of people who'd clearly seen the clown girl. I caught a glimpse of her purple wig heading out the hotel's front door.

I dashed outside into the chill of the evening air.

She was standing on the edge of the curb. When I caught up, I recognized the Uber app on her phone.

"Cancel it," I said.

"I can't."

"Yes, you can."

"I have to go, Max. Don't make this more difficult than it already is."

"You caught me by surprise, that's all. With your..." I pointed to her wig.

"I wasn't planning on turning up here like this. The models were hogging the makeup remover. One thing you don't prepare for is having half a ton of waterproof clown makeup smothered all over you."

"I always have some in my glove compartment," I joked. "But that's just me."

She didn't laugh. "I figured I'd take it off in your room."

"Okay, I take it back," I said with a smile. "This dare really is the most hazardous one so far."

"Why did you invite me to dinner with a beautiful woman? It doesn't take a genius to see why I wasn't even told."

"I didn't know she'd be here."

"So, you do find her beautiful, then?"

Oh, shit, I'd walked into that one.

"You know what I was thinking when I saw you, Daisy?"

She threw up her hands. "Go on, then, tell me."

"That you were still the most beautiful woman in the room."

Her eyes teared up. "I don't believe you."

"Why would you say that?"

"Because you've lied before."

"When?"

"That's the kind of woman your mum wants you to marry. I can't compete with those upper crust types. It's not who I am."

"I'm not asking you to compete with anyone."

"You could have warned me."

"I started to..."

"You've been lying all this time."

190

"How?"

"The invite to the Dare Club. It came from you."

My shoulders slumped as I realized how all of this must look, now with the added complication of another woman being thrown into the mix.

Her lips trembled. "Did you switch out the invite to Bar Ibiza in Soho with one for The Dare Club?"

"Listen, I—"

"You replaced it, didn't you?" Hurt shimmered in her eyes. "Then signed me up for the club online?"

"It's not how it looks."

She stepped back. "You think I'm boring. You want to change me. You want me to be like Morgan or that woman in there. I was never going to be good enough for you."

"No, that's not it at all."

"Did you actually think I would sit down with your mum while she paraded a perfect woman in front of you so you could compare me with her?"

"Daisy, please, come inside so we can talk."

"Why should I?"

There was nothing I could add at the moment that wouldn't hurt her more. When I'd first met her, I'd seen how hesitant she was to have fun. Nick had hinted that she needed to be more outgoing, and on our first meeting she'd appeared shy and reticent. I hadn't wanted her to miss out on the best life had to offer. I'd wanted her to come out of her shell.

And I'd thought maybe, just maybe, Nick might want Daisy back if he saw her playful side...if he saw her trying new things and being more adventurous.

But I hadn't counted on falling for her myself.

Daisy looked away and gave a nod of defeat.

"Don't go like this," I said, my heart aching.

She was already walking away. I watched as she climbed into the back of an Uber, a Ford Escort, and slammed the door shut.

I drew in a sharp breath of regret. Of all the people in her life, it had been me who'd let her down the most. I'd put myself forward as her knight in shining armor and all the while I was the one who was destined to destroy her.

A whiff of Gucci hit me at the same time I saw Mum hurrying toward me.

"Well, that was strange." She was out of breath.

I glared at her. "I can't believe you treated Daisy like that."

"She was dressed like a clown! At the Waldorf!"

"She's a member of a Dare Club. They help people find courage to stretch out of their comfort zone."

"Coming here was a dare?"

"No, Mum," I snapped. "She modeled that dress in a fashion show for a children's charity. They made her up like that, obviously."

Her eyes widened in horror. "She was your someone special who you invited tonight?"

"Yes."

"You can't be serious?"

"Daisy and I have been dating. I really like her."

"That strange little girl?"

"She's a beautiful woman. And your youngest son was an idiot for letting her go."

"You haven't stopped to ask yourself why he left her."

"Yes, Mum, and the conclusion is that my brother is an ass who became besotted with another woman who has no soul. He deserves someone a lot better. In fact, I suggest you introduce him to Cresilla and her Carrot Tops."

"Turnip Toffs. I went to all this trouble for you, Max."

"I didn't ask you to. And you know what? Those Turnip Toffs can fuck right off." It felt good to say it.

She gasped. "We're talking royal connections."

"Listen to me, Mum…when I marry it will be for love." I raised my hands in the air to make my point. "For love!"

My heart was breaking for the one I'd lost too soon.

"Where are you going?" she asked, as I stormed off towards Drury Lane.

"To take a walk and get some fresh air."

I needed to think…needed to decide if Daisy would be better off without any of us in her life. She deserved better.

A woman like Daisy deserved the goddamned world.

Chapter
TWENTY-THREE

Daisy

AFTER LAST NIGHT, CREEPY CLOWNS WERE GOING TO be a trigger for me forever. Every time I thought about turning up at the Waldorf Hotel in clown makeup, only to be confronted by Max and his dinner guests, hives appeared on my neck.

Max's mum was probably permanently scandalized.

I was actually happy to be back at work, here amongst the zoned-out shoppers and my moody co-workers. One person who never changed her attitude was my friend and colleague Amber. She worked in the same department, and if anyone could shake me out of this post-traumatic nightmare, it was her.

I'd spent the last hour moving items from one end of the gown department to the other—mainly because shoppers had this annoying habit of picking a dress off a hanger and, halfway to the changing room, deciding they didn't want the dress after all. Thankfully, most of the customers had thinned out since we were closing soon.

My feet were sore from walking around the vast showroom for eight hours straight. I was glad we only had fifteen minutes to go before I could go home and watch some mind-less TV.

But sometimes, working at a major retail store could be kind of fun…when my heart wasn't breaking—mainly because I got to hang out with Amber.

I found her in one of the back rooms, looking miserable as hell, sorting through returns—a job we hated, therefore, we took turns doing the dark deed. Basically, the only way you could tell if an item could go back on sale after a buyer had re-turned it was to sniff the damn thing—no kidding.

I watched as Amber sniffed the armpits of a Victoria Beckham gown. It would of course be dry-cleaned to remove the lipstick stain on the collar, but if it was worn it couldn't be sold as new.

"Want some help?" I asked, with a please-don't-say-yes expression on my face.

"Almost done."

"We deserve danger pay."

"I know." She slid the gown down the rack, and then turned to me, giving me a look I'd gotten used to over the last few weeks. "How are you, Daisy?"

"Fine." I forced a smile.

"A few of us are going out after work for fish and chips. Come join us."

"No, thank you." I wasn't ready to be social.

"Are you getting out at all?"

"Yes." I rested my hands on my hips. "I joined a Dare Club."

Because some trickster bastard had signed me up—the man I missed, the man I hated and yet adored all at the same time.

Seeing her confused expression, I added, "It's a club where

a bunch of us get together and do things we wouldn't normally do. You know, to shake us out of our comfort zone."

"How did you find out about it?"

"A frenemy."

Amber raised her eyebrows. "That was nice of her."

"It was a him." I pretended my emotions weren't scrambled. "Nick's older brother. The invite came from him."

"That wasn't weird?"

"No." It was the *way* he'd done it that was weird.

"What sort of things do you have to do?"

"Hang off buildings. That kind of stuff." I grinned at her. "It's liberating."

"Oh, my God, seriously?"

"The guy who runs it is super cool. It's about pushing yourself beyond what you believe you're capable of doing." Might need a lifetime membership at this point.

"Good for you."

"As long as it's not flying, I'm fine."

"Right, well, if they try to make you do that, tell them to F-off."

"I doubt it's in the budget."

"I have a mannequin I have to slip this on." Amber picked a dress off a hanger. "Come with me and tell me everything."

"Is that Versace?" I reeled at its beauty.

She ran her hand over the silk. "Even with fifty percent off it would still cost me six months of my salary."

"I've got a girlie crush on a dress in the window," I admitted.

"I've been drooling over those shoes, too." She pointed to the high heels. "I feel like I knew them in another life."

She made me laugh. "Isn't it funny that we both work in a store where we can't afford to buy anything?"

Amber beamed at me. "We can afford a cupcake from the café."

"True."

She pulled the strappy shoes out of the box and held them up. "Love at first sight."

We headed out onto the showroom floor.

I helped Amber redress a mannequin with the Versace gown. She took her time to fluff out the skirt.

On the other side of the divider was *the* dress I coveted, in the same display I always stopped to stare at after work.

A memory of me and Max at the Victoria and Albert Museum flashed into my mind—him knowing they had a shop window display that would wow me. Even though he'd hurt me, he'd done so many wonderful things, too.

Don't think about it.

He'd tried to change me. I was never going to be good enough for his family. Our romance had been a mistake.

The showroom window entrance was hidden behind a fake wall.

The handle turned and I entered the display. Beyond polished glass, pedestrians streamed back and forth along the pavement, all of them in too much of a hurry to look my way.

As though I were paying homage to a rare artifact, I held my breath in awe. Up close, the gold braiding and twinkling crystals on the bodice reflected the light with shards of color—blues, pinks and muted greens.

The ballerina pumps on the mannequin went perfectly with the style of the evening gown, a sheer skirt over a mini, the delicate material falling like water.

My fingers tingled as I touched it.

I pretended this was all part of my job should some pedestrian look my way. I trailed my fingertips over the shining crystals. Then, moving closer, I traced the edge of the bustier, admiring its beauty.

A camera flashed, blinding me, and my foot slipped off the stand.

I grabbed the mannequin's arm to steady myself, and it came off in my hand.

I stood there staring down at the dismembered arm I was holding, trying to feign to the gathering crowd that this was all part of my window-dressing routine.

I attempted to reinsert the arm into the shoulder socket.

It wouldn't go.

Another shove made the mannequin rock unsteadily. I let out a howl, reaching for it as it tipped over. I lost my balance as I grabbed it and landed on my back with my legs splayed, the thing lodged between my thighs like it was shagging me.

Fuck my life.

A crowd on the other side of the glass was riveted to the unfolding drama inside the shop window. Like I was a show-girl, and this was the main act.

"Daisy, are you okay?" Amber rushed in to help.

I nodded, still feeling winded.

She glanced at the many faces looking in. "Are you trapped?"

"I'm just going to lie here until my luck changes for the better."

She looked amused as she hurried forward. "You really do love this dress, don't you?" She gripped the mannequin by its waist and pulled it up, placing it into its pre-Daisy disaster position. She easily re-inserted the dismembered arm.

"Want to try it on?" she asked. "It's your size."

"What's the point?"

"It'll be fun!" Amber began unhooking the dress.

I climbed to my feet. "We'll get in trouble."

"I'll say I spotted a moth. Was pulling the dress out until I'd hunted down the insect. I'll be awarded Shop Assistant of The Month! Grab a dress off a hanger."

Within minutes, we'd switched out *the* gown for a little black dress. Not quite as glamorous but at least we'd not left a naked mannequin in the window for the wierdos to gawp at.

I followed Amber across the showroom floor toward the changing rooms. She chose a cubicle for me.

"I'm not sure about this," I said, nervous about touching the dress again.

She threw her hands in the air. "What else would you be doing?"

I'd be on the Tube with my head in a book, trying not to think about how my life was always so calamitous. Trying not to think about *him*.

Trying on this dream gown was probably the only thing that could cheer me up. I kicked off my shoes and stripped down to my underwear.

Within the cubicle, Amber helped me step into the dress. She fastened the catches on the back and then gestured for me to step outside. "Go see yourself."

I left the cubicle and waltzed up to the full-length mirror on the wall.

The gown fit perfectly, the bustier pushing my breasts up and making my waist appear smaller. It was fun to imagine wearing this dress at some posh party, the other guests throwing me admiring glances. Lifting my hair above my head, I turned this way and that to see the gown from all angles, the crystals twinkling hypnotically beneath the lights. It could have been made for me.

Amber looked me up and down. "Yeah…wow."

My shoulders slumped at the realization that my dreams would never become a reality. The woman who would wear this dress one day belonged to a different world.

"You need shoes! Let me get my favorite ones from the back." She scurried away.

The quiet was a welcome change from the constant humming of voices and music that went on throughout the day. The throng of shoppers that usually buzzed around us were gone, just a few stragglers and staff were left.

I needed to get out of this dress. I reached for the catch at the back, but it was too low. I stepped out of the changing room.

"Amber, forget the shoes."

The place was deserted.

Turning, I let out a surprised gasp.

Max was standing there, dressed in a leather jacket and jeans, the beauty of his features belying his sexy ruggedness.

"You really are versatile," he said. "One night a clown, the next night a princess."

"Go away or I'll call security."

"Daisy, you've not been answering my calls."

"My phone's been off."

"The dress looks better on you," he said.

"As opposed to…?"

"The one-armed mannequin." He gave me a crooked smile.

My eyes closed for a beat in embarrassment—he'd been one of the onlookers in the crowd.

His admiring gaze traveled up and down my body. "You look stunning."

"I'm not supposed to have it on."

"You should wear it all the time," he said softly, his deep voice sending tingles down my spine.

"My friend will be back any second," I said breathlessly. "She's going to help me out of it."

"Is that Amber?"

"Yes, how do you know her?"

Max's gaze devoured my figure, roaming down to my bare feet before returning to my flushed face. "I was worried about you. That was quite a fall in the window."

"I was more worried about the dress."

"The dress can be replaced."

I shook my head. "Not this one."

His expression softened. "I'm glad you're not hurt."

"I'm very flexible."

"Hmmm, yes...I know."

I glared at him to let him know I didn't think his comment was funny—even though it was.

He moved closer. "I wanted to explain something."

"No need." I turned to go.

"Daisy, please. Last night, I meant what I said—even with all that clown makeup on, you were still the most beautiful woman in the room."

"You tried to change me."

"That wasn't my intention. Look, I really care about you. Please believe me. We're not ready for those words, those rare and precious words that say so much more, but I know we could be saying them to each other soon."

I placed a hand on my chest, trying to remember how to breathe.

Max let out a sigh. "When I helped you move into your aunt's home, I got to see where you'd be living. You and I had those few moments of reflection, sitting together on your bed while I looked around at that room. I saw your sadness and it broke my heart. I wanted to do something wonderful for you."

"Why?"

"You deserve the best that life has to offer. I want you to take the kind of chances that will lead to happiness. I want you to follow your dream, and if it happens to be designing shop windows, I want that for you. I want to see you in there doing your thing. Not on your ass, obviously. Though it might bring in more shoppers."

"Are you saying you weren't trying to change me?"

"Never. When I came back to offer you new glasses to replace the ones I broke, your aunt told me that all you'd been doing was staying in your room."

"You felt sorry for me?"

He shook his head. "I wanted you to thrive. I didn't want to walk out of your life and leave you feeling that way."

"What am I to you, Max?"

"You got inside my heart, Daisy. You did what I believed was impossible. You gave me hope that my life could be more than work and loneliness. I felt compelled to spend more time with you…"

I took a deep breath. "I'm not boring now, am I?"

"Oh, Daisy," he said, his voice wavering, "you have never been boring…you were just afraid of being hurt."

I gave him a tremulous smile. "Can you help me out of this dress, please?"

"I can do one better." He stepped forward and lifted me into his arms.

He carried me through the showroom and past the few remaining shoppers who gawped at the handsome man carrying the girl in a posh dress. A few of my co-workers who saw us walk by smiled and gave me a thumbs-up.

"Where are we going?" I asked, as we headed towards the exit.

"Back to my hotel."

"But the dress! I have to take it off."

"You're currently wearing my latest purchase, so I have no choice but to bring you along."

My face flushed with the realization that he'd bought this beautiful gown for me.

Amber caught up and handed me my handbag with my shoes sticking out of the top, laughing as she waved me off.

I buried my face in Max's neck as he carried me outside to the waiting town car.

Carl was holding the back door open for us.

Before releasing me, Max dipped his head, his lips finding mine. As we kissed, the world slipped away.

In that moment, all that mattered was *us*.

Chapter
TWENTY-FOUR

Daisy

I, DAISY WHITBY, WAS GIVING *THE GREAT BRITISH BAKE Off* a run for its money. I'd poured my heart and soul into baking something special for Max. The feelings I had for him were so intense, all I could do to endure them was to keep myself busy—while trying to suppress a nagging fear it was all too good to be true.

I took a deep breath, feeling a rush of excitement that he'd be here soon.

Yesterday, he'd carried me out of Harvey Nichols while I was wearing the most beautiful gown in the world—the same one I'd been ogling through the shop room window after work each day for weeks.

Turning my attention back to baking, I checked the pot filled with boiling water, watching it steam around the pudding. The dish had been baking for over an hour and its sweet smell filled the kitchen.

Still wearing my oven mitts, I tried to pinch myself. When that didn't work, I looked up toward heaven in awe. I'd never met anyone as amazing as Max. And he'd told me he felt the same way.

This was all so new, but it felt so right.

When the doorbell rang, I sucked in a nervous breath, pulled off the oven mitts and threw them on the countertop.

Still overwhelmed with how my life had gone from crappy to incredible in a few short weeks, I wanted to hold on to these magical feelings.

When I opened the door and looked at Max standing on the top step, I almost forgot how to breathe. He was holding a bouquet of white lilies, looking sexy in his jeans and leather jacket.

"I wanted to buy you the entire flower shop. But the florist told me that was a bit stalkerish. Wouldn't be a good look on me, apparently."

"They're beautiful." My eyes stung with tears of joy.

He gave me a crooked smile. "Can I come in?"

"Of course." I stepped aside.

"What are you cooking?"

I glanced down at my flour-covered apron. "A surprise."

He followed me down the hallway and into the kitchen. "Is the surprise for me?"

I grinned at him. "You introduced me to Brazilian cuisine. I want to introduce you to the delicate art of British baking."

I found a vase and filled it with water, and then set about arranging the flowers, admiring the white leaves bursting with life.

"Well, I have tasted British food before." Max looked amused as he shrugged out of his jacket and laid it over a barstool. "I spent my summers here, remember? Not that I'm not grateful."

"I bet you've not tasted this delicacy."

"Something tells me I'm going to be blown away." He leaned in and trailed kisses along my neck, moving to my chin.

The press of his lips to my mouth stilled my reeling thoughts, his firm body trapping me deliciously between him and the countertop. Being in his embrace made all of my concerns, all my worries, slip away. His tenderness gave me the faith I needed to trust in our happiness.

The timer buzzed.

"It's ready," I announced.

He continued kissing my neck. "I don't mind it being a little overcooked."

I moved away from him towards the oven. "Not with this. I have to take it out of the pot." I pulled on the oven mitts and waved them at him playfully. "I can't wait for you to taste this."

Reaching into the large pan, I removed the dish and carried it carefully over to the plate waiting on the central island. Tipping the porcelain dish upside down, I let the dessert slip onto the waiting plate. The fluffy sponge was perfectly formed and covered in currents, their sweet scent wafting around us.

Max gave me an uneasy smile. "This isn't what I think it is, is it?"

"Don't knock it til' you've tried it."

He backed up a little. "No way."

I reached for a teaspoon and scooped out a mouthful from the top of the sponge for him to taste. Max raised his hands in the air, shaking his head and playfully declining.

"I baked it especially for you."

"You went to all this trouble, for which I am grateful. Can I just admire your talent from here?"

"You can't say no."

"This is me saying no." He stepped back farther, laughing.

I raised the spoon toward his mouth. "You have to eat the spotted dick!"

"I'm not eating anything that has the word 'dick' in it."

I chased after him down the hallway with the spoon. "Pretend it's called something else."

"It doesn't work like that." Max pivoted and burst into the living room.

"Where are you going? I baked this for you!"

"Help!" He laughed raucously as he backed up against the couch.

I waved the spoon in front of his face. "Eat it."

"What have I ever done to you?"

"Close your eyes if that helps."

"It doesn't." He fell back onto the couch.

Straddling him, I pressed the spoon to his mouth. "Humor me."

He let out a sigh of frustration. "Only because you baked it, Daisy. This is me proving how much your happiness means to me. And I'm not promising that I'll ever eat this or any other British food again."

"Max!"

He opened his mouth and let me ease in the spoon. He chewed slowly, his expression changing from one of doubt to delight.

"It's good, right?" I coaxed.

"Delicious." He sounded surprised.

"I'm so happy!"

"Why did they have to call it that?"

"They called puddings 'dick' back in the nineteenth century."

"I'm sure that piece of information will come in handy one day." He pressed his lips to mine and smiled against my mouth.

I eased back a little. "See, it's good to try something new."

Huskily, he said, "I want to watch you eat the spotted dick now."

I squealed with delight at his double entendre and we burst into laughter. He twisted me around on the couch so that he was lying on top of me.

"You know what happens now, don't you?" he whispered, easing the spoon out of my hand and tossing it onto the coffee table.

I played innocent.

"Who knew British cooking could be so arousing," he teased.

Lifting my hips, I let him tug my jeans down until they reached the top of my thighs. He leaned low and pressed his mouth to my panties.

"Max," I said wistfully.

He raised up onto his elbows. "What's wrong?"

"You and me…"

"I promise I won't hurt you," he whispered.

I cupped his face with my hand. "I feel like I'm dreaming."

"This is very real."

"Thank you for the flowers. They're beautiful."

"You're beautiful, Daisy."

The press of his lips to mine sent a shudder of delight through me as my fingers trailed through his hair. He unbuttoned my blouse next, peeling it open and tugging down my bra. His tongue circled my nipple and then drew it in, suckling, sending a jolt of bliss. His kisses trailed south, and he pulled down my panties and jeans, easing them off. My heart raced as his hands pushed my thighs apart, and I felt his tongue lick the folds of my sex.

His tongue trailed kisses down my leg to my ankles, and then he worked his way back up. "Every part of you is perfect."

"I don't like my knees," I admitted.

"I can assure you there's nothing wrong with them." He sat up. "Your Honor, I would like to submit into evidence these two gorgeous knees. Along with these silky soft thighs." He kissed my inner thigh. "I rest my case."

Easing myself up, I leaned toward him and unzipped his jeans, watching his reaction as my fingers eased out his erection. He was firm and hard and felt amazing in my hand as I stroked its length.

Kneeling before him, I drew him into my mouth and took him all the way to the back of my throat, worshiping this man, thanking him for all he'd been to me.

"Daisy," he said, sucking in a breath. "That feels incredible."

I let out a long moan at the sensation of having him fill my mouth with his girth; he moved me in endless erotic ways.

"I need to be inside you," he growled, flipping me over and shoving me toward the end of the couch.

My gasp of surprise caused him to chuckle.

On my hands and knees with him behind me, I jolted when his fingers traced along my sex, parting me there, and then entering two fingers inside me. He tenderly strummed me until my body was pushing back against him, needing, wanting more of him.

"You're always on my mind," he said gruffly. "I can't stop thinking about you. Can't bear to be away from you."

My back arched when he thrust in deep. Max pulled all the way out and then shoved himself all the way inside me again. My body exploded with pleasure, causing ripples of lust that stole my next breath. My hips moved fiercely against him, pushing back, while I begged him not to stop. He reached around, the tips of his fingers finding my clit and rubbing it, sending me over as he came with me, catapulting us both into a blinding climax.

He collapsed next to me and I fell on top of him, my head resting on his chest, hearing his heartbeat, and quickly being lulled by it.

Chapter
TWENTY-FIVE

Max

I ONLY HAD MYSELF TO BLAME.

Had I been more present for Nick during this visit to London, had I insisted he spend more time with me than that new girl of his, this would never have happened. He'd have completely focused on his training and his head would have been in the game.

It felt like my fault that Nick had been injured and hospitalized. The details were only to be revealed when we spoke with the specialist in person. Nausea welled up in my throat as my imagination took off—maybe the coach had pushed him too far, too fast? Maybe Nick had clashed with another player?

My phone pinged. The text was from Daisy, but I'd have to answer her later. I had to see Nick first and make sure he was okay.

This London facility, with its sprawling campus and state-of-the art medical care, specialized in sports medicine. Nick would be distressed to find himself here.

At the end of the hallway, I saw Mum sitting in a chair.

I rushed toward her. "What happened?"

Gillian looked pale. "The doctor's in there with him now."

"Can we go in?" I stared at the door across from us, fearing what I'd find on the other side.

The door opened and a doctor in a white coat appeared, his expression dour.

Mum pushed to her feet. "How is he?"

The orthopedic surgeon approached us. "I'm Doctor Patel."

"Max." I reached out to shake his hand. "I'm Nick's brother."

Dr. Patel gave a nod. "Nick's given permission for me to talk with you. His anterior cruciate ligament, which crosses in front of the kneecap, is torn. It helps control mobility of the knee."

My mouth went dry. "Nick tore his ACL?"

Shit.

"What does that mean?" asked Mum.

"It will affect his ability to play football," said Dr. Patel.

A somber silence played out until the doctor cleared his throat.

"I'm sorry it's not better news," he said. "I'll operate as soon as we confirm a theatre is available. Until then, he's NPO." His brow furrowed. "That's nothing to eat or drink."

"They pushed him too hard." I leaned against the wall. "They did this to him."

Patel gave me a curious stare. "This injury wasn't sustained during training, Max. It happened early this morning during a scuffle."

"What the fuck?" I hissed under my breath.

"Max!" Mum frowned at me.

"Are you saying he got into a fight?" I asked.

"Go see him," the doctor replied, compassion in his tone. "Nick will explain."

211

I gave a nod and walked over to my mother's side. "Mum, after you."

"You go," she said, tearfully. "He'll need to talk."

"This is where big brothers come in handy." Patel patted my shoulder. "It's a long road back and he'll need emotional support."

That gesture of kindness helped me focus. I entered the private room.

Nick was wearing a hospital gown. He sat up in bed with his right knee resting on a pillow and wrapped in a bandage. A discarded icepack lay beside it. Dark shadows blemished his eyes and his pale face wore a desolate expression.

I pointed to the icepack. "Shouldn't that be on your knee?"

"Intermittent icing," he replied. "They don't want to freeze my leg off, apparently."

Leaning forward, I patted his back before pulling a chair closer to the bed.

"How's it going, bro?" I asked, after taking a seat.

He looked around, lifting his arms in a frustrated gesture. He was here and not on the pitch where he belonged. The stone-cold fear of a sportsman shone in his eyes.

"I heard the doctor talking to you." Nick pushed himself up a little. "You can hear everything in this place."

"Athletes come back from injuries like this all the time."

"My stock went down." He squeezed his eyes closed. "MU's coach is on his way in right now. No doubt to deliver the news that I'm cut from the team."

"You don't know that."

He gave me a look that told me he expected the worst case scenario.

I looked around for a piece of paper. "I want his name, Nick. Whoever did this to you."

"Max, don't make things worse."

How the hell could I make things worse? I suppose he understood why I had the urge to find the bastard—I'd make him pay for what he did to my brother.

"Where's Morgan?" I tried to change the subject, for now at least.

"She's shaken up that I'm in here. She's with a friend."

"She's not hurt?"

"No." His jaw tightened. "She's fine."

"What happened, Nick?"

He rested his head back against the pillows, looking defeated. "We were at a pub, me and Morgan. The Spread Eagle… you know it? It's on Woodstock Street. We were just having a drink. I had no idea…"

"No idea of what?" My body chilled as I watched his face turn grey.

"The place is full of Liverpool United fans."

Jesus, the arch enemies of MU were Liverpool fans.

"There was nothing in the place to indicate it was their hangout," added Nick. "This guy just walks up to me with his mates. I didn't know him. Found out afterwards he's Hugo White…Morgan's ex. She dated him right before me."

My back stiffened. "Did he pick a fight?"

"He and his friends started throwing beer mats at us. They were drunk. We went to leave. Got outside the bar and he tried to get Morgan to stay. He wouldn't let go of her arm."

"Who threw the first punch?"

He sighed. "It was all very quick."

"What was White saying, Nick?"

He shrugged. "He insisted they were still together."

I started to ask if they still were, but then thought better of it.

213

I rubbed a hand over my face. "Was this reported to the police?"

"There were no other witnesses. It's their word against ours."

"Street cameras?"

"Maybe."

"We'll look into it." I could sense he thought the effort would be futile.

We'd all invested our hearts into getting Nick to the top, and in one evening his universe had been tilted off its axis. Ours, too...

His eyes filled with tears. "I've thrown it all way."

"You're getting the best care possible. We'll have you running around in no time."

He nodded, a hopeful expression appearing on his face. "Dr. Patel's the best there is. Mum made sure of that."

"We're here for you, Nick. Whatever we can do."

"I'm such an idiot," he said. "I had a few drinks and wasn't thinking straight. We should have just walked away."

"What was Morgan doing during the fight?" I asked softly.

Nick shook his head, refusing to answer. I didn't want to go there, didn't want to think of her making the scene worse.

I rested my hand on his shoulder. "Are you in pain?"

"I'm taking hydrocodone." He gave me a tired smile. "Mum's scared I'll get addicted."

"No, because we won't let that happen."

"Thank you for coming here."

"I'm in England for you, you know that."

"But apparently you've met someone?"

I frowned at him. "Who told you?"

"Mum."

I studied his face, waiting for him to say *her* name.

He smirked. "When do I meet her?"

"Soon?" It came out as a question. "I'm going to stay another week."

"For me?"

"Let's get you through surgery and go from there."

"You can afford to take more time off?"

"My team will handle everything." And they could. It was time to share the workload a little more.

Nick's gaze flitted to the door. "Daisy!"

She paused in the doorway and gave me a questioning look.

Concern must have flashed over my face because she said, "I came as soon as I got your text, Nick." She glanced at my phone hinting she'd tried to get in touch with me.

Nick patted the bed, inviting her to sit near him. "Come here."

She approached him with a bright smile. "I can bring in chicken soup."

"You're so cute, Daisy." He reached for her hand. "This place costs a fortune so they'd better have soup." He paused. "Thank you for coming to see me."

"Of course." She glanced at me for reassurance. "What happened?"

"I was attacked."

She looked horrified. "Did the police arrest them?"

"They're investigating it."

She stared at his knee, swallowing hard at the sight of his injury. "You'll be okay though, right?"

Nick swapped a wary glance with me. "You've always been there for me, Daisy."

"So…you've been messaging each other?" I tried to sound casual.

Nick brought Daisy's hand to his chest. "I didn't know

who else to call. I texted Mum and you—" His affectionate stare fell on Daisy. "And then you."

She was probably wondering where Morgan was, too. "It's going to be okay, Nick."

"I fucked up." He shifted to get comfortable.

"One day at time, buddy." Reaching over, I rested my palm on his shoulder and squeezed.

Nick turned to look at me. "We were groomed by our dads to keep their dream alive. I just hope I haven't blown it."

A cold sweat formed on my brow.

We had been groomed and at no time had we been asked what we wanted to do with our lives. Still, Nick was obsessed with football and I'd once believed law was my destiny. It was in our blood, at least…though my heart fought against the urge to fulfill someone else's ambition.

"Shall I get your mum?" asked Daisy.

"Yes, let her in. I've got to face her sometime." Nick shrunk back in the bed. "I've let everyone down."

"That's not true," I said. "You were doing what you believed to be right. Sounds like you were trying to protect…"

"And now look at me." He cringed. "I've thrown it all away for someone who doesn't appreciate it."

My heart stuttered as I saw how Nick's focus had returned to Daisy.

"On a happier note, Max met someone in London," Nick told her. "He's dating."

She swallowed hard but didn't break his gaze. "He deserves to be happy."

"I can't wait to meet her," he said.

I pushed to my feet. "Mum wants to see you."

"I should let you have some time alone with her." Daisy rose. "I'll go get you something to drink."

"I'm NPO. I'm not allowed to eat or drink until after the surgery."

Daisy's gaze fell on his leg again, her expression showing that she now realized the seriousness of the injury.

"I'll be right back." She fled the room.

Nick's gaze followed her out. "This is hard on her...to see me like this. She still has a thing for me."

"You'll bounce back." My gut wrenched at the fact Morgan had pissed off into the ether when he'd needed her.

Mum came in showing the kind of brightness a mother forces to give her child courage. I made some excuse that I wanted them to have time to talk.

And then I went after Daisy.

She stood at the end of the hallway looking out at the miserable view of the medical building opposite. I walked over to her. I hadn't expected that the next time I'd see her would feel this strained.

"I texted you." She looked up at me.

"I'd just arrived when I got it. Sorry I didn't call you to explain. I should have."

"It was understandable. You wanted to see Nick as soon as possible."

"Still..."

She reached for my hand and then withdrew it quickly, glancing down the hallway as though she feared getting caught. "He doesn't know about us."

I shook my head. "Unless Mum's telling him. I doubt she would, considering."

"When should we tell him the truth?"

My shoulders slumped. I'd been holding on to this tension since getting the call he was here.

"It can wait," she said, reading my reaction.

Don't ask the question.

Don't doubt what you have with her.

Fuck it.

"How did you feel walking in there?" I watched her carefully.

Her frown deepened.

"I mean, Nick really did look happy to see you."

"Which was a surprise considering he's been avoiding me for the last few weeks." She reached out and took my hand. "You have nothing to worry about, Max. My feelings for you will never change."

I should have called her. "I'm sorry you have to see him like this."

"How does his future look?"

I shrugged, doubt all over my face.

"Oh, God." She closed her eyes.

"One day at a time. We need to get him through surgery before we make any major decisions."

"He's spent his entire life getting here and now this…" She looked up at me. "What really happened, Max?"

"He got in a fight with Morgan's ex-boyfriend outside a pub."

Daisy's eyes widened in shock.

"Sometimes it sucks to be right." I paused, trying to find the right words. "Daisy, listen…"

She took my hand and kissed my fingers. "I'm here for you."

She meant all of us but was kind enough not to say it.

"I'm glad." I studied her reaction, looking for any seed of affection for Nick that might have still been buried deep, listening for quiet whispers of her heart that might reveal her true feelings.

Nick's relationship with Morgan was fraught with complications. That girl had potentially ended his career.

Staring at Daisy, I wondered if all this chaos would ricochet back on us, shattering our newfound happiness and breaking our hearts.

"Don't look at me like that," Daisy snapped. "It's you. It will always be you for me, Max." She changed her footing, looking up at me with soulful eyes.

"I'm sorry." I dragged her into a hug and held her tight, sending out a silent prayer.

Down the hall, my injured brother was fighting for hope, fearing his life's dream might be in ruins. I just hoped the world didn't ask the impossible of me.

I'd always been the good brother. I'd always tried to do the right thing and put myself last. If fighting to keep Daisy meant destroying my brother, I wasn't sure I could be that man.

But how could I ever bring myself to let Daisy go, now that I'd found her...

Chapter
TWENTY-SIX

Daisy

"COME ON! LET ME SEE YOU!" MAX CALLED through my bedroom door.

"I'll be down in a minute!" I listened to his footfalls heading back downstairs.

I wanted nothing more than to fall into his arms, but I needed a few more minutes.

I can do this.

I could play happy family with Max's relatives. I could face his mum again...see Nick with Morgan and finally tell him about us. There was nothing to it, really. All I had to do was walk back into their grand mansion in Hampstead and pretend that the last time I'd been there I hadn't almost drowned in their family pool in front of all their friends.

The good news was I doubted anyone would recognize me anyway. Hell, I hardly recognized myself. After I'd shared with Max that I was thinking of getting my hair and makeup done, he'd arranged for a professional to visit the house. She'd spent the last couple of hours styling my hair and beautifying me. She'd made my eyes pop with eyeshadow, eyeliner, and then applied a pretty shade of lipstick. A hint of blush and I was ready.

I was going to enter Nick's family home feeling that I deserved to be there just as much as Morgan. After all, she had singlehandedly threatened Nick's career and she was still around.

Nick was recovering well from his surgery. It had been good to hear he was feeling optimistic, and he was eager to begin physical therapy.

Tonight, he would finally see me and Max together as a couple. It would feel good not to have to hide our relationship from him anymore.

All that was left for me to do now was don the gown Max had bought me at Harvey Nichols. This was like one of those fairytales that never happened in real life—except it was happening to me.

All those times I'd stuck my nose against that shop window, and not once had I ever believed this dress would be mine.

After leaving the bathroom, I eased on a pair of delicate heels and then approached the dress in awe. Maybe we could just pull up a couple of chairs and stare at it all evening—it was seriously that stunning.

I eased the gown off its hanger and over my head, pulling down the wispy skirt and adjusting the sparkling bodice. I gazed at my reflection in the tall mirror, admiring the way my styled brunette locks tumbled in shiny waves over my shoulders. This was a big, bold improvement from my crazy clown look.

I, too, can rock the glamour.

Holding the fitted bodice to my chest, I descended the stairs.

"I need help fastening my gown," I called through the kitchen door.

"I'm ready," said Max.

I went on in with a big grin on my face, but then my breath caught when I saw how incredible Max looked. He was wearing a tuxedo. If it was even possible for him to go from dreamy to devastating he'd just managed it.

Max's jaw went slack as he looked me up and down, his expression going back and forth from looking awestruck to looking mesmerized.

"You like it?"

"It's…um…" His grin widened. "Wow."

"I was thinking the same thing about you." I let out a whistle.

He raised his hands. "You've seen me in this tux before."

Yes, but I'd been distracted with trying not to drown that night.

"I've never owned anything like this," I admitted breathlessly. "Thank you so much, Max."

He came around behind me and helped fasten the hooks of the bodice. "Daisy, this dress was made for you. It would have been a crime to deprive you of it."

"I look okay?"

He turned me around to face him and stared into my eyes. "Absolutely stunning."

"Thanks to you."

"No, it's all you, trust me." He smirked. "I'm going to have to stay close to you all evening."

"I like that plan." A nervous tingle shot down my spine.

He helped me with my silk shawl, gently pressing his lips to my shoulder before we headed out to his car.

During the journey out of London, Max weaved his fingers through mine and we held hands. I settled next to him, staring out the window and enjoying the classical music he played to relax me.

I no longer had a hole where my heart should be. Instead, I had butterflies buzzing around in my chest and stomach, setting off the kind of fluttering reserved for…

I wasn't going to say what this felt like…wasn't even going to think it. The emotion was different to how it had ever felt before. What we had was more precious, more powerful—a palpable connection that went soul deep. Max had stolen my heart and hijacked my every thought. Being with him felt so right and I couldn't get over how lucky I was now. I wanted to go back in time and tell myself that all that pain, all that heartache, would soon be forgotten.

Life felt magical.

We arrived on time, driving up to those familiar brass gates. Max navigated his car toward the house, its familiar grandness looming large, reminding me of the kind of family event I was stepping into.

He parked beside Nick's Range Rover.

"Ready?" asked Max.

"What?" I said with a smirk. "No valets?"

"This is a private family affair." He switched off the engine. "I told Mum to keep it simple. Just invite our closest family and friends. Nothing showy."

"Oh, that will be much better."

"I knew you'd agree." He shuddered as though all that pomp and ceremony didn't agree with him either. "Ready to face the dragon?"

"Your mum's not that bad."

"I meant Morgan."

"I know you did. Of course I knew, because your mum—"

He grabbed hold of my pointing finger and gave it a shake. "Let's stop there, Daisy. Or would you like me to get you a shovel?"

"I'm all good."

"Don't be nervous. We'll just walk in and hold our heads up high. Everyone will be able to see we're together. We won't have to say a thing."

"You're right." This was going to be me returning to shake off the girl I'd been before. I would create new memories and we would officially start our lives together with nothing to hide.

After stepping out of the car, I let him take my hand again and lead me inside.

I paused in the hallway, the marble and gold and shiny everything causing me to shiver. My feet froze as though this was my first time entering their intimidating manor home. This opulence was so foreign to me. I was going to have to watch everything I did and try not to embarrass myself or Max.

He glanced at me sideways. "Let's go in here first."

Max guided me into a room, and I recognized it. This was where I'd first caught sight of the family photo that had made me realize this was Nick's childhood home. Max's too, even though he'd only visited in the summer.

He followed my line of sight and looked up at the photo. "I was having a bad hair year."

"You look cute."

"Yeah, well. It's my shame to carry."

"Silly." I punched his arm.

"I'm going to get you a drink." He backed up. "Some liquid courage before you face the dragon." He waggled his eyebrows playfully.

My hand slapped to my mouth, stifling a giggle.

He grinned and then disappeared out the door.

I let out a long, deep breath.

Neither of us had anything to worry about, I reassured myself. We weren't doing anything wrong. As far as Nick was concerned, he'd moved on with Morgan. We'd both moved on, and now where that dull ache had been I felt nothing but gratitude.

Strange, how you can look back on your life and feel that way.

I stepped closer to the family photo, staring up at it as though seeing it for the first time—they had somehow made it work, this stepfamily. The two sons had gone on to have successful futures.

"Daisy?"

I spun round to see Nick in the doorway—a tuxedo-wearing hunk of a man, his hair a rebellious ruffle, his grey eyes bright and familiar and knowing. He stood there on crutches, his expression so different than how he'd looked at me last time I'd visited.

"Hi," I said weakly.

"You're here." He hopped into the room using the crutches like he'd had them much longer.

"You invited me."

"Yes, but after everything, I didn't think you'd come."

I opened my arms in a welcoming gesture. "Ready to party."

"I hardly recognize you." He closed the gap between us.

I ran trembling fingers over the soft material of my gown. "It's new."

"I can see that." That voice, his voice…it once did things to me.

Now, it filled me with memories that spilled over like a fountain of hurt. The spell of infatuation had faded.

He reached out and trailed his fingertips through a loose lock of my hair.

I stepped back. "I got my makeup and hair done."

Nick towered over me. "You look incredible."

"You've seen me dolled up before."

"Not like this."

I glanced toward the door, half expecting Morgan to burst in.

"She's not here." He'd read my nervousness.

"Oh?"

"Me and Morgan...we're over." Nick shuffled to get comfortable on his good leg.

"I'm sorry. When...?"

"A few days ago. I found out she was still seeing her ex-boyfriend, after that fight inside the Spread Eagle. They were photographed together."

"As good as admitting it, then?"

He nodded.

"I don't know what to say." I reached out and patted his arm to reassure him. Obviously, I'd not liked her. But seeing him sad was somehow worse.

"You did try to warn me, Daisy."

"I had no right to interfere—"

"Look, the way I've been treating you lately, you didn't deserve any of it. I mean, here you are, supporting me even now. After everything we've been through."

"Um...well..." I shot a glance toward the door. "Hi, Max."

Nick's eyes flashed with disappointment and then he brightened. "Hey, bro. Glad you're here."

Max walked in with a cocktail in each hand. "Hey." He flashed a glance my way. "How does a martini sound?"

"I'd love one." I took it from him. "Nick just shared his news."

Max gave a nod. "About Morgan? Sorry it didn't work out, buddy."

The alcohol burned my throat as I took a gulp.

Nick chuckled. "Slow down, we don't want you in the pool again."

"I'm trying to forget that," I said.

"You went to all that trouble to confess your love and try to protect me." Nick smirked. "That's pretty romantic."

Max was stone-faced, sipping his drink like this wasn't awkward and we weren't all on the edge of reason. I gave him a reassuring smile.

Tell him, Max.

Nick pointed to my drink. "That was nice of you, Max. Thank you for making her feel welcome."

Max gave him a nod and then took a sip of his drink. What followed was a troubled moment of silence.

I smiled at Max again. *Please, tell him.*

"Well, I should, um…" Nick pointed to the door.

"We have something to tell you," I burst out.

"Oh?" Nick flashed a wary look at his brother.

Max gave a nod. "We, as in Daisy and I…"

"You're here!" said Gillian.

We turned to look at the strikingly beautiful presence in the doorway. Their mum was dressed in a long red gown that hugged her tall, lithe body. "You're all hiding in here." She narrowed her gaze on me. "Is that Daisy Whitby?"

"Yes, it's me." I tried not to wince.

"Didn't recognize you at first. I do love that dress."

"Thank you, Mrs. Banham."

"Please, call me Gillian."

"Or you could call her Mum." Nick howled.

Max and I both cringed.

"Come on," insisted Gillian. "Come join your guests. They're wondering where you are, Nick."

Max and I swapped a knowing smile.

We left the room to rejoin the party.

With Nick and Max on either side, I was introduced to their friends and family. If they recognized me from my previous disastrous visit, they were all kind enough not to say anything. Not to my face, anyway.

After an hour or so we joined a crowd who'd gathered in the kitchen, a more intimate group of friends who were amiable and welcoming. Included were some of Nick's football buddies and an aunt and uncle who were a big deal in the music industry. The atmosphere buzzed with excitement—the thrill of old friends being together again.

There'd been no good moment to tell Nick. Still, he was going to hear it soon. Or maybe he'd guess.

I couldn't stand being this close to Max and not touching him. Not having him reach out and wrap his arm around my shoulder. From the way Max was frowning at me, he felt this same frustration, too.

Nick hopped up close to me. "Daisy, are you going to tell me what you've been up to lately?"

"How do you mean?"

"You seem…different."

The room hushed and all eyes turned my way. I felt an uncomfortable sting of self-consciousness. Though this time, instead of getting looks of disapproval as the girl who'd been bouncing up and down on the cover of the family swimming pool, these were looks of expectation.

"Tell them what you've been doing, Daisy." Max raised his glass to encourage me.

"Wait, how do you know what Daisy's been up to?" asked Nick.

"I joined a Dare Club!" I burst out.

Nick looked intrigued. "That explains your Instagram. I thought you'd lost it for a minute."

Laughter rose up around us.

"Actually," I said. "I've hung off buildings, been a fashion model for a day—" I threw a smile at Max's mum. "And done things I believed I'd never do. Tomorrow, I've got one more dare. They don't tell us what it is until a few hours before."

Max shared a proud smile with me.

He piped up, "Daisy has been inspirational for me, too."

Nick swallowed hard; we both caught it.

"She's influenced me," added Max. "I have her to thank for helping me see life differently."

"Max," his mum hissed in warning.

He held her gaze for a long time and then peered down at his shoes, his expression conflicted. "I have an announcement."

I stepped toward him in support. We were ready. We would be open to questions and we would still be here for Nick, who we expected might need some time to adjust to our news.

"This is all very exciting," said Gillian nervously.

"I've been thinking about my future," said Max. "How I want to spend the rest of my life."

Oh, my God…

Here it comes…

Gillian set her glass down on the central island. "This feels like one of Daisy's dares," she said.

Max snagged another champagne glass off a tray. "I'm making a career change. I'm going to become a civil rights lawyer."

My breath left me, my heart hammering at this near miss. I was happy for Max. How could I not be? Still, I'd been digging my fingernails into my palms waiting for an alternative announcement.

"That's amazing," I said.

"But you love the firm!" said Gillian.

"My dad's company will continue to thrive," added Max. "I'll still be part of it. Only I'll be doing what I love. I'll be taking on cases for those who can't afford an attorney like me. I'll be fighting for justice."

Nick wrapped his arm around his brother's shoulder. "That's amazing news, Max."

"It's what will make me happy." Max gave his mum a reassuring glance.

"I can see you've given it a lot of thought," she said. "I'm happy for you. If it's what you really want."

"It is." He gave a nod of conviction.

A staff member sidled up to Gillian and whispered to her.

Gillian came over to talk with Max. "Can you sort this out?" She kept her voice low. "Apparently, the pastry chef is drunk. We need to call him an Uber."

"Sure." Max threw me an apologetic smile. "I'll be right back."

I felt the loss of his presence from the room. And I sensed it was going to take more thought and a lot more time for us to come out with the truth.

Nick smiled at me. "Do you want another drink, Daisy?"

"No, thank you." I reached for a handful of crisps.

"Don't be nervous." He hopped closer. "You're here because I want you here. I need you here."

I swallowed, and said, "I'm glad to see you doing better."

"There's something I want to ask you."

I gave him a nervous smile. "I think we should just focus on having a good time."

"You really like salt and vinegar crisps, don't you? You always eat like this when you're nervous."

"But I'm not. I'm happy. Really."

"You know what, I'm just going to say it in front of everyone. You deserve a public apology."

"What? No…"

Ding. Ding. Ding.

Nick tapped his champagne glass with the back of a teaspoon, and then set them on the center island.

He looked around to make sure he had everyone's attention. "Thank you for coming to show your support. Now cover your ears, Mum." His smile was full of sadness. "I've fucked things up. I've probably ruined my chance of playing football professionally. I've pissed away years of training. All because I made a snap decision to do the right thing outside the Spread Eagle. It's a pub, by the way, for those with dirty minds. Anyway, I took on a total git to protect the woman I was with at the time. Huge mistake…which is why I'm on crutches. I've made a lot of stupid mistakes lately." Nick fixed his line of sight on me.

I recognized that look, and I almost snapped the stem of my champagne glass. I hadn't seen that kindness in his eyes for months…that boyish charm directed at me.

"Daisy, I'm so sorry for what I put you through. You're beautiful, funny, and kindhearted. You tried to warn me about 'you know who'—and even after everything, you're still here. You were one of the first people to visit me in the hospital. I've been an idiot." He scanned the many faces in the room to see their reaction.

All of their expressions were full of hope for him. Hope for his recovery and for his future—and so many of those gazes were filled with love.

"Daisy, come here." Nick gestured for me to step closer.

My mouth went dry and I couldn't move.

Gillian stared at me.

She had to know I loved her oldest son more.

I'd been moving rapidly toward a brilliant future, a place where true love reigned and where hearts were safe. It was a place of trust.

I loved my new life.

Nick moved closer, raising his glass in a toast. "To the most amazing woman in the world!"

The crowd shared the sentiment, raising their glasses and beaming at us both. The only face in the crowd that looked concerned belonged to Gillian, her eyes widening in warning for me not to say anything contradictory.

My attention snapped back to Nick.

"I'm sorry, Daisy."

"It's fine, Nick. I'll always care for you—you know that. Me almost drowning in your swimming pool proves it."

Laughter rose and we shared a cheeky grin with everyone.

"I've lost everything," he said, becoming emotional. "Because I lost sight of who I was. I forgot what's important. But through it all you were there."

My throat tightened and I threw a glance toward the door hoping to see Max. I hoped he'd stride in and say something that would take this conversation in another direction.

"After the accident I hated myself," added Nick. "I couldn't bear to look in the mirror. Then you came to see me in the hospital, Daisy." He lowered his voice. "I'd get on my knees to beg you to take me back but that's not possible right now."

My heart pounded furiously against my chest and I felt dizzy and lightheaded.

"It's a lot to take in," whispered Nick. "But I wanted to do it in a place that's special to me."

The place I'd never seen the whole time we'd lived together. A soft, panicked murmur escaped my lips. Looking around, I tried to find Max in the crowd again, tried to find the only man who'd know how to handle this without embarrassing Nick or hurting him any worse.

"Daisy?" Nick rested his right crutch against the center island and took my hand.

I blinked, feeling like I was having an out-of-body experience.

A roar erupted from the crowd as Nick pulled me into a hug.

Wait…

I broke away, my cheeks flushed. Movement in the archway caused my freaked-out stare to move away from Nick's face over to where Max was now standing.

I could see words trying to form on his lips, but he couldn't say them.

Instead, Max rushed forward and embraced Nick. "Well done. You did the right thing."

"She's amazing, isn't she Max?"

"Of course she is." Max turned to me, leaning over to kiss my cheek—though he failed to make eye contact. "Congratulations, Daisy."

"Max," I said, sounding panicked.

He broke away, strolling back through the archway and out of the kitchen.

A flash went off near my face and I blinked away the stars.

Remember to breathe.

"I'll be right back," I told Nick, fighting back tears.

He blew me a kiss.

I hurried out, scurrying down a long hallway, pausing to peek into each room as I went, hoping to find Max. I had to catch him and explain…I didn't want to be with Nick. I wanted him. From the first moment we'd met it had been him.

233

Pushing open a door, I found Max standing at a window, texting.

I ran toward him.

He raised a hand to warn me not to come too close. "Someone might see."

A thousand tons of pressure pushed against my chest. Drawing in full breaths was impossible. "Did you hear his speech?" I asked.

He let out a sigh. "This is what you wanted. What you fought for."

"No, Max you and I—"

"I'll always be here for you. You know that. But I have to return to Brazil—I have a situation in São Paulo."

He was steadying his emotions.

Pushing me away.

I reached for his arm. "Please, Max—"

He brushed off my hand.

The door flew open. "Daisy!" Nick appeared on his crutches. "We have to take more photos."

"I was just telling Daisy how happy I am that you came to your senses," said Max. "You're a very lucky young man."

Nick hobbled closer. "Come get in the photos with us, Max."

"I have to answer this." He raised his phone. "Work always comes first with me. You know that."

"I'm glad you're finally following your dream to practice civil rights law." Nick gave his shoulder a manly slap. "It's what you were born for."

I gazed at Max with tear-filled eyes, willing him to tell Nick the truth and admit we were in love.

He turned to Nick. "You've been through so much. Daisy really is the silver lining for you. You're a lucky bastard."

"I know, right?" Nick's eyes crinkled with happiness.

Max didn't have the heart to tell him.

He'd always put his brother first...

But surely, I meant more. Surely, I was worth it.

Max raised his phone in the air. "Reception is useless. Excuse me, I have to step outside."

My throat tightened as I watched him go.

Nick was watching me. "You really like him, don't you?"

I nodded, not trusting myself to speak.

"He's quite protective of you. He made me swear I wouldn't fuck things up with you again, Daisy. I promised him I'd take good care of you."

I stared at Nick. "When did you talk with him?"

"After you arrived. You were chatting with Mum. I told him the truth...that for a while there I'd been depressed and not sure if I could go on. Told him the way you fought for me proved how much you love me."

I did love you...once.

"Are you okay?" he asked. "I know you must be feeling a bit overwhelmed."

"I don't want to live with you," I burst out.

"We can take it slow. I won't let you down. I promise."

"I have to go." I hurried out, turning right and heading toward the front door, assuming Max had gone that way.

Standing on the front steps of the manor, I peered into the darkness, panic piercing my heart when I saw that his car was gone.

I could hear it speeding down the driveway toward the gate.

Clutching the hem of my dress, I kicked off my high heels and bolted after Max, hoping he would look in his rearview mirror and see me...hoping he would stop. I wanted to climb back into his car and go home with him.

The gates swung open and Max's Tesla sped through them.

Out of breath, my chest tight with dread, I walked back to the house. I retrieved my shoes and slid them on, taking a few seconds to look at that intimidating door I would soon have to walk through, returning to their world alone.

I hated the thought that I would have to rely on Nick to take me home.

I entered the mansion, keeping my head low so I didn't have to look anyone in the eye.

Gillian met me in the foyer. "Is he gone?"

I nodded, and met her gaze.

She gave me a thin smile. "Max didn't say goodbye."

The void he had left behind felt like a black hole, sucking all the oxygen and joy from the world. The cold air wafting in from the open door chilled my bones.

Gillian stepped forward and closed the door. "It's for the best."

"You don't really believe that?"

"Daisy, Nick needs you now more than ever."

I sighed. "I still care about Nick, but I'll never stop loving his brother."

"It's over." She gave an elegant shrug. "He's gone."

"I need to talk to him."

"He'll be fine. Have you seen Brazilian women? They are incomparable."

"Why would you say such a thing?"

"My youngest son needs you more. Don't let him down."

"You've always preferred Nick."

"Max is the strong one. The wise one. The one who can look after himself. Max doesn't do love. Not even with me."

"That isn't true. He adores you."

"Deep down he hates me for what I did to him."

"You're wrong. He's forgiven you."

"You have no right to express any opinions about my family."

"Max and I—"

She gripped my arm. "You're a passing infatuation. Nothing more."

"Let go of me."

Her hand slipped to her side. "Do the right thing."

"That's just it, Gillian. Max *has* done the right thing. Again. He's put himself last. He's stepped away so that everyone else can be happy at his expense. When are you going to let him have his happiness?"

"There you are—" She looked down the hallway at Nick, who was coming toward us. "Nick, dear, we were just talking about you."

"I thought I'd get some fresh air." He nudged up beside me. "Daisy, want to come with me? We can sit by the pool." He gave me a mischievous wink. "I promise to hold onto your hand so you don't fall in."

"She'd love to." Gillian's glare let me know she insisted I go with him.

She had long ago put aside her conflicted emotions and done the wrong thing.

And now she was asking the same from me.

Chapter
TWENTY-SEVEN

Max

GROWING UP WITH A FOOTBALL LEGEND—DAVID Banham, Nick's dad—you soon learn how obsessed British fans are. They attend every match, whether at home or away, proudly wearing their colors and buying all the team merchandise.

Take Manchester United, for example. Their emblem is a red and yellow crest featuring a devil with a trident. It's easily distinguishable from the bright colors of Liverpool F.C., which stand out at a game, the blood red shade that marks their passion. The fans wear this coat of arms with pride.

Having popped into a store that sells tourist memorabilia, I'd purchased a nice-looking scarf with Manchester United's team colors.

Of course, I'd have to be crazy to walk into the Spread Eagle Pub with this item on display while a game was going on between Liverpool and Manchester, broadcast in high definition on all of the wall-mounted big-screen TVs.

Especially since the only fans in the place were here supporting one team—Liverpool. The rowdy lot, predominantly men who were trying to drink the barman dry, didn't even notice me entering. And they wouldn't see the offensive scarf tucked inside my coat pocket.

"I'll have a beer," I told the bartender.

While sipping my drink—which would have tasted better chilled—I took my time scanning the crowd for Hugo White, the asshole who may have destroyed my brother's career.

There was still hope that Nick would make a full recovery. The doctors were optimistic, and so were we. But the damage done was potentially catastrophic. Hugo had known what he was doing that night. Even with alcohol on board, he should have had better control.

And there he was, sitting at a table in the center of the pub drinking his beer. He was of medium build, handsome in a way, though his jaw was too square and his eyes were too close together. His lips formed a too-thin line, showing the bitterness of man who believed the world owed him.

All eyes in the pub were on the TV screens. Liverpool was winning. Everyone in the place was happy.

Except me, of course.

Hugo had caused more devastation than he'd ever know. Not only had he attacked Nick, he'd kicked my brother when he was down. Seriously injuring an exemplary sportsman.

The fallout from that incident outside this pub had reached me and Daisy, destroying everything we could have had together. Hugo had set my brother back in more ways than just his health. He'd weakened Nick's resolve. He'd taken a swing at his ego and come out the victor.

I nonchalantly walked behind Hugo, my hand inside my coat pocket gripping the scarf, casually sipping my drink.

Hugo's coat hung on the back of his chair and slung on top of it was his fan-boy Liverpool scarf.

Liverpool scored again and everyone roared.

Acting like a long-time fan, I raised my drink in a salute.

Hugo had jumped up to applaud, causing his scarf to fall off his coat onto the floor. I kicked it under the table. Reaching into my pocket, I drew out the Man United scarf and laid it over the back of his chair.

Then I returned to the bar to watch the rest of the game. Those players really knew how to protect the goal, how to forge ahead and score, how to help an opponent up after he'd fallen in true sportsmanlike behavior—pity none of that had rubbed off on Hugo.

With the match over, the place erupted in wild cries from the winning side.

I strolled toward the exit, feeling justified in my quest for justice.

Outside, sitting at a table surrounded by sycophants, I saw *her*.

I strode toward her, all smiles. "Morgan, how are you?"

From her expression, I could tell that being confronted by the big brother of her ex was not how she'd thought her afternoon was going to go.

At her stony-faced response, I asked, "Nick is doing much better, thank you for asking. He's looking forward to starting physical therapy."

"Good." She gave a nod as though she cared.

"And how have you been?" I peered past her through the pub's window and saw Hugo put on his coat, wrapping the Man United scarf around his neck.

"I'm coping," she said with the quietness of the guilty.

I saw another man push Hugo, saw them arguing, and to my utter surprise, a fight broke out.

"There's your boyfriend," I said with forced brightness, pointing at the pub's window. "Always causing trouble wherever he goes." I stared down at her. "At least this won't be on your Facebook or Instagram page, since they've been taken down permanently."

Morgan looked up at me in disbelief and then whipped out her phone. For an attorney with friends in high places, getting a Facebook or an Instagram page pulled is as easy as it sounds. One phone call was all it had taken to erase Morgan's social media presence.

It was a small gesture, but it might help another unfortunate victim who was being led by his ego—a potential boyfriend who wanted to be seen with an Internet star.

That shit was over.

Morgan looked dumbfounded.

"Well, if you'll excuse me." I gave a nod and walked off toward my SUV.

When I climbed into the backseat, Carl turned around to look at me. "We should make Heathrow in good time, sir."

"Thank you, Carl." I sat back and pulled out my phone, turning it off to keep myself from calling Daisy. All I wanted was to hear her voice. My heart ached to say the words I should have told her before I'd walked away.

I wanted to turn this car around and find her.

"Advise my mother that my phone died," I said.

"I can charge it for you, sir, on the console."

"That won't be necessary," I said, wanting to get out of London as quickly as possible.

Because Daisy lived in this city—and I didn't trust myself to stay away from her.

Chapter
TWENTY-EIGHT

Daisy

"**W**ELCOME, DARE CLUB MEMBERS!" TED STOOD on a chair at the front of the bar so he could see us all, peering down with the kind of respect usually reserved for heroes.

We'd gathered in the bar at the Waldorf Hotel, where it had all begun, taking advantage of the plush seats, flowing beverages, and endless supply of crisps and dips.

This was it—we'd proven to ourselves we could push our limits past what we thought possible. I'd watched my friends overcome their mental roadblocks, seen them make decisions that would change their lives.

I tried to focus on what people were saying around me, engage in conversation and ignore the fact that my mind and body felt numb.

Max was gone and he wasn't coming back.

I hadn't wanted to come to the meeting tonight.

Ted had insisted that being here was all about supporting our teammates and celebrating their breakthroughs. He was right, of course.

His speech was inspiring, and he teared up when telling

us how proud he was of our accomplishments. He invited us all to move forward in life with what we'd learned, with our new-found courage. Our life coach had given us the tools we needed to chase our dreams.

Returning to university and finishing that degree seemed like a real possibility for me now. I felt an eagerness to see myself the way Max sees me. He'd given me more than affection... he'd given me a way forward, too.

Ted sat beside me. "How are you, Daisy? You're a bit quiet."

"I'm glad I completed each dare," I said.

"Bet you never expected to tackle an Army assault course." He laughed.

"I'm still aching."

"I always knew you had it in you."

Yesterday, we'd all met up in Beare Green where we'd tested our fitness and been put through our paces like military recruits. Most of all, we'd laughed our way over each obstacle. I was feeling sad that it was over, as this was our last dare, but all of us were still hungry for more adventure, which was the point, I suppose. We all promised to keep in touch.

"Keep doing what you're doing, Ted," I told him. "You're changing lives. Giving people the courage to make big life choices."

"That courage was always inside you, Daisy, just waiting for you to tap into it."

"I'm willing to believe that now."

"I'm glad." He pushed to his feet, peering over toward the door. "That guy's familiar. Do you know him? He keeps staring at you."

I followed Ted's line of sight, and swallowed hard.

"That's Nick Banham," he said in awe.

I hurried over to greet Nick. "What are you doing here?"

"Didn't want to miss your big night."

"I wasn't expecting you."

"My girl's graduating from the Dare Club. Of course, I want to be here."

When he reached for my hand, I pulled away. His gaze narrowed as he processed my need to take things slow.

I wasn't ready for any show of affection. I needed more time. I felt like I was betraying Max, even though we were over now.

Within minutes, a crowd had gathered around us, football fans who had recognized Nick. Ted was beside himself, acting like the biggest fan boy, throwing me glances that said, "Why didn't you tell me?"

I let Nick have the limelight. It took the pressure off me. I sat sipping my white wine quietly in an armchair.

On the back wall, the Dare Club's logo lit up a big-screen TV. It was a man's silhouette taking a leap off a cliff.

"What's that?" I asked Ted.

"We've put together a montage filmed during the dares." He nodded toward the screen. "This should be fun."

There came a continuous flow of images, edited with dramatic music as a backdrop to our adventures, as the team members moved through each dare.

There was me sliding down the glass chute, me heading in for a night of ghost hunting, sharing my feelings on Instagram about my challenge being thwarted by the swimming pool incident. And then there I was dressed as a clown.

I put my hands over my eyes when that segment came on.

The last dare saw me elbow-deep in dirt as I dragged my body along a ditch and then clambered over a wall. I crawled under a barbed wire with my face covered in smudges of green camouflage.

Everyone featured in the footage cheered when they saw themselves. The images rotated to show each dare, coming back around to me and Max…

Both of us stood side by side atop The Shard. The chemistry between us was more pronounced than I'd realized. The footage had been filmed when neither of us had known the cameras were on us. It showed the affectionate glances we'd shared, those quiet moments where we touched hands, our fingers intertwining.

Nick had taken a seat to watch the montage. Now he pushed himself up out of the chair and grabbed his crutches.

I rushed after him as he hobbled towards the door.

When I caught up, he shot me an annoyed look. "It just kind of happened, I take it?"

"You were with Morgan."

"Daisy, do you love him?"

"We've only known each other a few weeks. But he made me feel like I was worthy of happiness."

Nick sneered. "So very Max."

"I love him," I blurted out. "I do."

"And you felt like keeping it a secret?"

"I was waiting for the right time to tell you," I said hoarsely.

"He left that night without saying goodbye, remember?" He let out a harsh laugh. "He didn't even look back."

"He did that for you," I said softly.

Nick's expression turned sad. "You and me, we're only good for each other when someone dies."

"Don't say that."

He headed toward the doorway, pausing when he got there to stare back at the TV screen, nodding at it so I'd turn and look at the footage they were showing.

There it was, me sitting astride Max after I'd shot out of the glass chute, having landed on top of him. What followed was that spontaneous kiss I'd shared with Max Marquis as he lay beneath me, our passion devastatingly real.

There was nothing more to say.

That kiss told the beautiful truth.

A shiver ran through me as I watched Nick leave.

Chapter
TWENTY-NINE

Daisy

BEING AT WORK WAS STIFLING, WITH EVERY TASK SEEMINGLY five times more tedious. I'd dragged myself around the showroom all day greeting guests, forcing myself to smile whenever a customer came in, trying to act cheerful when they wanted to try on a dress.

But I couldn't shake this heartache.

Losing Max had been worse than losing Nick, or my home, or the life I'd known.

I recalled Max's expression at the party a week ago, as he looked at me and Nick standing side by side in the kitchen—and now I saw it through a new perspective.

Max had ended our relationship earlier that night for Nick's sake, and yet he'd remained by my side. Even then he'd been strong.

Not being able to talk with him was the hardest thing I'd ever experienced. That text Max had sent me saying we should catch up next month was his way of distancing himself.

I missed him.

I'd been wearing my favorite gown when Max had left me back at Hampstead after the party. Funny how I'd thought that glamorous gown would bring me happiness.

Nothing would...not really.

That night, I'd had to face off with the "dragon" and then wrangle with Nick afterward, trying to avoid any physical contact. My loyalty to Max would never waver.

For the thirtieth time today, I hid away in a changing stall, burying my face in my hands, lost in my despair, trying not to let anyone see me like this.

I couldn't wait to get home, even though my bedroom was small, the walls too close. But even that place held loving memories of Max.

Nick and I had no love left between us. I'd stood in the same room with him and felt nothing. We'd been together for all the wrong reasons.

A voice rose from the adjacent cubicle. "Where's that shop slave when you need her?"

I heard hysterical giggling from the two girls.

Pushing to my feet, I left my cubicle and knocked on theirs. "Can I help you?"

I heard sheepish laughter and then the door opened.

A pretty twenty-something handed me a dress on a hanger. "I need this in a ten."

"Got it," I said with a fake smile, hoping it looked real.

Within a few minutes, I returned with the dress in the requested size and gave the cubicle door another knock. "Here you go."

A hand appeared from inside and snatched the hanger like a Golem grabbing the golden ring. The door slammed shut.

"You're welcome," I whispered.

I leaned back against the wall, waiting for them to come out and prance in front of the mirror.

Don't think about the dress you fell in love with. Or Max carrying you out of this store in his arms with you wearing it.

The two women emerged from the cubicle, one of them wearing the dress I'd found her. She spun around, looking at her reflection in the long mirror.

"You look beautiful," I said, and meant it. "Let me know if I can help in any way."

"Don't rush me," she snapped.

She needed help with a personality upgrade, that was for sure.

"I shop here so much…" She turned to look at her butt in the mirror. "I should get a discount."

I stepped back a little.

She pivoted to look at me. "You can't make that decision?"

"No, sorry," I said flatly.

She turned to her friend. "You don't think it looks too…?"

"I kind of like it," her friend admitted.

She wrinkled her nose. "I don't know…"

"The dress is from Mimi Trent's Magic Unleashed Collection," I told her. "Mimi's husband left her after her daughter Lilly was born. Mimi was a single mum living in a counsel flat in Brixton. You can only imagine the stress she endured having to care for a child alone. She persisted, though, and her daughter grew to love fashion, too, eventually joining Mimi's empire. They're the most respected designers in the world. That dress you're wearing has a piece of Mimi's soul stitched into every seam. Look closer, you'll see how she honors the feminine curves of a woman. She gets it. She gets life."

They both stared at me, dumfounded.

She turned back to her friend. "I think it's pretty."

Her friend agreed. "It does fit nice."

My eyebrows rose and my lips quivered with amusement.

Their eyes widened at something they had seen at the end of the hallway.

Gillian's reflection appeared in the mirror.

She stood there looking as pristine and elegant as she always did, her handbag resting on her arm with the sophistication of the Queen. Her expression was hard to read as she fixed her intense gaze on me.

I gave her a nod. "Mrs. Banham."

"Max told me that you work here." She glanced at the two girls standing before the mirror.

They scurried back into the cubicle like vampires looking for shade.

Gillian's focus returned to me. "Hope this isn't a bad time?"

It was never a good time to be chewed out by a dragon in front of other humans.

"We can talk in here." I gestured for Gillian to join me in a private area down from the changing rooms.

"I do love Harvey Nichols," she said.

My heart hammered at the bollocking I was about to receive. She'd obviously heard about me and Nick and that awful evening we'd recently shared at the Waldorf's bar.

"How long have you worked here?" she asked.

"A year."

"I had a job in a shop once. A cake shop in Copacabana. It's where I was discovered. A year later, I was strolling down catwalks in Milan and wearing Givenchy."

She was still beautiful in her blue Chanel suit and Tiffany jewelry. Her eyes shone brightly, hinting at the girl she'd once been.

"How can I help you, Mrs. Banham?"

"What you see—" She opened her arms, her Gucci bag hanging from her wrist—"is a woman who grew up running barefoot on the streets of Rio. A girl who dragged herself out of a slum to become one of Europe's most beloved fashion icons."

"You're still perfect," I said, my tone sincere.

Her expression softened. "I'm flawed." She gave me a sad smile. "Don't look so surprised."

"You're always so…"

"Well put together?" She gave a nod. "I've always leaned on Max. He was always the strong one, too good for this world."

"I couldn't agree more." I stepped toward her. "He's like no one I've ever met."

"I only want the best for him."

"Of course you do."

"It's a revelation, isn't it?" she said. "How you have affected both my boys so deeply."

"I never meant to," I said, letting out a shaky breath. "It all happened so fast. It was unexpected, me and Max…"

"Hmmm." She looked at me with a curious expression on her face. "Do you ever eat here, in the Fifth Floor Café?"

I hesitated, surprised by the abrupt change of subject. "Um…I usually bring a sandwich."

"Right. Well, I've heard they serve a nice Spotted Dick." She winked.

My eyes widened. *He'd told her.*

"Apparently you baked one for him?"

It made me smile, remembering how he'd reacted.

"When he was little, I used to bake for him back in São Paulo, before I left him there…"

I felt a stab of pain in my heart for Max—even for her, too.

I realized that small thing I'd done for him had meant so very much.

"I've never seen Max like this," she continued with a

sparkle in her eyes. "When I saw you together at the hospital while we visited Nick, the way Max looked at you revealed how he felt."

He was far away now. Too far.

Talking about him brought everything back. The laughs, the tender moments filled with smiles, our indescribable passion...a romance that would never be forgotten.

"Nick was foolish." She shook her head. "He's like his father. Someone who goes after what they want with that basic instinct to win. That's why he's a successful sportsman, I suppose."

"I didn't mean for it to end the way it did between us."

"Nick walked out on you." She tilted her head. "I know that hurt you."

"Still, I messed everything up."

"You humiliated yourself in front of our guests. You almost drowned in my swimming pool. That was what you were willing to do to save my youngest. Though it was what you did afterwards that is more compelling. You and Max walked away from each other, so Nick didn't get hurt."

The walls seemed to close in and I found it hard to breathe.

The voice on the overhead speaker announced that the store would be closing soon. It said something else, something I didn't catch.

Gillian raised a hand. "You can only imagine how I feel knowing that Max has spent years in a profession only to keep the memory of my late husband alive, never once thinking of himself. He did it for me and for his father, too."

I took a deep breath to steady my voice. "He'll make a wonderful civil rights attorney."

"He will." She looked thoughtful. "Do you have a passport?"

"I never use it. I don't fly."

"That's easy to fix."

"How do you mean?"

"I've requested a private plane be made ready at Heathrow."

My flesh tingled at the thought of flying. "To where?"

"Brazil, of course."

The room started to spin.

Chapter
THIRTY

Daisy

"**M**RS. BANHAM, WE'VE BEEN CLEARED FOR takeoff." The middle-aged pilot had addressed Gillian, but he was staring at me with a concerned look on his face.

I was sitting on the metal steps, not moving, trying to remember how to breathe. "I just need a second." It was a lie.

I wasn't getting on that plane.

Not now.

Not ever.

The pilot went back inside the jet.

We'd arrived at Heathrow half an hour ago and I'd gotten a taste of how the other half traveled. There were no long lines for customs, no sitting in crowded waiting rooms. I'd been directed right to my flight after a five-minute check-in—all the while trying not to throw up on Mrs. Banham's Louboutin pumps.

I couldn't bring myself to walk through the door of that plane—which meant seeing Max wasn't going to happen. My heart squeezed with the agony of knowing I wouldn't be able to leap into his arms.

Carl had driven me to my place in Richmond. We'd stopped off just long enough for me to pack a small suitcase and find my passport—a futile half-hour that had been a waste of time, because I was too petrified to move.

Gillian walked down a few steps and sat beside me. "This is because of what happened to your brother, isn't it?"

Hives scorched my neck, burning my skin.

She wrapped her arm around me. "What can I do?"

"I'm sorry you went to so much trouble." I rested my palm over my rapidly beating heart, willing it to slow to a normal pace.

"It's all right," she said. "I feel the same way about spiders."

Okay, that was not really the same, but I didn't say so, as she was clearly trying to comfort me.

A sports car zoomed around a hangar. It came to a stop thirty feet away from the plane, and I saw Nick open the passenger door. I recognized Carl, who'd driven him here.

After a brief struggle to get out of the low-slung automobile, Nick had his crutches beneath both arms and was hopping toward us at a dangerous pace.

He stood at the bottom of the stairs. "Can I have a minute with Daisy, Mum, please?"

She stood up and gave me a reassuring nod before ambling off toward the car, presumably to speak with Carl.

"Mind if I sit a minute?" Nick hobbled up the steps.

I helped him by grabbing his crutches and holding them for him.

He let out a frustrated sigh. "This is getting old. I mean the crutches. I'm going to lose my mind if I can't kick a ball soon."

"Maybe you can bounce it off your head?"

He burst out laughing. "I do miss you."

"Sorry about last night," I said.

"You have nothing to apologize for. I shouldn't have walked off like that. It was your special evening, Daisy. You achieved something amazing and I should have stayed to help you celebrate."

"I never meant to hurt you, Nick."

He rested his face in his hands. "I've been such an ass."

"I couldn't find the right time to tell you about…"

"I wondered why Max wanted to talk about you so much." He gave me a wry smile. "He kept bringing your name up in conversation. I think he was feeling me out, seeing if I'd be okay with you two being a couple." Nick nudged against me. "He's kind of goofy when he's happy."

"He's fun to be around."

"You both are."

I couldn't look at Nick. God only knew what he thought about me getting on a plane for Brazil to see Max.

"You two started spending time together," he said. "You grew to really like each other." Nick reached for my hand. "Then I went and injured myself and you both felt sorry for me."

"We didn't want you to have anything more to worry about."

"And here we are."

I sighed. "Yeah, but I can't get on that plane."

"It's better than first class."

I stared at him. "Why did you hide your family from me? Why hide all this?"

"It was something I'd always done. Dad insisted we go to a regular school, a regular college. No private education for us. He didn't want us to be snobs. There was a part of me that feared that any girl that got to know me would like me for all the wrong reasons." He cringed. "And Mum was always on my case about…"

"I saw her do that to Max, too. She only wants the best for you both."

"The thing is, Daisy, you are the best. You proved that time and time again. I proved I'm an idiot."

"It's going to be okay, Nick," I said softly. "You'll bounce back from this. I know it."

"I'll give it my best try."

"I'll cheer you on as I've always done…as a good friend."

"Daisy, I can't believe I'm saying this," he paused for a beat. "But you should fly to São Paulo to see Max. It's the best way for you to prove how much you really love him."

"Nick, I don't think I can bring myself to board this plane."

He sat up straight. "What can I do to make it easier?"

"I keep thinking of Liam." I bit my lip to suppress the panic I was feeling. "What he went through. How scared he must have been."

"It happened fast, Daisy."

"I want to believe that." I turned to face him. "You were there for me. When I needed you, Nick. I'll always be grateful. I couldn't have made it through without you."

"You were there for me, too, when Dad died. I don't know how I would have coped without you. I pushed everyone else away. But you, you knew what I was going through. You got me."

I squeezed his hand.

"When I was injured you were there for me, too." He shook his head. "You came to the hospital. Maybe you should have told me about Max then."

"I know. We wanted to protect you."

"Can I do the same for you now, and give you some advice?" He turned to look at me. "Liam would want you to go after the man you love. He'd never want to think that what happened to him had stopped you from finding happiness." Nick wrapped his arm around me. "Max is as good as it gets, Daisy. We have to get you on this plane."

Tears stung my eyes. "Tell him...tell Max..."

Gillian headed back towards us. Nick gave a shake of his head to let her know it wasn't happening.

She gripped the handrail and looked at Nick. "Dear, will you let me talk with Daisy alone?"

He gave a resigned nod, pushing himself up and navigating down the steps with his crutches like a pro.

Gillian sat beside me again. "Max is the practical one. The methodical one. He is changing careers because he wants his life to be different. I believe that he was ready to have a serious relationship and give it the time it deserves." She reached into her handbag. "It seemed like a small thing—" She held something in her palm. "Maybe with some afterthought, it's a big thing."

"What is it?"

"Max left his tuxedo jacket behind when he rushed off the night of the party. I know he'll regret leaving you like that for the rest of his life. He believed he was doing the right thing. He always does—to his own detriment."

She opened her hand. Resting in the center of her palm lay my tiny ladybug button—the one that had popped off my blouse the night I'd slid down the glass chute and landed on Max.

He'd kept it.

Minutes later, in the elevator, he'd tugged at my blouse telling me I'd lost that button. All the while knowing he had it in his pocket.

Max had fallen for me that night...

Just as I'd fallen for him.

Gillian dropped the ladybug button onto my palm. "He was carrying this with him."

All those times he'd turned up at the same events with some excuse or other, he'd been feeling the pull toward me, too.

"He was willing to walk away for you, too, Daisy," she said softly. "He thought you may still have a fondness for Nick."

I shook my head, denying it.

"I know that now. And you need to let Max know. What are you willing to do for him?"

I hugged my knees, resting my head on them.

"You've proven yourself very brave over the last few weeks." She rubbed my back with the affection of a mother. "Go to him."

Chapter
THIRTY-ONE

Max

AHEAD OF ME LAY AN ENDLESS STACK OF PAPERWORK and an infinite number of tension-filled hours spent in chilled courtrooms.

São Paulo, my favorite city, had opened her arms to me upon my return two days ago, as though I'd never left. I'd craved the climate, the people, the remarkable landscapes, and the warm ocean.

Home.

I'd been craving coconut truffles, or more specifically, the woman I'd once fed them to. I missed Daisy so much.

This was the most I'd ever exposed my heart to anyone. And it had felt so good. I'd willingly let myself fall for her, daring to think love was a good idea.

My office walls now made me feel claustrophobic, the clean lines of the classic décor had grown stale, the air conditioning bitterly cold.

Daisy had changed me irrevocably. I was never going to be that man who sat behind this desk going through the motions of court dates, client appointments, and tackling endless paperwork.

All of it to grace my ego.

Even knowing Daisy for such a short while, I grew to care deeply for the woman who could make me laugh like no other person on earth. I had finally experienced London through a romantic's eyes. Our time together was a memory I'd always cherish.

Doing the right thing sucked.

A knock on my office door shook me out of my day-dreaming, and Gylda's smiling face appeared. "Olá, Maximus."

"Olá, Gylda. English, please."

"Why?"

"I'm homesick for London." I leaned back in the chair with my hands behind my head.

"This is your home."

"Humor me."

She shrugged. "Fine."

"I got you this." I reached for the paper bag I'd brought with me—all the way from the Quinto Bookshop.

Gylda eased the book out of the bag. "William Waterhouse's paintings!"

"You like?"

"I love." She clutched it to her chest. "Max, how did you know I would?"

"I had a little help." My smile shimmered with sadness, but she didn't catch it.

"How was your trip?"

"Good and bad."

"I'm sorry to hear about the bad. Why?"

I let out a long breath.

"If you want to talk…"

Her eyes saw too much in the face of the man she'd known since boyhood. I never wanted to burden her. She had her own family to think of, her own life with its ups and downs and everything in between.

"You look tired." She came in and sat in the chair opposite me.

"This trip was different."

"You met someone?" She gave a nod. "That's it, isn't it?"

"It's complicated."

She gasped. "*Ela é casada.*"

"No, she's quite single. Or she was." I shook my head. "She's Nick's ex-girlfriend. We connected on a deep level. We spent time together. I fell hard, Gylda."

"Well, that is good, right?"

"Nick injured himself and…"

"She went back to him?"

"They were dating for a long time. They lived together. He left her for another woman."

"You were there for her?"

"Her name's Daisy…" I let out a wistful sigh. "We've only known each other a short while, but…"

"But you know. You always know when it's right."

"It was…so very, very right, Gylda."

"She felt sorry for Nick. Is that why she went back to him?"

"I forced her hand." I reached for a pencil and tapped it on a stack of folders.

"Why?"

"Nick needs her."

"Don't be stupid. No one needs to be in a false relationship." I rubbed a hand down my face.

"Has she reached out to you?"

"I'm afraid to check my phone. I texted Mum that I'd landed safely and then I turned it off."

"Well, look now."

I gave a shrug. "What if I see a photo of them together? I don't know how I'm going to feel about that...or the thought of going back to London and having to be in the same room as both of them." I paused, swallowing hard. "Or worse, being invited to their big day." I leaned forward with my face in my palms. "Oh, God. Can I decline a wedding invite when it comes from my own brother?"

"Holy shits."

"You don't need the 's' on the end."

She shot to her feet. "Look at your phone!"

"No."

She leaped forward, grabbing it and waving it in my face. "Max, what if it's the answer you want?"

I snatched it back—and tossed it in the bin beneath my desk.

She reached down and retrieved it. "Your father would want you to look, Max. Do it for him."

"My father lost the love of his life."

"More reason to look," she said softly.

She was right...

Swiping the screen, I saw a slew of messages had come in from my mum. No surprise there. There were five texts from Nick, which was kind of unusual.

And one from Daisy.

I stared at the screen.

"What does it say?" Gylda's expression was full of hope.

"I have to go back." I slammed my palm to my forehead. "I have to go back right now."

Gylda let out a delighted squeal, and it matched my inside voice.

I'd been too distraught to think straight, to think we had

a chance. My life was flashing before my eyes—because that's how much it hurt to think I'd almost lost her.

There was still time…

A company car was put on standby to take me to the airport. Gylda arranged for a private jet to fly me back to London.

Not caring that I had no luggage, I grabbed my passport from my desk drawer and hurried down to the waiting car.

Gylda escorted me down and waited with me on the curb.

Before getting into the car, I hurried back and pulled her into a big hug. It felt like she'd saved my life, and in many ways she had.

"Call Maria Alves," I told her. "The woman looking for a Civil Rights Attorney. Tell her I'll represent her brother."

"I remember her." Gylda's eyes watered with emotion.

On the backseat I checked my watch a hundred times a minute. It was going to take me a lifetime to get back to Daisy.

A confirmation email came in that a plane was ready. I'd have jumped on a regular flight—I didn't need the luxury of a private jet. What I needed was to get back to London.

The car pulled through to the VIP parking area.

Within the airport, I hurried through the pre-flight check-in. With no baggage, I made it through security quickly and was escorted to a private jet at the end of the runway.

I'd call Daisy once the plane was in the air, hear her voice again. Reassure her that everything would be fine and I was on my way back.

Reaching the metal steps of the plane, I took two at a time, hurrying as though take-off was imminent. I willed the pre-flight check to go quickly.

"Mr. Marquis," said Angus Baxter, one of our loyal pilots, greeting me warmly at the top of the steps.

"Thanks for this," I said. "Sorry about the short notice, Angus."

"We can't take off yet, sir."

"Why not?"

"This plane just landed from Heathrow. The last pilot advised us we have a passenger still onboard."

"Who?"

"Your mother—"

"My mum's on here?"

"No, she gave instructions to make sure you were notified when they landed. I'm glad we finally reached you."

I glanced toward the private cabin. "My phone's been off." I felt a jolt of disbelief. "It's not…?" No, that was impossible.

"I'll send Katarina to wake her?" said Baxter.

I waited for the stewardess to pass by me and followed her toward the cabin, peeking through the door to see who the mystery guest was who'd hitched a flight.

I inhaled in a rush when I saw Daisy.

She had flown to Brazil.

She remained fast asleep, lying with her brunette locks curled on the pillow and her arms above her head, looking restful and not like someone who was terrified of flying.

"I know her," I whispered to the stewardess as I entered the small space.

She stepped back.

Katarina waited in the doorway. "I gave her a drink to calm her nerves, sir. She spent the first half of the flight curled up in a ball."

"What did you give her?"

"A shot of whisky." She grimaced. "Well, two, maybe."

My eyes widened at her confession, but clearly it had worked as Daisy looked serene.

I sat on edge of the bed and glanced back at the stewardess, who was lingering in the doorway protectively. "She slept the rest of the way."

It worried me that Daisy had been so stressed. Though, selfishly, I was glad that I didn't have to wait a minute longer to hold her in my arms. I should have been with her during the flight, holding her hand and saying the kinds of things that would have made this trip bearable for her.

She'd faced her biggest fear...for me.

I leaned low and pressed my lips to her forehead.

Daisy's breathing lightened and she stretched languidly, sleepily opening her eyes and brightening when she realized it was me.

She took my hand. "You came back to me."

"That was the plan, yes, but you beat me to it."

She gave me a sweet smile. "I'm so happy to see you."

I glanced back at the stewardess to let her know she could leave us. With a nod of understanding, she closed the door and gave us privacy.

I reached for the bottle of water on the side table and handed it to Daisy. She drank thirstily and then looked around.

"Where am I?"

"You don't remember?"

"Am I on a...?"

"You've landed now. Obviously."

"Don't let it take off again."

I squeezed her hand. "You were very brave."

"I might have had a drink. That stuff tastes nasty."

"Whisky?"

"The stewardess told me it costs three hundred pounds per glass. You might want to get your money back."

Same old Daisy. I wouldn't have it any other way.

"Your mum offered me a free flight to Brazil. I couldn't say no."

I shook my head. "My mother's incorrigible."

"I didn't need much persuasion." She pushed herself up. "Well, maybe a bit, at first."

"That old dragon." I smirked at Mum's cheekiness.

"Gillian did something right. She made you, Max."

"Well, there is that." I grinned and then reached out to stroke her cheek. "I should never have left England so suddenly. Forgive me."

"You did it for Nick."

"It's been my job to protect him."

"He's fine. I spoke with him before I left."

I swallowed hard but the truth came out anyway. "I missed you as soon as I drove through those Hampstead gates. It hurt more than I care to admit."

"Leaving me?"

"That will never happen again." I played with her hair. "Just say what you want, what you need, Daisy. I swear if it's the moon and stars, I'll get it for you."

"Just you, Max. I only need you."

I smiled. "And maybe some aspirin? How does your head feel?"

"I feel fine." She looked around. "Are we in São Paulo?"

"We are."

"That's where you live."

"It is." I pulled her into a hug, wanting to make her feel safe, relaxing only when I heard her sigh of happiness. "I want to show you the city I love."

"I know I'll fall in love with it, too," she said, looking up at me. "We found each other again, Max."

She rested her head on my shoulder.

Daisy was back in my arms—and it felt like she had always belonged there.

Epilogue

Daisy

Eight Years Later

THE ELABORATELY DESIGNED WINDOW DISPLAY looked fantastic.

Standing back, poised to get into my Jeep, I admired what I had created in Braga's shop window. An elegant manne-quin wearing beachy attire standing atop a generous sprinkling of sand straight from the beach. The store was nestled within the leafy streets of Ilhabela. Known as a green oasis, Ilhabela was filled with stylish stores, elegant restaurants, welcoming bistros, and chic fashion boutiques. It was also the place we called our weekend home.

I'd be taking a break from this part-time work for a while, for months, really. Resting my hand on my baby bump, I knew time would fly and also be filled with joy.

Music rose from my handbag.

My new favorite song. I grinned. It was *him*. Max had changed my ringtone to Frank Sinatra singing "The Girl From Ipanema."

I answered. "I'm on my way."

"Time to take a vacation," he said. "Come home."

"Did you see the photos I sent?"

"The window display looks great." He chuckled. "I know you're obsessed, but we want you home."

"I'm not obsessed."

"Remember that time you tried to shag a mannequin in Harvey Nichols?"

"She fell on me!" I laughed. "It was her dress I was after."

"So you say."

"If you let me get off the phone, I'll be on my way to you."

"I see a foot rub in my future."

"Wait a minute, you told me if I made it home before dinner, I'd be getting the foot rub."

"Your word against mine."

"I'm getting in the car now."

"Drive safe."

I was less than a half hour away from our home. The ocean views were spectacular. I'd never ceased to be awed by the sight of the endless blue sea, or the feel of the warm air on my skin. I inhaled the fresh ocean breeze with gratitude.

Once inside the house, I heard Max's voice coming from the garden. He was out there playing with our sweet six year old, Ava. She took after her daddy with her big brown eyes and luscious dark locks. We adored our beautiful, smart little girl. She easily switched back and forth, fluently, between English and Portuguese. It was a joy to be excited about the way she would continue to shine in the world.

Changing out of my skirt and blouse, I happily climbed into my yoga pants and roomy T-shirt, and then headed for the door. One of the drawers in Max's bedside table was slightly open. I went to push it closed and then recognized a small object that Max had kept—Max had kept the ladybug button he'd carried around since our first kiss.

A shiver went through me; even now it meant something.

He was a little greyer now around his sideburns, though his eyes were just as bright and full of life. I'd fallen head over heels in love with that romantic and sentimental soul who made every moment special.

"Ouch!" Max's yell came from downstairs.

I hurried down the winding stairwell that led to the living room. "What happened?"

Max was barefoot and hopping around the living room, clearly in pain.

Seeing me rush down the steps, he gave me a disapproving look. "Careful!"

"I'm totally capable of walking. What's wrong?"

He pointed a finger at his foot. "There's no worse pain than this."

I rested my hands on my hips. "Hello, you forgot childbirth."

"Not even close." He rubbed his sole.

I rolled my eyes, trying not to smile. "You stepped on a Lego again, didn't you?"

"This is not funny."

"I'm not laughing."

His lips curled at the edges. "I didn't know fatherhood could be so dangerous."

"Wearing shoes is an option."

"I was playing football at her age." He wandered over to me. "This is how the best players train."

I glanced out the large glass window and saw Ava kicking a ball—with her shoes on, at least.

Max wrapped an arm around me. "Maybe we can switch out her Legos for a puzzle."

"She takes after you."

He wagged a finger in my face. "Being artsy comes from you."

"What's she wearing?" I looked closer. "Is that a Manchester United T-shirt?"

"Nick sent it."

"How's he doing?"

"He's never been better, he says."

Max looked me up and down. "You look extra pretty today."

"You say that to me every day."

"That's because—" His lips found mine and we shared a passionate kiss.

Ava ran in. "Mummy!"

She looked adorable in her football shorts and T-shirt.

Leaning low, I dragged her in for a hug. "Ava, you're a professional player now."

Max and I shared a smile, a look of pride. I rested my hands protectively on my swollen belly.

Ava gripped Max's leg. "Daddy, let's play again!

I followed them outside, sitting in my usual spot in one of the wicker chairs. On the other side of the veranda, the spectacular view of the city was like a painting. Our five-bedroom home was perfect for Max to work from when he took a break from the office. His career as one of the most distinguished civil rights attorneys in the country continued to flourish. He'd have made his father proud.

We also loved this location for its accessibility to the beach. Every weekend we were swimming, building sandcastles, or watching Ava's daddy surf. We savored our time together as a family.

Max was kicking a football around the garden and Ava was trying to intercept it. I cheered her on as she grabbed the ball and then kicked it into the goal. Again, Ava dribbled the ball toward the net, moving around Max who was trying to defend it. She threw a goal in the center.

We cheered like she'd won the World Cup—like she hadn't used her hands, either.

Max looked ecstatic. "It's in her blood."

I wasn't surprised.

Afterward, we settled in the sitting room.

Max and I huddled close together on the couch while Ava ran around the living room, mimicking her Uncle Nick playing football as she watched him on the big screen.

Nick's match was live on TV. He was playing with the talent that had earned him fame and fortune, his old knee injury never once obvious.

We'd have been there in person, but with me heavily pregnant and about to pop any moment, I wasn't allowed to fly—which was as good an excuse as any not to do my least favorite thing.

I'd flown since that first flight on Max's private jet all those years ago, but if it was possible to find another way to travel, I preferred it.

Ava was doing her favorite thing in the world—watching her uncle's team, Manchester United, play Liverpool F.C.

At halftime, the match was evenly scored. Nick was going to have to draw on all his passion and drive to see this through. We wanted this win for Nick as much as he did.

Ava slipped off the couch and hurried over to pull something from behind a seat cushion.

"What have you got there, baby?" asked Max.

"I found a toy."

Max and I swapped a wary glance, and then saw what she was holding. It was Pelé, the collector's statue that Max had once entrusted me with on the day we'd first met.

Max sat up. "That's not a toy, Ava," he said. "That's the greatest football player in the world."

"Can I keep him?" she asked.

"Yes," Max said, glancing at me first. "Just remember, he's very special. He needs to be handled gently."

She hugged him to her chest. "What about Uncle Nick? Does he play as well as Pelé?"

"Well, um…" Max deferred that one to me.

"They play differently," I said with a smile. "Pelé…"

"Careful," said Max, amused.

Gesturing to the TV, I said, "No one will replace Pelé. He will always be in our hearts. But Uncle Nick is talented, too."

Ava waved the figure's arm. "I want ice cream."

"Yep, takes after her mum," said Max.

I nudged him in the ribs with my elbow. He squirmed, and both of us ended up in one of our usual embraces.

Sitting with my head on Max's shoulder, I remembered what he'd once told me: *One day you'll find your happily ever after.*

Turns out, he was right. Max and Ava filled my heart and my life with light and love.

My happily ever after.

Manchester United vs. Liverpool F.C.

News Report:

Manchester United knocked Liverpool F.C. out of the League following a 1-1 draw between the old rivals. With the crowd cheering, Nick Banham bent the ball into the top right corner. The goalie didn't even see the ball coming. The match was won by this seasoned player with a gift that would make his dad proud.

Next, onto the World Cup.

Birth Announcement:

Max and Daisy Marquis

Welcome the birth of their son and brother to Ava,

Oliver Liam Marquis

Also from Author
VANESSA FEWINGS

PERVADE LONDON and PERVADE MONTEGO BAY

&

PERFUME GIRL

&

THE ENTHRALL SESSIONS: ENTHRALL, ENTHRALL HER, ENTHRALL HIM, CAMERON'S CONTROL, CAMERON'S CONTRACT, RICHARD'S REIGN, ENTHRALL SECRETS, and ENTHRALL CLIMAX

&

THE ICON TRILOGY from Harlequin: THE CHASE, THE GAME, and THE PRIZE

Vanessafewings.com

About the
AUTHOR

USA Today Bestselling Author Vanessa Fewings writes both contemporary romance and dark erotic suspense novels. She can be found on her Facebook Fan Page and in The Romance Lounge, Instagram, Twitter and Goodreads.

She enjoys connecting with fans all around the world.

Made in the USA
Coppell, TX
24 March 2022

75502022R00166